The Ice Between Us

Celina Trotzki

ISBN: 978-3-9824737-0-3

THE ICE BETWEEN US

FOR EVERYONE WHO SHARES THE DEEP
LOVE TO FIGURE SKATING

1

SLOANE

The accident was now three months ago. Today is the first time I am setting foot on the ice.

Figure skating has always been part of my life. I started it when I was a little kid. I can't even remember the first day I have been on the ice. I have always wanted to do this professionally. I always dreamed about going to the Olympics.

Nothing is more important for me, so I took some time off from college. I had just finished high school, and instead of going to college, I decided to concentrate on figure skating.

There is only one problem right now. I don't have a partner anymore. This is the part that hurts me the most at the moment. This is what kept me from skating for three months.

Since I started skating, I have had the same skating partner. I had never seen myself as a solo skater, so I started skating with my best friend.

We met at the rink when we were little and bonded immediately. This was years ago, and ever since that day, we've been a team.

I take a deep breath as I have a look over the ice. No one else is here. As always, I am early. I, in fact, wanted to be alone. I wanted that no one was going to see me right now.

It hurts to know that I can never skate with Flynn again. This alone is a reason to give everything up. There is no way I will find a new partner, someone who is as good as Flynn.

We were the perfect team.

I take another deep breath and step onto the ice. I just stand there, not moving a single bit.

I forget how to breathe, the accident right in front of my eyes for a second. I can see it happening. Every time I returned to the rink, I saw it.

I see Flynn fall. I see the blood spreading over the ice. I was the first one by his side when it happened. I was the one who held his hand the entire time until we arrived at the hospital. It was just a typical training day for us.

I shake off the memory and the terrible feeling. I grab my AirPods and put one of my favorite skating songs on. With another deep breath, I finally start moving.

First, I am not doing much. I just skate along the edge. I missed this feeling more than anything else in this world. There is nothing better than being on the ice. It makes me feel free.

Without even noticing it, I start moving to the music I hear. A spin here and there, some easy jumps. It happens automatically.

I shut the world out and concentrated on the ice beneath my skates and the music in my ears. Everything could be so perfect right now. Flynn and I could be here together, preparing ourselves for the next competition.

Now there won't be a competition. Not for me, at least. Maybe there won't ever be a competition for me, ever again.

I gain speed. I let out the anger and frustration I am feeling right now. Everything inside me is screaming. I hate what happened. I wish I could turn back time and make everything different.

Why did it happen? Why do I have to give up the thing I love most? I can't skate without Flynn. It feels wrong to even think about it.

I remember every critical moment. Every success, every time we laughed and cried here. I trusted Flynn with all my heart. There won't ever be a person I will trust as much as him.

And trust is the most essential thing when you are skating with someone.

I stop entirely breathless. I don't feel better in the slightest bit. I know that it's only going to be more challenging from now on.

Irina is going to find a new partner. We have to start from the very beginning. If she can't find someone and if I can't adjust to the new situation, I have to give it all up.

This is the one thing I have always wanted to do, and if I give up, I have nothing left.

I hear someone clapping as I stop in the middle of the ice. I nearly can't hear it because of the AirPods inside my ears. I look around to see Flynn standing at the barrier, clapping at me.

„What are you doing here?" I ask him, already skating toward him. I remove my AirPods slowly and put them back into their case.

„Your mom told me that you went to the rink this morning, and I just had to see it with my own eyes," he replies with the sweetest smile.

I know that there is a lot of pain behind it. I know it hurts him that he can't do it anymore. He was living for it, and now he isn't allowed to be on the ice anymore.

Maybe he can skate one day again. But he will never be able to do figure skating again. He could lose his ability to walk if he gets hurt again.

No one wants this to happen, and the risk is too high. Irina told him that she would not coach him anymore, and even though he was an adult, his parents forbid him to skate.

„I just wanted to try it. It's not working the way I want anyway," I sigh and leave the ice quickly. I sit on the bench and start untying my skates to remove them entirely from my feet.

I am angry and frustrated. I want Flynn back as my partner. I want to turn back time so that this stupid accident never happened.

„What are you talking about? It was perfect! With a new partner by your side, you will win every competition," he encourages me.

I know that he wants to make me feel better. Maybe he thinks that it is going to be easy for me.

„There won't be a new partner, and there won't be any competitions. You know that there is no one out there who will be as perfect as you had been," I tell him a bit harsher than I wanted to.

I take a deep breath and look at him. His brown eyes are staring back at me.

„You can't just give up! You're the best skater I have ever met! You have to find someone else, and I know someone is out there. Maybe he is an even better match for you than I ever was."

Flynn drives his hand through his red hair. I know I drive him absolutely crazy. Everyone tried to bring me back onto the ice for the past two months.

Everyone told me that I should just keep going. My coach Irina isn't happy at all about my little break. She thinks that by now, we could already find a new partner. When it comes to her, there wouldn't have been a break at all. She wanted me to be a part of this season.

„I'm going home. It was a mistake to come back here," I sigh and grab my stuff.

Other skaters are entering the hall to start their training, and I don't want to be here anymore. I don't want to see how everyone can be happy except me.

I can't skate happily without my partner. I am not a solo skater, and I'll never be one. But I can't find a new partner either. It seems like giving up is the only choice.

„Sloane, wait!" Flynn yells behind me. I should stop and wait for him. He can't walk that fast since his accident, but right now, I don't want to stop and wait for him. I don't want to hear that I make a huge mistake.

2

SLOANE

I waited for Flynn. I can't just leave him behind. He is my best friend, and he can't drive a car at the moment. I bet someone dropped him off here. I have to take him home again.

„You can't just give up!" He says for the millionth time in the past ten minutes.

I groan, trying to concentrate on the road ahead of me.

„I can't skate without you! It just feels wrong! There are also too many things speaking against it," I reply this time.

It feels like I am betraying him. He can't skate anymore, so why should I do it? It feels so unfair.

„God, what is speaking against it?" He rolls his eyes at me. I know he wants me to skate more than anything else. He always told me.

„There isn't a single person I trust as much as I trust you. We're the perfect team. There can't be another person as excellent as you. You're literally the best skater," I point out. There are way more things I can think of.

„Hold on, first of all, I was the best skater. I am not anymore because I am not going to skate anymore. And there is someone who is working perfectly as your partner. You will learn to trust him," he replies, and I automatically feel bad.

He was the best skater. I know that he still wants to be. I can only imagine how he feels. Just thinking that I might not be able to skate again pains me. If I got hurt and someone told me I couldn't skate anymore, I would surely die.

„I'm sorry. I know that you still want to skate. I just can't skate without you," I shrug my shoulders.

„I know that you hate adjusting to something new. I hate that I can't skate anymore, but it hurts me even more that you're not skating anymore. It kills me that you think about giving up!" He replies calmly.

„I know it is hard, but you have to try. You have to go out there and be the best for me. You have to go and win the Olympics for me," he adds slowly.

This makes it even harder. It feels like Flynn is putting me under pressure now. It was our dream. We wanted to win the Olympic Games together.

But he knows me too well. I can't stay away from skating. Even though I hate that I lost my partner, I loved it on the ice today.

„I can't be a solo skater. I am horrible as a solo skater," I reply slowly.

„You would be a great solo skater, but you are the best skater with a partner at your side. We both know that Irina is going to find someone new. She is the best coach and only accepts the best skaters as your partner. You don't have to worry about a single thing; if everything turns out worse, you can still give up. You have to at least try."

Flynn, his words are balm to my soul. Even though I know the situation pains him, he is too good to me.

When someone is addicted to a sport, they are in pain when they have to give it up.

I think about his words. Even though we both already know my reply. I can feel the desire inside me. I want to try it. I want to go back to skating.

„You have to say that it felt good on the ice today, " he adds slowly.

I stopped right in front of my house and looked at him.

„You know that I won't give up. I will try it, but let me tell you that I am not going to skate with some idiot" I sigh, and Flynn already starts cheering.

„You won't regret it. The minute you get back into training, you are red-hot for the ice again" Flynn chuckles about his choice of words.

I roll my eyes annoyed, but the smile on my face tells otherwise. I know that everyone is going to be happy about my decision.

I gave up college for this. I gave up everything to have a career as a figure skater. I wanted to try it and had to use every chance to succeed.

„I am going to tell Irina right away. I also told her that you were on the ice today, and she said it was about time. She wants to see you and start with the training again," Flynn says as he already grabs his phone.

I sigh, walking inside my home with him together. Silence is meeting us. My parents are probably still at work. I guess I have to tell them later that I am returning to training.

„Irina set you up, right? She told you to talk to me?" I ask him slowly. He can't lie to me. I always know when he is lying to me.

„Maybe…" he looks at me apologetically, „well, I also want you to return. We all want that. And Irina wants her student back. I guess she is afraid of losing her best chance and job."

This clearly is the truth. Irina is losing her job when I'm quitting, and she told us several times that we have been her best students.

Irina doesn't have any other students. She gave up her second student when everything started working well with us. She said she only wanted to concentrate on us and that we deserved all her attention.

„Now, I at least know that she will call me later," I sigh.

I love Irina, but she is a strict coach and very eager too. If she has something inside her head, it must happen the way she wants. Irina is a former figure skater from Poland, and I know she was the best long ago. Her strong accent is only one of the things I have always loved about her.

She can't skate anymore because of an injury. But the skating experience she gained indeed formed her into the best coach.

I am sure that she can't wait to dive right back in. I let her wait for way too long. I didn't even go to the gym. She is going to kill me.

3
SLOANE

I was right, of course. Irina wants to see me the following day. She called me, yelling at me for the long break I had taken. Before hanging up, she told me politely to come to the rink the following day.

And here I am, my pulse racing. I am a little bit scared of Irina and her reaction. I know that she can be hard on me sometimes. She wants me to be the best, so she must be strict.

I'm already wearing my skates as I sit on the bench. I wait for Irina before setting foot onto the ice.

I take a look around the rink. Literally, everyone is here, and it makes me even more nervous. We're living in a small town in Canada. Everyone knows everyone here. Some are waving at me, a friendly smile on their lips, while others watch me curiously. They haven't seen me in quite a while now. I bet they are surprised I am back, and I know they are most definitely talking behind my back.

„Have you already stretched, girl?" I hear Irina with her polish accent. I quickly turn around to face her and nod with a smile.

„What are you waiting for then? Go and warm yourself up on the ice."

Her facial expression is stone cold, and I think she hates me for my break. She possibly thinks that I am weak and a nobody. I know the break was a mistake, but I can't change it anymore.

I slowly turn away from her, kind of happy to now go on the ice. She can't yell at me for the few rounds of my warm-up.

„Wait!" She instructs right before I put my first foot down on the ice. I turn around to look at her.

A soft smile is lying on her lips, and she opens her arms, welcoming me. I am now confused, but she already steps forward and pulls me into a tight hug.

Her hugs remind me how strong she actually is. She squeezes me tightly.

„Are you feeling good?" She asks me right after she lets go of me.

„I think I do," I reply, unsure of how I feel.

„Good, because I won't take it easy on you. We have to get you ready for the new season and a new partner. It won't be easy," she tells me, and with that, she points at the ice.

I slowly nod and do as she tells me to. I slowly skate my warm-up rounds to get used to the feeling. Then I gain speed for a couple of rounds to get warmed up.

I don't know what our training session will look like today, but I am excited. I am thrilled to be back for the first time in a while.

It is weird because I don't have a partner anymore. There is no one skating next to me. I won't practice lifting figures or pair spins. I don't have to skate synchronously with someone.

It is just me on the ice, and somehow this doesn't satisfy me. I know that I am not as good alone as with a partner.

Irina is watching me skeptical as I perform our latest choreography for her. I can only do the solo elements.

I come to a halt as soon as the song ends. Flynn is standing next to Irina. Both of them are watching me. And as soon as I am done, Flynn starts clapping his hands.

He smiles so widely that I think I might have done an excellent job. Irina nods slowly. Her face is severe and cold. I don't know what she actually thinks about me.

„We have a lot to practice. For now, I think it's best to leave the ice and try some usual ballet practices. You need to work on your posture," she sighs.

I can hear the disappointment in her voice. I was not doing good enough. Maybe I am not the best anymore, so I am not getting an excellent new partner.

I don't want to fall back in the competitions. I need to keep going with the best score.

„You are still outstanding, but the break didn't favor you. We have to bring you back into form and find you a new partner," Irina thinks aloud as I remove my skates.

I slowly look at her and nod. I know that I could've been more active. I did nothing except for running a couple of times.

„There are a couple of good skaters looking for a new partner right now! I am sure there might be the right one for Sloane," Flynn smiles softly.

I hate that we're talking about a new partner. I know every skater here, and I don't want them. They are not good enough. Taking one of them as my partner would mean I would fall back.

„I already have someone in mind. I talked to him and his father, and it is looking good now. I will introduce you to each other when it is final," Irina nods firmly.

She is already turning her back toward me and starts walking away. She is not waiting for me to be ready. She expects me to be done by now. I quickly shoot Flynn a look and grab my stuff.

I will have a new partner very soon, and I have no idea who it will be.

It already seems final to her. There is no way out for me. She makes the decision without asking for permission. I can't say anything against it. I know that it is my time to obey her. I can imagine how she yells at me as soon as I say anything against my potential partner.

She wants the best for me. She wants us to be the best. She doesn't care if we get along.

It only has to work whenever we're having a competition. We have to bring home the victory, and anything else just doesn't matter.

My new partner is all I can think of while practicing some easy ballet figures. It drives me absolutely crazy that I have no idea who it will be.

„Sloane, you have to be more concentrated! It will not work like this," she yells at me. Her polish accent only makes her sound angrier.

I look at her and nod slowly. I know this is not working like this. I can't concentrate ideally, even if I want to.

„I try my best," I press out, still holding the pose I am in right now. I am standing on one foot, the other up in the air. My arms are in front of me in the most elegant position possible. It might look elegant but is hard to hold. My muscles are tense, and I try to get my leg even higher.

Figure skating has a lot to do with body tension, and we skaters have a lot of muscles. They might not always be visible, but we're actually pretty strong.

„Maybe we should just stop for today," my coach sighs, and I look at her.

I don't want to disappoint her. I don't want to disappoint anyone. This is why I shake my head.

I told everyone that I could do this. I threw away my chance to attend a good college because I was sure I could be the best figure skater.

„No, I'll do better!" I tell her, still in my position.

„But you're missing a part. We can continue training with your new partner. You have to start from the beginning anyway," she tells me.

I give up this time and stand up straight. My coach turns away from me and grabs her stuff.

„I'll see you tomorrow with your new partner," she tells me, and with that, she leaves the room and is gone.

I am more than disappointed right now. It feels like I did something wrong. I am not good enough anymore, and it has only been three months.

„It'll be fine! Today had been the first time" Flynn starts slowly. I bet he can see how bad I am feeling right now.

„No, it's not okay. It'll only get worse with a new person by my side." I grab my stuff and look at Flynn.

I wish the accident would have never happened. Everything would be okay right now. We would try our best to get into the Olympics.

I don't even know if I can make it to the next competition. I am going to lose the points I gained. I will drop in the ranking.

I have to start from the beginning because of my new partner.

„Who knows, maybe you're doing more than good together!"

I love Flynn for his optimistic mindset. Right now, it is not really helpful. I know that it's not going to work with a new partner.

I have never seen a skater as good as Flynn. There are not a lot of couple skaters here anyway. We have tons of solo skaters and a hockey team. Switching from solo skating to couple skating is the hardest thing possible. A solo skater doesn't depend on anyone, and mostly it's hard for them to learn how to trust a partner.

„I just wanna go home right now," I sigh and leave the room. Flynn walks behind me, a bit slower, but he follows me outside. I wish I don't have to come back here tomorrow.

„You're coming tomorrow, right?" I ask my best friend as I am zipping up my jacket.

He nods slowly, a broad smile lying on his lips. His brown eyes are watching me. „Of course, I'll be there like always!"

„Would you mind coming earlier? I want to skate a bit before I meet him," I ask him, and he nods again.

„Sure."

„Great, I'll see you tomorrow then."

And with that, our ways part. Flynn's parents are picking him up, and I am driving home alone.

4

ASHER

I watched her today. I had noticed her before. Of course, I did. Everyone knows her. She is one of the best skaters, and everyone is talking about her bright future.

Well, she can afford it in the first place. Her parents are paying a lot, and she always has the newest and best stuff. And now it seems like she is my miracle, my ticket to the upper skating class.

A couple of days ago, her coach asked me to be her new partner. She even talked to my dad, who pretended he didn't care about it.

In fact, it made him so mad that I wanted to spend even more time at the rink now. My father thinks I should choose a college and do something for my future. He wants me to stop skating. He always wanted me to stop.

My father has been unbearable since my mom died, but somehow I survived his behavior.

I agreed immediately. Sloane is the best chance I have now. I imagine that working with her is not going to be easy. She is the ice princess here. She has everything she wants, and I am just a regular skater. I am no one special. But she has access to stuff that I would never have access to.

For the first time today, I came to the rink to watch. I left my skates home, knowing I wouldn't need them today.

I sat in the back, where I could see the whole ice, but I stayed invisible to the others. Sloane started her training with some warm-up rounds.

I watch every move she makes. Sloane looks like she is made for the ice like she is born to do this. Her movements are so smooth and perfect. It seems like she is flying across the ice.

Every spin is perfect, and every jump is on point, yet she seems unhappy with everything.

She and her former partner had been the best in town. Everyone talked about how they are one day going to win the Olympics. There is no way that I can keep up with that.

I can't afford to be in the upper skating class, so I am more than happy that Sloane's coach told me that I don't have to pay for anything. I only have to bring my skates and my talent. *My talent.* This makes me laugh out loud. I don't think I am that talented. I never had a good coach. I learned everything I could by myself. Before the deal, the coach I had was not the best you could get, but it was the best I could get.

I won some competitions with my partner. Olivia is a good skater, but she could also do much better. It sounds stupid, but I know she is better off without me.

Now I am watching my new partner down there. I heard all kinds of things about her, which hasn't been good.

But she is eager to win, which I am here for. I want to be the best, which might be possible with her by my side. I don't need to be her friend. We just need to win.

She leaves the ice soon after her performance. The atmosphere seems to be tense, and even her coach seems unsatisfied.

I follow the two blondes and the red-haired boy. The ballet room has a glass window to look through.

I might seem like a creep right now, but I watch her. Her movements are confident and strong. She is not struggling the tiniest bit. I can tell she has a good posture, even after her long break. Defined muscles are visible under her tight shirt.

I know that she has been doing this her whole life long already. Her clothing looks expensive, and it might possibly be the newest collection. Her blonde hair is in a ponytail, away from her face.

A storm is brewing in her sapphire-colored eyes. I hope that she will be in a better mood when I meet her for the first time.

We're going to have a hard time. We must get used to each other and find a way to trust each other.

I don't trust her, even though I don't know her.

I was so deep in my thoughts that I didn't even notice how the door opened. Her coach Irina steps outside. Sloane storms out next, and her blue eyes meet mine. Her facial expression is ice cold, even when she sees me. She doesn't say anything. Instead of that, she keeps walking past me.

Before anyone else leaves the room, I quickly turn around and go.

I have seen enough for today anyway.

5
SLOANE

I couldn't sleep at all. All I could think about was my new partner. I don't know who it is going to be. Not even Flynn knows who it is, and he is the one who has a better relationship with Irina. He is the chatty one of us, and he mostly knows everything.

I am tense when I put on my skates the following morning. Flynn is already encouraging me.

„Can you please just put on a good song and stop talking? It makes me nervous, and I just want to calm down for a second" I stop him before he can say even more.

I don't think I can listen to much more. Flynn nods,

„Sorry, I am just so excited."

He follows my wish and puts on a song. No one is here so far. We're alone, and I think today will be a closed training session for the professional skaters.

As soon as the music starts, I step onto the ice and start skating. I do whatever I feel like. I do whatever the music tells me to.

For at least a minute, I feel free and happy. All the weight gets lifted for just a couple of seconds. Everything around me is a blur. There is just the ice and me.

I don't even notice that we're not alone anymore. I soak in any minute I get alone on the ice right now.

I am not ready to meet my new partner. I am not prepared to see him. It means that I have to train every second with him together.

I know that I am not going to like him. I don't know who he is, but I know I won't like him.

And as I stop and turn around to see Irina, I know that I won't like my new partner.

Next to her is no one other than Asher Williams. Everyone knows him in this small town. Every girl wished for him as their partner, not because of his skating skills but because they hoped to get laid.

Even I agree that he might be the hottest skater in this little town. I don't know if he is a good skater, though. I have never seen him skate before, but I know his looks are why I hate him. It's one of the reasons.

There are no pretty privileges when it comes to competitions. Asher's look won't get us anywhere. That everyone wants to have him will make it a lot harder. I know how everyone is looking at him. I know how much he likes the attention.

I groan out loud as I slowly skate closer to them. God, I hate today already.

„Sloane, this is your new partner, Asher," Irina greets me, this time with a smile. It was so unusual to see her smile on a training day. She wants to make a good impression on the new team member.

„Asher, this is your partner Sloane. I am sure you will make a great team," she tells him, and Flynn is holding up his thumbs. It seems like he is pretty happy with the constellation.

„I want to see you skate," I say without greeting him.

We don't have to build a relationship here. This is only professional, and who knows, maybe it doesn't work between us, and Asher won't stay anyway.

He nods, slowly stepping onto the ice next to me. He doesn't waste time and starts right away. As if he waited for me to say this. I watch him as he skates. It is the first time I have seen him on the ice, and I am surprised that I haven't noticed him before.

I never noticed him and his former partner. I am sure that he was there quite often. We share training sessions with other skaters, and I bet I shared quite a few with him.

He is good, better than anyone else here, I guess. His movements are smooth and confident. He knows what he is doing and is not shy to show off.

I like his techniques. They are similar to mine. For a second, I think that this really might work. I shake off this thought quickly because I don't want this to work. I want Flynn and no one else. Especially not Asher.

„Good enough," I reply as he comes back.

„I know, no one is as good as you. I get it, princess," he replies, slightly annoyed. I am surprised by his words.

He doesn't even know me. He just thinks what everyone else here thinks, that I am the wealthy princess. My parents are paying for everything, supporting everything that I want to do. My life is so easy and perfect. I never have to worry about anything. No one really knows me, but at least they can talk about me behind my back. Sometimes I wish they would see the pressure I'm putting myself under. Maybe they would understand me better if they knew how hard it is for me to have the urge to be absolutely perfect.

„Well, I am sure you'll find a way to work together," Irina sighs. I guess that everyone can feel the tension right now.

The mood is anything but not good. I want to go home. It is the first time in my entire life that I hate being here.

„For now, I want you to skate together. Nothing special, no lifting," Irina starts. She grabs her iPad and shows us a video.

She shows us an easy choreography, including one jump and two spins. It's the easiest thing that we could do. We have to be synchronic. Everything has to be smooth and at the same time.

With the right partner, a choreography like this looks outstanding. But it's one of the hardest things to do. Some of the best can't skate synchronic.

We watched the video as often as we wanted, and then for the first time, I was standing in front of Asher in the middle of the ice. We have to skate together now.

He holds out his hand for me, and I take it. I try to remember what to do now.

I have watched the video intensely, and I remember every single step.

He nods as a starting sign, and I nod back, signaling Asher that I understand. He seems to get that because we both start skating. He is the first, and I follow right in.

Isn't it quite impressive that we just communicated without using words? I could use this as a good sign, but it is something I overlooked quickly because I definitely don't want this to work.

We are still holding hands, gaining some speed as we skate. I let go of him. We're skating solo yet still as a team. While I try to remember the video, I go into my first spin.

I try to always have an eye on Asher. We have to be synchro. I don't know what it might look like, but it seems like the best we can offer.

From the corner of my eye, I can see that Asher is also moving into the spin. The spin starts slowly, getting faster as we pull our arms closer to our bodies. We exit the first spin, putting our right foot harder into the ice while lifting the left one up. We skated backward with our right arm in front of us and left to the side.

The choreography is filled with easy movements. From backward now to forward, into small jumps. We're doing another spin, and then we're gaining speed. The axel is the most challenging jump we're trying in this choreography. I don't know if Asher actually knows how to land an axel.

If he can't, he has to learn it quickly. Flynn and I included triple axel jumps into our performances, knowing it would improve our ranking.

Landing the jump perfectly makes me feel better. I see that Asher is still skating beside me. It is at least not completely hopeless.

Our performance is finished with a side-by-side spin.

We both come to a stop, immediately looking over at Irina. I see how Flynn whispers something into her ear, and she nods eagerly.

„Not that bad. I knew you two might work well together!" She smiles proudly.

I hear Asher exhale, and as I look at him, he seems slightly relaxed. Irina loves him, which means that we're now indeed a team. I watch him as he gets off the ice first. His toffee-colored hair is a mess from our skating performance. His green eyes are sparkling, and his chest moves quickly as he tries to catch his breath.

He has an athletic shape, not too muscular. Like most skaters, he is tall, with broad shoulders and a muscular body. His waist is slim, and his legs are long.

I stand right next to him now. Irina is now explaining her plans to us. She wanted to see us skate today. Irina wants to know what she is working with from now on. So we have to do it over and over again.

The closest thing we have to do is hold hands to get a feeling for each other.

She wants to give us time to get to know each other and build trust. Today we're only doing the easy stuff. Easy spins, single jumps, and no lifting.

Tomorrow we're going to meet again. We'll see each other without the skates, off-ice training.

After tomorrow we have some time off. We can use that time however we like, even if Irina told us we better spend that time together.

There is no way I will spend my free time with him. I don't want to build up a personal relationship with him. It's enough to see him here.

Next week we're going to start with lifting. It's what I am most afraid of. Getting lifted by someone you don't really trust is a stupid thing to do.

I don't know how this is supposed to work. I can't imagine being in a team with Asher, and I can feel he doesn't like me. He is not really talking to me. He doesn't want to get to know me either.

Irina is ending our training session today, and as soon as she tells us we're done, I am leaving. I say goodbye to her and look at Flynn. I don't want to talk to Asher, and this is why I am leaving without saying anything to him.

„You both are fantastic together!" Flynn says with a broad smile. He has a lot to say about Asher, only positive things.

„I don't like him," I finally say aloud as we hop into my car. „This is so not going to work out."

„What, why? He is fantastic! You both are perfect together. I have never seen this, the way you move, and you both had been totally synchronized today, and this was your first time together! And you have to say that he looks soo good!" Flynn can't stop talking.

He is so excited now, and I wish I could share this feeling.

„Careful, or your boyfriend will be jealous." I sigh and start the engine.

„Ugh, you could at least be happy that you have a good partner. He is your best chance to win every upcoming competition."

„I know, I know. I just hope that it'll work. Maybe he gets sick of it or falls in love with someone and wants to skate with her. He indeed finds a reason to ditch me" I shrug my shoulders.

Maybe another good offer has him running away.

6

SLOANE

God, it drives me crazy. More than five girls sent me a message because of my new partner. They asked me if I liked him and what he was like. They saw us skating together today, and they wanted to let me know that they wish they could skate with him.

I absolutely hate this. Maybe Asher is leaving anyway. Perhaps he doesn't really want to skate with me.

It at least seems like he is spending his money on other things. His skates are old and worn out. He could really use a new pair and some new training clothes.

Flynn loves him, of course. Everyone loves Asher, even Irina. But nobody really knows him. He is an asshole, in my opinion. He wasn't talking to me, he wasn't talking to anyone, and his face was saying enough already.

It looked like he didn't want to be there.

This night I couldn't find any sleep. How am I supposed to win any competition if we hate each other? I think at least that we hate each other. It indeed feels like it. Why am I so confused about my feelings?

I don't know how this is going to work. We have to trust each other and somehow build up a relationship.

Right now, I am not even happy thinking about training with him. I wish it still would be Flynn. It's hard for me to accept that I won't ever skate with him again.

I don't want to see anyone else besides me. Especially not Asher. I am mad at him for several reasons.

I look at him as he enters the training room this morning. I am early as usual, and I have already started stretching. I pray that Irina is coming too now. I don't want to be alone with him.

Flynn would make this a lot easier, but he has other things to do today, which leaves Asher and me alone.

I turn away from him, my back toward him. I don't want to talk, so I will make this as clear as possible to him.

He doesn't say anything as well. It makes me even more furious. Before I can even think about saying something to him, Irina enters the room and greets us.

Today is going to be easy. We're not doing much. We don't even have to touch or look at each other. Irina tries to keep up a conversation. She wants us to talk about our private lives.

„What are you doing in your free time?" She asks Asher first. I look to the ground while I wait for his reply.

„I'm here skating," he replies.

I know this is not true. Even I have other hobbies, and I am always here.

„And you, Sloane?" Irina looks at me. It seems like Asher his answer is enough for her. Not for me. He is hiding something.

„I run," I reply as shortly as possible.

„Okay…" Irina sighs, turning back to Asher. „Since when do you skate?" She asks him slowly.

„Since I am eight. I had to learn everything by myself, which took a while, and then when I was fifteen, I had my first coach," he explains in a short sentence.

This is the first sentence I heard from him. His deep voice is cold and uninterested. It bothers me that he doesn't seem to care at all.

„And you, Slo?"

„Can't remember. Since I am a baby, maybe," I shrug my shoulders.

„She and Flynn started together. I started coaching them when they were thirteen," Irina replies.

I don't want him to know anything about me. I don't want her to talk about Flynn.

„Okay, guys, you need to speak to each other. I want you to be ready for the next competition in three weeks." Irina her voice shifts. It changes into a more tensed tone. I know that this situation is bothering her. Neither of us is behaving maturely.

„In three weeks? We have to start with the lifts and everything, and then we have to learn a choreography. How should this work?" I ask her as I relax and stand up straight again.

„You would have never asked that question before you took your break. Make it work, girl. It's all on you two."

I don't reply, and he doesn't either. We both know that it is going to be a challenge. I know it is not going to work. It's not going to be an excellent start to this season. There is no way that we will win the next competition.

No one is saying anything optimistic, nothing encouraging. Asher is not saying a single word.

This is not going to work.

7

SLOANE

I am more than happy that we have the weekend off. I don't have to train with Asher. But I am still at the rink. I want to skate on my own this weekend.

I want to clear my head, which works best on the ice. Flynn had been there a couple of times. He thinks I am overdramatic and that Asher and I will work things out.

I was here the whole weekend and haven't seen Asher once. He wasn't here. So it seems like there is another hobby. Something that is not related to skating.

I thought that he might take his chance and train every minute. But he wasn't here. I look at Flynn as I take off my skates this morning. I skated a couple of rounds to warm up and eliminate the tension.

„I don't understand what Irina is seeing in him. He obviously doesn't take this seriously" I huff and look at my best friend.

Today we're starting with lifting elements, and this makes me nervous. I don't want to work with someone who doesn't take this seriously. Asher has something else on his mind, and it seems he doesn't care about anything related to figure skating.

„He is a good skater. Who knows, maybe he had family business," Flynn shrugs his shoulders.

„We have to make this work, and he doesn't care. I noticed it the last time. He is not talking to anyone and seems so uninterested," I tell my best friend.

„You never judged someone so quickly. Why can't you just get to know Asher and see how good he is! You both have a massive chance of winning. You know well enough that you wouldn't have this chance with anyone else."

I know that Flynn is right. I wouldn't have the chance of winning with someone else. He is a good skater, his technique is similar to mine, which might make us a perfect team.

But it seems like we're not working on an emotional basis. I can't get warm with Asher. He is not talking to anyone, and I sure don't want to talk to him.

„Try to get to know him better. Maybe he isn't that bad after all," Flynn smiles at me, and I shake my head.

„Irina gave him a huge chance. It's his time to make the first step here," I reply to him.

„You are so damn stubborn. It doesn't matter who starts talking," my friend replies, and I roll my eyes at him.

I hate that he is trying his best right now. I hate that he doesn't hate Asher as much as I do. I hate that Asher is here because Flynn can't skate anymore.

I don't say anything else. I am afraid that I am going to say something wrong. I don't want to hurt Flynn's feelings, and I don't want to ruin this day.

I grab my stuff and walk straight into today's training room. Irina is already waiting for us. Asher is not here.

I sit down for a moment, catching my breath from skating. My heart is racing, possibly because I am nervous. I have never been scared to do lifting elements, but I never had issues trusting my partner.

„Are you ready? Have you spent the weekend with Asher?" Irina asks me. She told us to spend some time together.

„No, I haven't seen him since our training session on Thursday," I shrug my shoulders.

Right now, it even seems like he is late. There is one thing that Irina hates, it's when someone is late. She hates it when someone is not taking things seriously.

I have been late once. I never made this mistake again. But I am also a person who takes this really seriously, and Irina knows that.

„Where is Asher?“ My coach asks me, and I shrug my shoulders once again.

„I don't know. But it seems like he is late,“ I reply, and at that moment, he storms into the room.

He is out of breath, possibly because he ran here. His toffee-colored hair is a mess. He looks around.

„I am so sorry. I'll never be late again,“ Asher quickly apologizes. Irina just nods and gestures to him to get ready.

She doesn't say anything. *She doesn't yell at Asher.* I look at her, more shocked than anything.

Before I can say something, she starts to explain today's plan. Basically, we're just trying some lifts. Luckily none on ice. I don't want to break a bone.

We start with some stretching, and then we just stand in front of each other.

„A simple lift. Nothing else,“ Irina gestures to Asher to lift me. He should just lift me above his head. It's the easiest thing we can do.

My heart is racing, and Asher is barely looking at me. I can feel his hands on my hips. He hesitates, unsure if this is the right thing to do. Well, he surely knows how to lift his partner. I am not his first one. Yet, he seems nervous, and his movements are too slow.

On the first try, he struggles to lift me. Maybe I jumped too early or too late. We try again.

I was nearly above his head when he dropped me again the second time. He puts me back onto the ground, and I appreciate that he doesn't just let me fall down.

„Again,“ Irina instructs, and we nod.

We take our position, and he tries to lift me up.

This time it works, but it is wobbly and unsafe. We can't do that on the ice. Asher is shaking, and I am back on the ground just a second later.

I stumbled backward, surprised to feel the solid ground underneath my feet. I wasn't prepared to be back down. That's why I look at Asher. He can't hold the position for long enough.

„Try again," Irina instructs, but I shake my head.

„He is going to drop me. I don't want to break a bone just because someone is not taking it seriously," I huff and shake my head.

„I do take this seriously. You are too tense!" He replies quickly, and I shake my head.

„I try to make this work. I try my best. I have been here all weekend to train and free my head. You haven't been here! You don't care, and you have tons of better stuff to do!" I yell a bit too loud.

„You don't know me. You have no idea why I wasn't here this weekend. But it seems like you are pretty good at judging me, " he replies calmly.

„I don't trust you. You'll let me fall, and I don't want to get hurt. I need to win a competition in three weeks" I sigh and cross my arms in front of my chest.

„Okay, let's take a break," Irina sighs as she throws her arms up.

I know that she is going to make us do it again. We can't win anything without the lifts. But I don't trust Asher.

I don't see how I can ever trust him. I leave the room angrier than ever. I need some cold water.

I storm off toward the vending machine to get some cold water. Luckily it's far away from the training room and in the tiniest corner of the hall. No one is here, so I have a minute for myself.

I take a deep breath and put the coins into the machine, waiting for my water.

„I would never let you fall," Asher appears behind me. His voice is tearing me away from my thoughts, and I turn around quickly.

„God, I can't even have a minute for myself."

„I would never let you fall," he repeats, ignoring my comment.

„I don't believe you. You nearly dropped me in there!"

„I didn't. I would never let you fall or hurt you. You can trust me, especially when it comes to skating," with that, he turns around and walks back.

8
SLOANE

I begged Irina to not try any more lifts. She is angry at me, but she follows my wish. She can't force me to do it. I told her I didn't trust Asher and that we couldn't do it.

We're going into this competition without any lifts. Every beginner can at least perform one lifting element.

„Okay, again!" Irina yells.

We're now practicing our choreography for the competition. Actually, we're at the very beginning of learning it. I have a hard time remembering the steps today. I don't know what is going on with me lately, but I am not on point anymore. I am not concentrating enough.

Flynn and his boyfriend Gregg are sitting behind Irina. They're watching us and cheer every now and then.

I wish there would be an actual reason to cheer. But there isn't. I am terrible, and everyone can see it. I have never been that terrible before. Not in the slightest.

„Take a deep breath and try to relax. You're too tense," Asher whispers as we're back in the middle of the ice.

I roll my eyes at him. „I know."

There is nothing that can make me feel better right now. The music starts again, and we start skating.

I hope we at least are through half of the choreography by the end of the day.

We can't win this competition, but I will try for the best rating possible. I think there is way too much between us, and we should not attend the competition.

Irina is sure that we can do it. She is a good coach, and I trust her. But this time, I think that Irina might overdo herself with this decision. She has way too much trust in us. We hate each other and can't even pretend to like each other or be a team in front of others. The judges are going to hate us, surely.

I am more than disappointed with everything. I want to win so badly. I want to keep going where I stopped.

Flynn was the best partner I could get. He was the best for me, and we had been the best team possible. We could have been at the Olympics one day. Now, it's all gone.

He can't skate at all anymore. Now he sets all his trust on me, and I know that he wants me to win so badly. Instead of that, I am just a massive disappointment to him.

The song is over, and I storm off. I need to leave the ice. I need a second for myself.

„Sloane!" I hear Flynn yell, but I don't stop. I storm right into the girls changing room. At least no one can follow me here. No Flynn and no Asher. I can be by myself for a second.

I went straight to the sink to splash some cold water into my face. I am so close to crying that it takes me everything to control myself.

„You're so damn stubborn," someone says behind me, and I turn around. Irina is standing at the door, leaning against the frame as she looks at me.

„I know it is hard to lose a partner. I went through it myself. But I have never met someone like you." She shakes her head with a huff.

„You have to open up toward something new. Otherwise, you're going to tear yourself down. We're getting straight kicked out if you're skating like this at the competition," she continues, and I turn back to the cold water.

„Not everything is my fault," I reply. I know that it is partly my fault. I could do better if I wanted to. But this is also on Asher.

„I never said that. But you're the one I know best. I don't know Asher much, and we all have difficulty getting to know him. You both have way too many preconceptions. You don't even try to get to know each other."

„I just want Flynn back," I whisper and let my shoulders sack. I don't want anyone else. I just want Flynn.

„That's not going to happen, Sloane. He is going to risk his life if he is skating again."

I nod. I know that, and I don't want him to skate again. I want him to be safe and as healthy as possible. But I can't imagine being with someone else. I hate it, actually.

„Please just try your best," my coach says, and I nod.

She turns around and leaves the changing room. Irina isn't an emotional person. She isn't here to hug me or be soft to me. I know that she is strict and focused on the goal. I always loved that. I hated it when people had a soft spot, but I want her to be different now.

I wish she would have a soft spot for me now. I wish she would take it easier on me. The pressure is growing each day, and it feels like I can't take it anymore. I want to be the best, but I know I can't.

9

ASHER

The competition comes closer. We practice every day, trying our best to make this performance work. Even our costumes are done by now. It might be too early for us to be part of the competition.

We are struggling too much to win anything. Sloane doesn't trust me, and she doesn't want me to lift her. We have a choreography without any lifts. We surely won't get many points.

Everyone can see how much we dislike each other. We can't even pretend in front of others. It's stiff and forced. I can see how disappointed Irina is. Maybe she is going to kick me out after this competition.

Sloane doesn't want me as her partner anyway. I am here because this is my dream. I am only doing this for myself. If this would only benefit her, I would already be gone.

It's hard to work with her. We're not saying a single word to each other. She is so distant that I blame her if we're not winning this competition. I try everything because I really want this, and she is not even trying to give her best.

„I can't send you into the competition like that!" Irina yells. She is angry with us, which I can totally understand.

She wants us to do better and give our best, which we are most definitely not. She wants us to act mature, which is also not happening.

Sloane looks at her and nods. She doesn't answer. I don't know what to say because I am already trying my best.

„It's an embarrassment after all this time, Sloane. People might think you lost your talent during your break!" She continues, and Sloane looks down to her feet.

„I don't care what other people think," she whispers, but everyone here knows this is false. She does care a lot about other people's opinions.

„I'll let you go to this competition because maybe you'll learn your lesson. Maybe after this, you'll try harder," Irina tells Sloane.

She raises her head to look at her coach. I can see the anger inside of her. I can see how her facial expression changes.

„Not everything is my fault!"

„I'm not saying that. You both could do better! You both are so damn stubborn, and you could be a great team if you want to, but neither of you is trying hard enough," she sighs and shakes her head.

„You know what? We're done for today. I can't watch this anymore. I'll see you two tomorrow for the last rehearsal," Irina turns around and leaves.

She just gave up on us. She is not trying anymore. She just accepted the fact that this won't work.

I look at Sloane, who is already looking at me. Her sapphire-colored eyes are blown wide in anger. „This is all your fault!" She yells.

„My fault?! I try my best while you're the one who doesn't want to get lifted. You're the one who isn't trying hard enough," I yell back. She can't put this on me. This indeed isn't on me. I try as hard as I can, and it isn't working.

„Yeah, because I can't trust you! We both know that this here is not your first priority!" She yells back.

This here is my first priority. Sloane just doesn't know the truth about my life. There are a couple of things that I won't tell her. She just can't find out the truth.

She is a little miss perfect. Her life is uncomplicated. She has wealthy parents who are also caring a lot about her. She doesn't have to worry about how to afford everything. She is talented and beautiful.

I am not going to tell her about my damn pathetic problems.

„Yeah, sure, go there again! Tell everyone that I am just doing this to get laid. You know what, maybe it's the truth. At least I get laid, after all, something you should try too," I yell at her. I am so fucking angry right now that I don't even care what I say.

„Maybe, you'll relax and pull that stick out of your ass."

She gasped after I said it. She looks at me in total shock for a moment, but she catches herself quickly. With another look at me, she turns around and walks away.

Now I really fucked up. I shouldn't have said this, and I made things even worse. There is no way that we're winning this competition. We're lucky if we're not getting kicked out.

Flynn and his boyfriend are looking at me, totally shocked. I don't say anything to them and turn around to walk away.

God, if she only knew what was going on in my life. She would hate me even more. I can't tell her.

10

SLOANE

I hate him. I hate him. I hate him. God, I don't want to skate with him anymore.

The only reason why I am still skating with him is that he is so freaking good at it. He is talented, and he is my only chance of winning anything.

But god, he is an asshole. After our last conversation, I am sure we won't win anything ever!

I want to get rid of him. I wish Irina would tell me that I have got a new partner. Someone, I might like more.

Today is our last rehearsal before the competition tomorrow. And now I hate Asher even more. This is going to be a disaster!

Everyone is going to be so disappointed after the competition. What do my parents think about me? I am sure they know that I could do better. Flynn… I don't want to know what he might think about me.

He can't skate anymore, and I am not even trying my best. I am going to lose. I will lose points and start worse than ever in this season.

My heart pounds heavily as I think about everyone's disappointment. It feels like I can't carry this weight anymore.

I want to be the best. I need to be the best. I need to show everyone that I can do this. I want to show everyone that I can do this full-time and professionally. Even though I am not really acting professionally right now.

Irina isn't in a good mood today. I can tell it as soon as she comes closer. She is possibly still pissed at us and doesn't even know what happened after she left.

I look at her carefully. I am kind of scared that she is going to kill me. She has been my coach for a long while, and she has never seen me like this. She never thought I would take a break either, and I did.

The break might have been the most idiotic thing I have ever done. Maybe I could be a solo skater by now. Even though I don't want to be a solo skater. Pair skating is something so beautiful and unique. I would never want to give it up, even though it seems the easier solution right now.

„I want you to pretend that this today is the competition. So you better get your best acting skill and put a damn smile on your face," Irina tells us as soon as Asher joins us.

I don't look at him. I don't want to see him at all. But yet, I smile at Irina and nod.

I try to give my best today, which means we have to pretend to like each other.

Asher is smiling, and we turn around to step onto the ice. I grab his hand as we're skating to the middle together. God, I hate this.

We look at each other with huge fake smiles as we wait for the music to start. I bet Irina loves teasing us as she takes her time to put the song on.

We really do pretend that this is the competition right now. The choreography is on point and absolutely perfect, and we smile at each other until the very end. The smiling part is the hardest thing about this. Not even the triple axel jump comes close to it.

As soon as we leave the ice, the smile fades. God, I am so happy when tomorrow is finally over. Maybe we get kicked out of this season because we're not good enough. I bet everyone can do lifting elements and perfect little spins.

Asher and I don't even have good chemistry. Everyone says we do, but everyone can also see that we dislike each other. I am sure this will be the most terrible performance of the day.

„It wasn't that bad. But please don't forget to smile the whole day tomorrow. The cameras and judges are everywhere. The correct presentation is the most important thing, just in case you forgot" Irina smiles at us.

„Yeah, we're going to be the perfect fake skating couple tomorrow," I promise her, and I don't want to disappoint her this time.

We need to make a good impression, this is about our future, and I hope that Asher takes it seriously. I have my doubts. I still think that figure skating is not his first priority, especially after yesterday.

It might have been a joke, but I think there is a little truth in this. Asher enjoys the attention. I know that he loves having so many girls at his feet.

„It's gonna be okay! You always did well," Flynn encourages me. I roll my eyes before I look at him. His optimistic side has been bothering me lately.

„No, it's not going to be okay. I have to spend the whole day with Asher." I reply and roll my eyes again.

We have to be together tomorrow, we're a team, and we have to present ourselves this way.

„It won't be that bad. Maybe you get to know each other better," Flynn smiles widely.

„Yeah, I hope not. I don't want to get to know Asher any better. I am looking forward to the day I never have to see him again," I tell him and stand up.

Why does he always see everything so positive? He had this terrible accident. Shouldn't he be sad and frustrated? I would possibly kill everyone around me and be in the worst mood forever.

As soon as we were done on the ice, I went home. I can't stay there any longer. Also, I am getting more nervous about the upcoming competition tomorrow. It's getting unbearable right now.

I know that we won't win, and it makes me frustrated. I am angry at myself and angry at the world. I wouldn't worry about anything with Flynn at my side.

11

ASHER

It's my first competition with Sloane, and I can't be more nervous. We met early this morning at the rink. Luckily, the competition will be in our hometown, so we don't have to travel.

It is the start of this year's season. Hopefully, we won't get kicked out by the end of the day. The most important thing is that we're in the ranking after all. There isn't a big chance for us to reach a higher place, so we must try our best.

Sloane isn't in an excellent mood. She is grumpy, and she still doesn't talk to me. It makes things easier because I don't want to talk to her.

We're walking inside together with massive smiles on our faces. Today we have to stay together and show everyone that we're the new perfect team. I guess that everyone is going to miss Flynn by her side. I know that they both were everyone's favorite.

I might also see Olivia here if she has a new partner by now. I feel sorry that I left her so quickly, without warning. I kind of really liked her. Now that I know what Sloane is like, I miss her even more.

We're walking around at first, pressing ourselves through the crowd of people. We have to find Irina. She will tell us when it's our turn to go onto the ice.

Right now, we're still in our tracksuits, hiding our costumes. I gelled my hair back, hoping it'll stay that way during our performance. Sloane already did her hair and make-up.

I carefully look at her, hoping that she won't notice it. Her blue eyes are even brighter with the eyeshadow that she used on her eyes. Her skin is glowing.

Her blonde hair is styled in a lower bun. I have to admit that she looks gorgeous like this. So flawless and perfect. If she now would look less tensed, it would be even more perfect.

I am nervous about our upcoming performance. I wish we would have done a bit better during the rehearsal.

It takes us a while to find Irina. She is currently talking to another trainer. Even though she is angry, she introduces us with the most extensive and proudest smile. I feel so bad about letting her down.

We're smiling, trying to put on the most significant act of our lives. Is that how my life is going to be from now on? A huge show just to do what I love? I can't even enjoy it that much with Sloane.

I thought it would be easier, I thought the pretending would be easier, but somehow I disliked skating with her most of the time.

„You're the third couple on the ice!" Irina tells us, and with that, she pushes us toward the skater's gallery. We have a perfect view of the ice, seeing the others skate.

But before we reach our seats, someone stops us.

„We wanted to wish you luck with your performance, sweetheart! We're very proud of you."

It must be Sloane, her parents. They hug each other before they actually look at me.

„You must be Asher. It's so lovely to finally meet you! Irina told us so much about you," her mother smiles at me.

Sloane looks exactly like her mother. Even though her mother looks a lot kinder than her.

„I am sure you both are a fantastic team! We're so excited to see you both," she continues, and they both squeeze my hand with a huge smile.

I feel uncomfortable. Do they know what really is going on between us? Is it just an act because we're surrounded by tons of people?

I can imagine that Sloane is actually talking honestly to her parents. Maybe she told them how much she hates me.

They smile at us one last time and then disappear into the crowd. Sloane and I sit in the skater's gallery, facing the ice. It takes a moment to realize that everyone she loves is here. Flynn and his boyfriend already talked to us. Her parents are also here, and I don't know if she has more family supporting her.

„Do they come to every competition?" I ask her slowly.

„Of course. I hate that they will witness this," she sighs, and I nod slowly.

„Where are your parents?" She asks after a while. I wish she would have never asked. This is a topic I don't want to discuss, especially not with her.

„Not here... obviously," I reply with a huff. She rolls her eyes at me, slightly annoyed by my behavior.

„Yeah, I can tell. But why?"

„What do you care?" I reply in the hope that she is going to drop it. And she does, she sighs, and I can tell that she is getting even more annoyed with every second.

„Right, I don't care," she replies and turns away from me. I hate that I am doing this. I could explain everything to her, but she hates me even more. I just know it. I know how people look at me after they find out the truth. I saw it way too often and don't want this to happen anymore.

So it is way better to let the silence sit between us. We're watching the first couple as they start their performance right now. They are actually already good. We don't have the slightest chance against anyone.

My heart is racing, and I know that Sloane is not feeling better than me. We're both scared and nervous. The only thing that matters now is to stay in the skating season.

As soon as the second couple is announced, we're standing up to get ready. We get rid of our tracksuits and show off our costumes.

It's nothing special for the first competition, nothing that catches everyone's eyes.

Usually, I would be more than happy right now. I would be excited about this competition. I have always loved competitions. I loved the thrill that comes with it. But today is nothing like it. I am scared and nervous.

I have a weird feeling inside of my stomach area, and I just pray and hope that we're still in the ranking.

I look at Sloane as we wait for our turn to get onto the ice. She wears a navy blue costume with silver pearls stitched onto the material. For a moment, I can't tear my eyes from her.

Please welcome our next pair, Miss Sloane Griffin and Mister Asher Williams.

We both are smiling as widely as possible. I hold my hand out for Sloane as we skate to the middle of the ice. Now we have to put on the best act. We have to prove to everyone that we can totally do it.

Our choreography is the easiest one. We have the most effortless performance, which is not getting us many points. The judges might expect something different from Sloane.

I saw her performances in the last two seasons; hers have always been the best ones. She is a fantastic skater, and there wasn't a thing that she couldn't do.

We're here, starting from zero with the most effortless performance ever. We even used the easiest spins.

We could save this performance with at least one lift. Sadly we never even practiced the lifts. We can't change anything about our performance right now. We get through it, trying our hardest.

And we do. We try our best with every lutz and every axel jump. Every spin was perfect, and none of the couples had been as synchronized as us.

I can see Sloane's disappointment as we leave the ice together. She excuses herself quickly and walks away, straight into the nearest women's bathroom. No one except me seems to notice, so she is utterly alone there.

It's our own fault that our performance has been like this. We wanted it to be this way, and I don't think anything will change soon.

We dislike each other too much. I don't think we can get over it and act mature enough to be professional.

It should be easier to be professional. We shouldn't have a problem with it because this is our job. But somehow, it is so hard when it comes to Sloane.

I move back to my seat by myself. I wonder if I should check on Sloane for a second, but I decide it is better to just wait for her to return. It takes a while, she misses all the other performances, and I even start to worry about her.

I don't know why she left in the first place. I don't understand why she just ran away. It's her fault that our performance was the worst one.

She comes right back before the results are out. My heart is racing; all that matters now is that we're still in the ranking. We need to reach the next round.

It isn't a huge surprise that we're somewhere between other skaters. We need to get better. We're so close to dropping out.

With that information, we part, everyone is going home, and we're not talking about what happened today. I know that Irina has a lot to say and possibly needs to make some changes. This, on the other hand, is a worry for tomorrow.

12
SLOANE

Pure disappointment keeps me up the whole night. We could have done better. We're lucky to be in the middle of the ranking and not at the bottom.

I hate the fact that I am going to see Asher again today. I wish I would never have to see him again. This is his fault alone. I wouldn't act like this with another skater. I wouldn't have to worry about anything. Somehow skating with Asher is complicated and, for me, impossible.

As I get up and ready for the day, I receive a message from Irina. She tells me that we're going to meet in half an hour. I better be on time. She indeed is mad.

I quickly get ready to get there right away. It's better to be early than on time now. So I put on my training clothes just in case we're starting a new training plan immediately. As soon as I am ready and packed, I leave the house.

My parents didn't talk to me at all yesterday. They know how I feel and that I don't want to talk about it. It's been a while since I had been that low in the ranking, and it makes me feel even more disappointed.

I regret taking the break. Even though it is not my fault, I regret that the accident happened, and I don't want Asher to be my partner. I want another partner, and I might have a better chance.

I am going to say that now. I'll tell Irina everything that has been going on in my head the past few days. Irina has to be on my side. She had been my coach for so long, and I know she has to stick with me. She doesn't know Asher, so it should be easy to kick him out and find someone new.

I have already tried to find the right words inside my head. I don't want to make Irina angry, so I must be careful what to say. She has a huge temper, and I don't have the strength to argue with her.

I look around as I walk inside. The rink is entirely empty. No one is here, possibly because everyone has a day off after the competition.

We always had a day off too. Mainly we celebrated, but this time there was nothing to celebrate. It is the first time that I should really worry about my future.

Asher walks inside next. He doesn't say anything to me. We both sit next to each other in silence, waiting for Irina. God, it's going to be terrible now.

My heart starts racing as we wait for her. I can already hear Irina as she steps closer. Her steps are heavy and angry.

And then she is standing in front of us. She looks at us, her anger clearly visible.

„This is not working. From today on, we're changing things. I hope you two learned a lesson yesterday, as we nearly dropped out," Irina starts yelling, her polish accent even more prominent now.

„Yes, it is not working! I want a new partner. I want to be at my best, which is not working with Asher," I tell her just as I wanted to.

Asher's face drops. He indeed wasn't expecting this from me. Maybe he is scared that Irina is going to kick him out.

„Then make it work with Asher, Sloane. Even if you're not seeing it, he is the best partner for you," Irina replies. She clearly is against my suggestion.

„You make it work, Sloane. I don't care if you like each other or not. This is your job, and it can't be hard to put on a show for the judges. I did this, and many other skaters are doing the same." She yells at us, and I know that she is right.

Not everyone has a good relationship. Some are really putting on a show; you'll just never know. I just can't pretend that easily. I can't skate with Asher.

„I give you two one last chance, and we're doing this my way this time. I don't want to hear you cry or complain. If I'm telling you that we're doing lifts, we're doing it. I don't care if you want to or not," she tells us, and I swallow.

I don't want to get lifted by Asher. I don't want to do this at all, but this time I have to. Giving up means that I'm quitting. And I don't quit. I won't find a better coach, and I won't find a new partner quickly enough. The skating season has already started, and I can't begin again with someone new.

„Our next performance is going to be different. I want you to work harder; if it is not working, we're out of this season. And I won't try again," Irina finishes her speech and looks at us.

All we can do is nod. I am sure that we both understand what this is about now. We have to somehow make this work.

„You're going to spend a lot of time with each other. I don't want any secrets. You are on time whenever I tell you to be here. And the next performance is going to be sexy and full of passion. Understood?"

The both of us nod again. A knot formed in my stomach area. I am going to hate this. Maybe this is the point where I lose all the fun in skating. I once had that passion, and now I am not even looking forward to skating with my partner. I am not looking forward to getting on the ice.

„We start now. Put your skates on," our coach tells us, and we're automatically moving. I get my skates and put them on. Even though I try to take as much time as possible. I don't want to be on the ice today. I am not ready to skate again.

„Asher, you need new skates. Yours are worn and partly broken." She tells him, and he nods. His facial expression is full of worry, and I wonder why he isn't just buying new ones.

When he loves skating as much as he tells us, why isn't he just buying new ones? It should be a priority.

„We start with the lift tomorrow, the next competition is in two weeks. Today you both get a bit closer to each other and get a feeling for each other's bodies. No distance, no space. You better get used to each other's touch," Irina instructs, and I swear she is purely evil right now.

I cringe on the inside at the thought of him touching my skin. It is something totally normal. When you skate with someone, you're automatically getting physically close to each other.

I look at Asher as we're both getting onto the ice. Irina tells us what to do. We start with pair spins, first next to each other. Then a pair sit spin, which forces us to hold each other.

It's weird to be so close to Asher, to feel his hands on my waist. I avoid looking at him. I try not to think about his warm hands touching me. I can even feel his warm touch through my clothes, a shiver running down my back.

We are glued to each other for the whole day. No matter how we're moving on the ice, we have to move together. Our bodies constantly touching, and I am more than glad to finally leave at the end of the day. As always, I won't say goodbye as I leave.

God, I hate Asher.

13

ASHER

Irina is not joking around anymore. We have a tight training schedule for the next fourteen days. Yesterday we started with some standard skating practices on ice.

Today is going to be a challenge. We're trying the lifting elements again. I am not a massive fan of the lifting parts. I know that Sloane isn't trusting me enough anyway.

We're in the same room as the last time, standing in front of each other. Sloane is waiting for something as she looks at me. Her blue eyes pierced right into mine.

I carefully lift my hands to her hips and grab her, just as it should be. It feels weird to lay my hands against her tiny waist.

I struggled to keep her up the last time, even though she was light as a feather. But I would never let her fall. We're trying the same lift again, which is also the easiest.

This time I don't struggle. I hold Sloane up without even shaking once. She isn't heavy, and she has a good balance herself. I concentrate on lifting her and nothing else around us, and after a while, I slowly and carefully let her down.

My heart is racing inside my chest. We have been partners for weeks now, and we got closer in the past two days than ever. Not emotionally, of course.

„I thought we could have dinner together after today?" Irina asks us, and I look at her, confused.

There is a reason why I can't go. I can't tell them I don't have enough money to go out with them. It is ridiculous.

I slowly shake my head.

„I won't accept a no. We're going out later," she tells us. No choice. I see where this is going. This is supposed to be some kind of team bonding thing.

„But for now, let us try different lifting elements," she gestures to us to continue. We do the same position again. I lift her straight up above my head.

It is always easier doing this with the solid ground underneath our feet. After that, we try another one, which gets a bit harder with each lift. We have to move quickly, and we have to concentrate.

We wouldn't have been that bad at the competition if we had started like this from the beginning.

„Are we done?" Sloane asks after I let her down from our last lift. She looks at Irina, but our coach shakes her head.

„We're going out now. Don't get your hopes up to escape, girl," she replies.

I don't want to have dinner with Sloane. I can only imagine what it is like to sit at a table with her. I sigh and grab my stuff. I don't have a choice.

Irina keeps talking the whole time. She starts explaining the plans she has for us. I like that she plans on keeping me and thinks we might have a chance.

I was praying and hoping she wouldn't start asking questions, but she did. As soon as we ordered food at the restaurant, she got to know us better. She tries to get to know me, and she tries to make Sloane talk.

„Your family hasn't been at the competition?" She asks me, and I shake my head.

I can't give her the same reply as I gave to Sloane. She is my coach, and I don't want to hurt her feelings. So I try to stick at least a bit to the truth.

„My mom died, and my dad hates that I skate," I reply slowly.

Irina nods. She notices this is a sensitive topic for me, so she stops talking about it.

I can see how Sloane shoots me a look. She indeed wasn't expecting this. And she sure as hell shouldn't know about it.

Irina turns to Sloane and makes her tell me about her family. I know that she doesn't want to tell me anything. But now I find out a lot about her parents and Flynn. Her parents are both working in a vast company. They always supported Sloane. And they are there at every competition.

Flynn is like a brother to her; they went through everything together. Flynn his most challenging time was when he came out and his accident. Sloane had been by his side the whole time.

I haven't really talked to him so far. I know he is just there for Sloane, and maybe he doesn't like me.

„Do you have a girlfriend?" Irina asks me with a smile on her lips. She tries to be super friendly, hoping we'll tell her even more now. She wants us to talk to each other, but it is not working.

It is quiet at the table, and we only quickly answer the questions.

„No, I don't do girlfriends," I reply and get an eye roll from Sloane. I once had a girlfriend. She never met my parents, my dad is an abusive asshole, and I never wanted to bring anyone close to him. I broke up with her shortly after we got together. I couldn't bear the secret-keeping anymore, plus she kept asking about my family. And I have never had another girlfriend ever since. The situation with my dad got worse, and I never had the time anyway. I tried to concentrate more on skating.

No one is replying to me. It's better if they think that I am an asshole. The truth won't do them any good.

I killed the conversation because Irina is not trying again. Maybe she is just giving up, thinking we should leave it like this.

There is a lot they don't know about me, and I want to keep it that way. My life is not as good as theirs, and I am not as good as they are.

They would hate me even more if they knew me better. Maybe they would even kick me off the team.

„Do you really take this seriously?" Sloane asks me again, and I nod.

„Of course! Skating is everything I have left," I tell her, and she nods slowly.

Part of me thinks that she still doesn't believe me. It doesn't matter what I am saying. She is never going to believe me.

14

SLOANE

I hated the dinner. God, I hate Asher. Something is wrong with him, and it makes me feel odd. But now I have to get through it.

The lifts are scaring me, but by now, he lifts me so confidently that I trust him somehow. I have to. I don't have another choice.

The next day we went onto the ice and tried the lifts. Some are working out well, and others need some more practice. Well, I need to trust him more to actually try these.

It's more dangerous on the ice. We could just slip and fall. It would hurt a lot more than on the solid ground, and I still have the accident in front of my eyes.

But it seems like Irina is actually pretty happy with them so far. Today she wanted to discuss the choreography. She is done creating it, and we need to start learning it as quickly as possible. The competition is not far from now.

This time we need a better rating. We need to climb higher in the ranking. I would never forgive myself if we dropped out. I can't wait another year to make up for this.

The ranking gets shorter with each competition. Only the bests are allowed into the next round.

I am already on my way to the rink as Irina sends me a message. We are going to meet tomorrow. Asher can't come.

Of course, he can't come. As I thought, skating is not his first priority. I am so mad. This is the most important thing in my life, and I can't afford to lose it. His mind seems to be somewhere else.

I don't understand what is going on in his head. Seems like there is something else, something more important for him.

Now that I am already on my way, I decided to skate anyway. I need to get rid of the tension. I need to let it all out.

For a second, I am debating on calling Flynn. Maybe we could talk, and he could help me clear my head. But I don't call him. I want him to have a day at home with his boyfriend. He comes every other training day, and I think he also needs a break.

Everything here must remind him that he can't skate anymore. It must be hard for him. The sad thing is that I don't really know how he feels. He is my best friend, and I am not taking enough care of him.

I only thought about myself, especially after coming back to the ice. I put on my skates as soon as I reached my usual place. I have a look over the ice and quickly grab my phone. I need to talk to Flynn. I feel bad that I apparently am not caring enough about him. I am the worst best friend possible. So I called him and asked him to meet as soon as I was done here.

„Go on and skate. I'll be there in half an hour," Flynn tells me and hangs up.

I didn't want him to come here. Maybe it isn't a good idea. I can't change it now, though. So I did as he told me. I start skating for a while. Every now and then, I check if Flynn is already here.

I don't really know what I am going to say to him. I have to find the right words to apologize to him, and I am not good with my words lately.

Now I concentrate on the sounds of the ice beneath my blades. I always loved the sounds that come with skating. The rink is still pretty empty, and I enjoy being alone here.

But as soon as I see Flynn standing there, I stop my movements and skate toward him. I leave the ice to sit down with him.

It's still quiet here, so we don't have to move to a separate room. I look at Flynn and sigh.

„I am sorry that I am such a terrible friend," I begin.

His brown eyes widen as he looks at me, surprised. „What?"

„I'm a horrible friend, and I am sorry," I repeat, and he shakes his head automatically.

„What are you talking about?"

„Well, I am such a bitch lately, and I should've checked on you more often. I mean, I never asked you how you're doing. You're here so often, and I can imagine it isn't easy for you," I explain and sigh again.

I am scared that he hates me. I should've asked him more often. I am his best friend, and I have only cared about myself lately.

„I'm good. I am happy that you're back on the ice, and I wish you would relax. Asher and you are a good team."

„No, don't lie to me," I whine.

„I am not lying! I miss the ice more than anything, skating and competitions. But I have to live with the fact that I can't do that anymore. But it makes me happy to see you on the ice and see you with a good partner," he tells me and smiles.

I don't understand how he is doing so well. I would be devastated, and he is absolutely fine.

„I feel terrible because I haven't asked you earlier."

„Everything is fine. A lot is going on right now, and I totally understand that."

I nod slowly, hoping that he really isn't mad at me. But he sits here and smiles at me so widely that I know he means every word he says.

„I am going to apply to some colleges. I might move away next year," he tells me after a while, and I look at him, totally shocked. I wasn't expecting this. I need him more than anyone else, which means he can't move away.

It sounds totally selfish, but I can't live without him.

„What? Since when did you decide that?"

„A couple of days ago… I am not sure what I am going to study, though. But I need a plan for my future, and this is a good beginning," he tells me, and I nod.

„I am going to support you no matter what. I am here," I tell him, grabbing his hands.

I'll always help him and be there for him, no matter what he does.

„Thank you, and you don't mess up with Asher."

„I think he is going to mess it up. It's his fault that we're not working today." I sigh and roll my eyes.

We could've come so far today. We don't have much time, and we need to learn the choreography. I am mad that he is not working as hard as me.

„But he is here, " Flynn says as he looks behind me, and I quickly turn around.

There he is. Asher is standing there with his skates in his hand. Seems like he came here to skate, which doesn't make any sense. He told Irina that he couldn't see us today. Anger is rising inside me, and I quickly walk over to him. I am so furious, and I think furious does not describe how I feel most slightly.

„What the fuck is wrong with you?" I yell at him, not caring if everyone can hear me now. Tons of people are turning around to see what is going on.

„What?" Asher looks at me in pure shock.

„Irina canceled today's training, telling me that you don't have the time to meet us, yet you're here! You don't take this seriously. I'm going to lose everything I love because of you, asshole!" I have never been so angry before. It feels like he is proving all of my thoughts right.

He shakes his head and sighs. I don't know why he is still so calm.

„It is not what you think. Skating is my first priority. It always will be, but not everyone has an easy life like you."

„An easy life? You have absolutely no idea what is going on in my life!" I yell at him, and he shakes his head. Now I notice how his anger is rising inside of him.

„Oh, and you know what's going on in mine?" He yells back, and now I am actually quiet for a second. I am surprised that he is yelling back at me, and I absolutely have no idea who he is.

„Yeah, everyone knows why you're here. You said it yourself."

„Oh yeah, I'm working every free day I have left just to get laid. All the hard work is paying off, just to get some lame attention from stupid girls."

He is working? He has another job to afford all of this? Usually, you get paid. The higher the competition, the higher the pay. We haven't won anything before, and it seems like he never actually made enough winning competitions.

Which now means that he can't afford all of this. I am surprised because I never thought about the possibility that he doesn't have enough money.

„You're working?" I ask him, this time a little bit calmer.

„Every second that I am not here, I am working. I needed this day to work, so I can buy new skates," he tells me this time calmer as well.

I bet he doesn't want anyone to know about this, and I totally understand. But I wish I knew that.

Now I don't know how to handle this information. I don't know what to say to Asher.

„I'm sorry," I whisper, and he shakes his head.

„Forget about it," he waves off. Asher turns around quickly and leaves, even though he just came here to skate. I don't stop him. I watch him walk outside and turn back to Flynn.

He looks at me, and I know that we both feel the same uncomfortable feeling right now.

15

ASHER

God, I hate Sloane so much. I hate that she is the way she is. I never wanted to tell her that I didn't have the money to actually skate. I can't afford a new pair of skates.

My dad can't pay our bills. He can't pay them for a long while now. I work as much as I can to get the money together. I buy our food and pay our bills, even though my money is not enough to cover every single one of them. There is not enough left for my skating essentials most of the time. I am far away from buying a new pair of skating shoes. They are hell expensive, and it's money that I don't have. But I know that I can't skate without them.

After my fight with Sloane, it is even harder to come back the next day. I never wanted her to find out what was going on in my life. I bet she is laughing about me on the inside. I am so pathetic. Poor boy doesn't have enough money.

Luckily she doesn't know a single thing about my family. If she knew what was really going on, she would indeed pity me.

As I arrive, I try to avoid her eyes. I don't want to look at her just to find her already looking at me. Irina doesn't say anything. She knows that I was working yesterday. She doesn't know why I have to do it, but she at least knows a little bit. Maybe Sloane had told her everything by now.

I reached my usual spot, and as I wanted to sit down to put on my skates, I saw something on the ground. A brand new pair of my typical black skating shoes. A note is sticking to them, and I picked it up carefully.

For Asher. Nothing more is written on it. This is precisely what should have never happened. I don't need anyone's pity. I don't need to be pitied.

I pick up the shoes and walk over to Sloane. This could only be her idea. She bought them for me. She is the only one who knows about it.

„I don't need your pity," I tell her cooly and hand her back the skates. She looks at me, pretty confused.

For a moment, I thought they were not from her. But maybe she is just confused because I am giving them back.

„What?"

„I don't want your pity. You don't need to buy shoes for me because you feel sorry," I tell her and hand her the skates, still.

She isn't taking them from me and takes a step back.

„They are not from me. I don't know who gave you a new pair, but it wasn't me," she tells me and turns away.

I am sure that it was her. She is the only one who knows about my problem. I wasn't speaking loudly to her. I know that no one else was hearing us yesterday.

I don't walk after her, but I don't put the new shoes on either. I put on my old skates and waited for Irina to show us today's plan.

„I thought about the choreography for a really long time, and I thought we needed to perform something sexy, but I was wrong," Irina starts, and I breathe out.

This gives me hope for a less touchy dance. Maybe we are going to be a bit distant from each other.

„I think that something dramatic is the best. Something tragic…" Irina smiles at us widely, and then she starts explaining what she wants to express with this performance.

It basically contains a lot of holding positions. Drama and romance are a nice mixture, which will be impossible for us. A couple who loves each other deeply but who are not meant to be together, this is how Irina described it to us.

We have to go onto the ice and start learning the choreography. The first figure we have to do is a sitting spin blending in with a lift.

Sloane shakes her head as we start gaining speed for the spin. I softly grab her as we should begin spinning together. We are slowly moving closer to each other. While we're spinning, we're moving down in a sitting position, still holding each other. My hand is moving from holding her to grabbing her leg. I am ready to lift her up, trying to pull her up, but she doesn't move.

I wasn't expecting this and fell backward, sliding over the ice. Sloane is losing balance herself, falling onto her butt. I look at her, pretty frustrated, but I get up without saying anything.

We try it again, and again, and again. Every single time Sloane stops as soon as I try to lift her. She screams out and gets up.

I watch her leaving the ice, walking toward the toilets with her skates still on. God, I can't do this anymore.

I can't skate with her. This is the first time I have thought about giving up. This is not going to work. She doesn't trust me enough to perform something. There is no way to win another competition without a lifting figure. We can't stick to spins only.

„Let me handle this," Flynn says and walks after her. I don't know what to do now, so I just leave the ice and sit down at the side, waiting for Sloane and Flynn to come back.

16
SLOANE

I follow Flynn back outside. I have no idea what he is doing now. He yelled at me for being so stupid. I yelled back at him that he didn't understand what I was going through. As soon as I said it, I felt guilty. I don't know what he is going through either.

He storms out. I follow him only a couple of seconds later. Those seconds are indeed enough for him to put on his skates. He didn't tie them correctly. He just slipped into them.

„What are you doing?" I ask him, scared and confused.

Why is he putting on his skates? What is his plan right now?

„Please stop! You're scaring me!" I yell at him and try to stop him.

But he gets up with his skates on and gets right onto the ice. Everyone looks at him in total shock. Irina tells him to come down from the ice. He could risk his life right now.

It's unusual to see how easily he slides forward on the ice. I can see how relieved he feels, how familiar this feeling must be. My heart is racing so quickly that I start feeling dizzy.

I bet that one round wouldn't hurt him, but it could be dangerous as soon as he tries to jump or spin.

He looks at me as he skates to the middle of the ice. He pretends to do something. I am scared that he will hurt himself.

I can see the accident happening as if it was yesterday. The way he fell after his jump. I can still hear how his head hit the ice.

„That's what you want, right? Get your ass on the ice and skate with me!" He yells at me, and I shake my head.

„I want you to come down from the ice!" I yell back, and he shakes his head. He is insane.

„You have been acting weird for weeks now. Simply because you want to skate with me again. So do it! If you don't want anyone else, come and skate with me" Flynn is angry.

I look at him and still shake my head. I want him to come back here. I am scared for his life, but still, he is skating around on the ice. It seems like he thinks it's all a big joke.

„You don't want anyone else, right?" He asks me again.

He is unfair to me right now. The pressure that he is putting me under is getting too much. I feel helpless, and I hate this feeling more than anything else.

I look at him, my head completely empty. I don't know what to say right now.

„Please come back!" I beg him. Tears are filling my eyes. I don't want to cry in front of everyone. Not because of something so stupid. Flynn is important to me, and I don't want to lose him. I don't want to see how he gets hurt again.

I was there the first time. I saw it and the blood. I saw Flynn lying there, and I didn't want this to happen again.

He looks at me for a while, and then he skates back. I miss him on the ice as much as he misses skating himself. But I can't change the fact that we'll never skate again.

Now I look at him and shake my head. „You asshole scared the shit out of me!" I yelled at him, hitting his chest with my hands.

I hate him for this. I hate him more than anything for this. I can't stop the tears anymore. They roll down my cheeks in hot streams.

„I saw the accident! I saw how everything happened! How could you do this?"

He looks at me with pure shock. I know that he wasn't expecting this reaction. He never thought about the fact that I saw everything. I never talked about the way it made me feel. I never talked about the trauma that came with seeing the accident happening in front of me.

„Slo, I'm sorry! I totally forgot about that," he tells me softly, but I shake my head.

„You have no idea. Everyone acts like I am the bad guy. As if everything is okay for me. It isn't!" And then I turn around and walk away.

I walk as fast as possible with my skates on. I run right into the changing room. I need to change back to my usual shoes.

I don't want to skate anymore. Not today. I need to go home and clear my head. This is not working for me.

17

ASHER

My eyes follow her as she runs away. Flynn really messed up with his idea. Irina yells at him for being so stupid. She had a shock herself. I can see that she really cares about Flynn and that everyone is scared that something will happen.

„I really messed up," he tells me as he removes his skates slowly.

I nod, „I guess."

„I totally forgot that she saw it. I was so caught up in my own thoughts. I wanted her to realize that she is wrong," he continues. He looks at me, and I don't really know what to say for a second.

„I'm sick of trying to fix this. You both don't want to skate with each other, and I think that we can't force you anymore at some point."

He seems to be disappointed about it. It looks like he really cares. I start to feel guilty. This is also my fault. I argue a lot with her, and I am not really open-minded. I don't want to talk to anyone, and I sure don't want to spend time with them.

„I should talk to Sloane, " I say to Flynn and walk toward the changing room. It's time to end this. It's not going to work, we can't even do a simple spin, and I am sick of trying.

I understand that this isn't easy for her, but there isn't a reason to make this even more challenging.

I walk into the girls changing room and look for Sloane. She is sitting on a bench, changing back into her sneakers.

„You don't have to skate with me if you don't want to. I'll tell Irina I quit," I begin and look at her.

She looks up as if she hasn't heard me coming. For a second, she is surprised. Maybe she thought I would come here to fight with her. I want to skate with her because she is the best chance. She is the only good chance I have.

I need the best I can get, but we have to be a team, and she makes it really clear that we'll never be one.

„What? You're giving up?" She looks at me, wiping her tear away.

„It's not giving up. I just can't waste my time. I need to be good and somewhere up in the ranking. I don't have the money or time to waste some years with a partner who doesn't want me," I explain, and she nods slowly.

„Do you think we could make it work?" She asks me slowly. Her questions surprise me. I don't know where this is coming from, but we never actually tried to make this work.

„I don't know. I'm trying, but you don't trust me, and this isn't working without trust," I tell her as I slowly sit down next to her.

„I guess I have to accept that you're the best skater now. I won't get Flynn back, and seeing him on the ice today made me feel so scared," she starts, and I nod slowly.

„I want to be the best again, and you're the only one who is as good as I am. I won't get a good ranking with anyone else. I am stuck with you."

„It won't work if you're forcing it," I tell her slowly, and she nods.

„I'll make it work. We're going to be the best team." Sloane nods, and I am surprised that she really wants to try again.

It wasn't really working the last time, and I don't know what changed within her.

„You sure?"

„Yeah, but I still hate you," she whispers as she looks at me.

„I hate you too, " I tell her and stand back up.

This just had been our first real conversation. Maybe this here is the first step toward a good relationship.

„Put your skates back on. " I tell her before leaving the room we have work to do.

„And you put your new ones on. It doesn't matter who gave you those. You have them now," she tells me, and I nod slowly.

She promised me to try. She wants to make this work. I guess I can put on the new skates and use them.

Even though I am still sure that she gave them to me. I couldn't know that it really wasn't her.

I can't make sense of her. She is a highly complex person. Part of me hates her, and the other doesn't want to hate Sloane. I want to like her, and I can feel a connection between us. I think.

18
SLOANE

No one said anything ever again. I tried as hard as possible to make it work between Asher and me. We have to make this work, and our conversation was the first step.

We went back on the ice. We don't have much time left, so we train every day. I hate the choreography. I hate how my heart jumps whenever I can feel his hands on my body. I hate the feeling I get when he lifts me or when we spin.

This is what I usually love about ice skating. It's the thrill. The feeling in my stomach, the excitement. Even though I don't want to feel all of this with Asher. The song is coming to an end. We're in our final position. His head against my chest. A bizarre feeling, but it's only for the performance.

Irina is clapping her hands together. „I'm so proud. This is a huge step," she smiles at us.

We finally got our shit together, and we can at least pretend for a while to like each other. It might be enough for the competition.

„Watch your facial expression! I want this to be tragic and full of love," she tells us, and we nod.

Our way parts as soon as we have solid ground beneath our feet. We don't talk much, but it somehow works better than before.

Flynn smiles at me, „That was great! You two are a good team," he tells me, and I nod slowly.

We're not a good team. We don't talk to each other. We are only performing, and being in a team with Asher feels like an everlasting performance.

„I wish you could see it from my point of view. You move absolutely perfectly with each other! The judges will love it," he tells me with a smile, and I nod again.

I don't really think we're getting much higher in the ranking. Something is missing, and I can't tell what it is.

„Again, guys, and this time with more passion!" Irina yells at us, and we get back into our starting position.

There is only a week left until we have the next competition, making me slightly nervous.

It's only one week, and there is still so much to do. We need new costumes, and our performance isn't perfect yet.

I don't want to disappoint everyone again. Asher and I start at the same time with the music. We gain speed and start with our pair sitting spin.

We go over the lifting figure.

Asher pulls me up onto his shoulder as he stands up from the spin. We're moving forward again. So far, so perfect. Asher lets me down softly, and we continue with our performance. Jumping triple axel and a lutz, hoping that we land everything perfectly. Like Irina told us to, we're telling a tragic love story. Full of drama and passion.

I think that this time I am fully into this performance. I feel the music, and I feel this choreography. I forget about my hate toward Asher for a couple of seconds.

I actually enjoy it for a while. It's my one and only love. Skating has always been the most essential thing in my life, and here I am, finally enjoying it again.

Every movement is smooth and perfect. It would be absolutely perfect if this is how we skate in front of the judges.

We're in our ending position again. Kneeling on the ground, Asher buries his head in the crook of my neck this time. The both of us were breathless.

We know that this time was perfect. A euphoric feeling is streaming through my veins, and for the first time, I am pleased. We could get a higher ranking and be back in the competition.

It's not a first-place performance. We have to practice and get better as a team, but we're making steps toward our goal.

„Bravo! Bravo!" Irina claps her hands. This makes me realize how long we're already in that position.

My heart skips a beat, and Asher quickly stands up. He holds out his hand for me. I take it with a soft smile on my lips. *Am I really smiling at him?* God, what happens to me?

19
SLOANE

Our first and hopefully last fitting for the next competition is today. I am nervous because Irina has already chosen the outfits. My coach is always quick in making these decisions.

She always tells us that it totally suits our tragic performance.

We get the costumes always in the same store. They sell the most beautiful costumes nearby our small town. I look at Asher, and he shoots me a look.

Irina has been in such a good mood lately that we think something might be wrong. We're not really doing good, but I guess that the progress already makes her very much happy.

Asher looks at me for a moment, but we don't say anything. We're not really the talking kind of people.

But it is the actual first time that I'm looking calmly into his eyes. He has stunning eyes. Green like the deepest forest during summer. His eyes are dark, and somehow I feel even more relaxed looking into them. It calms me like I am standing in the middle of nature.

Irina pulls me out of my thoughts, away from the eye contact we held. She hands me the dress and gestures to try it on.

I have my first look at it. It is a soft lilac dress with spaghetti straps, and it seems to be knee-length.

The material is really soft, and the skirt seems to be really thin. It's simple without glitter or other details. I put this on with my transparent skating tights.

It doesn't look bad, but this may be too simple. Irina really wants to put us out there by keeping the focus on our performance. This is going to be a mistake. We're not that good.

I look at Asher as we both stand in front of the mirror. He is wearing a grey shirt. It looks similar to a button-up dress shirt. I guess that it is made of a more stretchable material, perfectly made for athletes

He eyes me for a moment, but he doesn't say anything. We look at each other in the mirror. It doesn't look bad, but it is really simple.

I wonder what is going on in Irina's head. We're not strong enough. Our performance is not strong enough. I thought that we would distract the judges with a nice outfit. Something with a lot of glitter and sparkle.

„Perfect!" She smiles at us and claps her hands together.

„You sure?" I ask her, and she nods.

She loves this outfit, and I better not start a fight with her. Everything is perfect right now, and I want it to stay like this. I want everything to be perfect.

Maybe the competition isn't going to be so bad at all.

20

ASHER

I feel good this time. Irina was driving to the neighboring town. It's where the competition is held this time.

We're wearing our tracksuits again, underneath them our costumes. We're both nervous, and we're scared of dropping out. I look at Sloane, and for a second, I smile.

I wouldn't describe us as enemies anymore. Maybe we're more on a professional basis now. It is at least working out most of the time.

We walk inside. It's already crowded.

I first don't know where to go. Luckily Irina is leading the way. She walks ahead, and we follow her like lost puppies.

„Asher?" Someone says behind me, and I stop to turn around. Sloane stops too. It seems like she heard the girl as well.

Olivia is standing there, alone, wearing her tracksuit.

„Hey, Olivia," I greet her, unsure what she might think of me now.

„I thought you wouldn't come here," she tells me with a smile on her lips.

I was always good with her. We weren't the best team, but it was always enough. We were there every season, somewhere in the middle of the ranking.

„Why?" I ask her slowly and confused.

„I heard you two might have quit, especially after the first competition. There is a rumor that Sloane can't deal with loss."

I don't know that side of her. I know her as a nice girl. But now, she is anything but friendly.

I know Sloane as well, and she has a hell of a temper. I quickly look at her. She seems calm for now.

„We haven't lost." She replies slowly.

„Yeah, but it wasn't good either." Olivia shoots back.

„Yeah, but we'll climb up the ranking again, unlike you. You have always been somewhere in the middle, not able to climb any higher," Sloane replies and turns around.

I am not sure if this was also against me. I was Olivia's partner, and we have always been stuck in the middle. It was also my fault.

I look at Olivia. She just rolls her eyes and disappears.

„Thanks," I say as I walk beside Sloane.

„For what?"

„For telling me that I am terrible. Olivia was my partner, and we always were stuck in the middle," I tell her, and she shakes her head.

„No, this is not on you. It's on her. She doesn't have any talent, and her skating skills are terrible. I bet that you're the one who saved it, " Sloane replies and surprises me entirely with it.

I thought she might say something mean to me.

„Don't let it go to your head. I still hate you," she quickly adds.

I chuckle at her words. Why do I think it is funny? Why do I think this is amusing at all? God, she is driving me crazy.

We sit down in the gallery. This time, we're one of the last couples performing. We have to wait for quite a while. The other skaters are good so far. There was only one couple who messed up. She fell, and it took time for her to get back up.

This gives me hope that we might not be the worst performance. We trained a lot, and I know that this will be better than the last time.

We get ready as it's our turn next. We stretch a bit and try to get rid of the nervous feeling.

This can't be that bad. It's going to work out perfectly. It has to be better than the last time.

We could perform this while we're sleeping. It's forever mesmerized in my head.

We wave to the crowd with a massive smile on our lips. We present ourselves pretty good right now, I guess. We get into position and wait for the song to start. My chest heaving up and down nervously. I'm praying on the inside that everything is going to be fine now. We have to just make it through the performance.

The judges have to like it, and no matter how much we despise ourselves, our movements are perfect and smooth. There is nothing to complain about because we indeed have an ideal technique.

We move forward, gaining some speed for the first element. I can feel the wind through my hair.

Then we move into our sitting spin, the first element of our choreography. We look at each other, making sure we're on time. Then I lift Sloane up, sliding forward with her over my shoulder.

I let Sloane down at the right moment, letting her slide backward until she turns around by herself.

Every jump and every spin is nearly perfect.

I bet that everyone can still feel the tension between us, the negativity.

I think that this time it was actually pretty good. We're not the winner of today's competition, but we're at least a bit better than last time.

I look at Sloane as we leave the ice with another wave at the crowd, and she stays with me this time. She isn't running away, which gives me the feeling that she has a good feeling.

Now we have to wait for the results. There are still three couple who needs to perform, and after that, we have to wait a couple of more minutes.

I can't wait to see the ranking this time. At our first competition, we were close to the bottom, and now I hope that we're closer to the top, somewhere in between all the other names.

„I hope we're better than that, Olivia bitch" Sloane sighs as she watches the other couple.

I laugh at her comment. This came out of nowhere.

„She is not that bad, and you don't even know her," I reply. Olivia is a good person. I never had a problem with her. She was always kind, and I know she worked really hard.

„I don't care. I don't like her," Sloane shrugs her shoulders.

I know where all the rumors and assumptions about her are coming from. I understand why so many are avoiding her.

She has a strong personality, and she likes to stay in her own inner circle. Sloane is not open to something new. I know that she isn't someone who goes out often.

I at least have never seen her going out. She is always on the ice or at home.

We're waiting for the announcement as soon as the performances are over. Even though I think we shouldn't get our excitement up. We might be disappointed when we see the results.

We look up as the announcement starts. They start from the bottom to the top. We're definitely higher than before. Our name isn't on the same spot anymore.

We made it. We were ranked much higher than before, but we're not celebrating. Not yet. We look at each other with small smiles.

Now we have to work harder, and maybe the next time, we can climb up this ranking. I want to be at the top with Sloane.

21
SLOANE

„I don't know what we're doing here!" I say as Flynn pulls me into the club. We have only one club in our small town, and it's always crowded.

„We're here to celebrate. You both climbed up the ranking pretty well!" Flynn replies as he pulls me deeper inside.

Asher is somewhere behind me. Flynn thinks that we need to celebrate this minor victory now.

I don't think it counts as a victory. I think that we could actually do so much better.

„Enjoy yourself tonight!" Flynn yells and walks straight toward the bar. He orders a drink for each of us, and I sigh.

„I won't drink that much! We have to start training for the next competition tomorrow," I sigh.

Irina told us that we couldn't afford a break. I won't drink much. This one drink is okay, but that's going to be it.

I can definitely enjoy myself while staying sober. We drown this one drink together, and after that, I move my butt to the dance floor.

I start swaying my hips to the beat. Actually, I really start enjoying myself. Pearls of sweat form on my skin as I move my body to the music.

I won't stop dancing for a while now. Flynn is constantly pushing another cup into my hand. And at some point, I stop caring that it is actually alcohol inside the cup.

I haven't been drunk for a long while, and I think this is one of the reasons why the alcohol is kicking in even more. I stop worrying and caring about everything. I lost my feeling for time.

I am still on the dance floor a couple of drinks later. I can feel a pair of eyes on me as I move my body to the beat. I scan the room and find myself in Asher his eyes.

He is still standing at the bar as he watches me. I don't mind him watching me. Actually, I quite enjoy it.

I bet it is the alcohol rushing through my veins. But I feel a thrill as I stare back into Asher's eyes. I can see how he watches the curves of my body and how they move to the beat of the song. He licks his lips, and his eyes dart back up to mine.

I smile at him. It's a soft and tiny smile. Maybe he will decide to join me. I wouldn't mind if he danced with me.

God, I am so wasted. But this brings me actually closer to my partner. He slowly stands up from his seat, pressing himself through the crowd. As soon as he is behind me, he lays his hands on my hips. We're now moving together to the beat. My ass against his front. And for a while, we dance like this.

I can feel his hands on my body, how they drive up and down my sides. Then they lay back on my hips.

Why am I so drunk right now? I shouldn't do this. I absolutely hate him. But yet, I enjoy this more than I thought I would.

„I'll get us another drink," he yells over the music and disappears with a smile. I keep on dancing, not caring if I get another drink.

It doesn't take long until I feel someone behind me again. But when I turn around, it isn't Asher. A handsome stranger is dancing up against me. I actually don't mind. Maybe this pushes Asher out of my head.

I lay my arms around the stranger and dance with him. It doesn't feel as good as it did with Asher. But it might distract me.

I am still waiting for the distraction because my skating partner is all I can think about. God damn, what's going on with me?

The stranger leans in to kiss me, and I let it happen. I close my eyes and lean forward. But before our lips meet, he gets pulled away from me. I open my eyes in shock and see Asher standing there. He pushed the guy back, and the next second he grabbed my wrists and pulled me toward the exit.

„What do you think you're doing?" He asks me, his green eyes blown wide.

„What do you care?" I spit back and try to free myself from him. I try to avoid his eyes, knowing that they make me feel weak.

„You can't kiss a fucking stranger!" He tells me, and I huff, annoyed.

„And why not?"

„Because you are my fucking partner, mine to kiss, mine to touch," and then he smashes his lips onto mine. It happened suddenly, and for a second, I didn't know what to do. But god, his lips are feeling too good on mine. They are pure and soft. He tastes like the latest drink he drank.

I pull him closer to my body, knowing that I long for more. He groans softly as he pushes me even harder against the wall. This is so wrong, yet it feels so right.

„Let us go home," I breathe against his lips, and he nods slowly. We part, and he quickly points to the next cab. This is where we hop in.

I tell the driver my address and wait to finally arrive at my home. We both know where this is leading us. Asher, his hand is driving up my leg. I can feel him touching my thighs, making me even more nervous and impatient. I want him to touch me. I want him to explore my body like no one ever did before. I am so wasted. This would have never happened if I had stayed sober.

I am not sober in the slightest bit. I smash my lips onto his soft ones as soon as we leave the cab. It's a good thing that my parents are gone for the week. I am thankful my parents are on a business trip for the first time.

I lead Asher inside, right into my room, where I quickly kick off my shoes.

My hands are roaming up and down his chest. I sigh as his lips leave mine. He gently sucks at the skin of my neck. Exploring my soft skin, licking over the spot he just sucked at.

We slowly walk backward until the back of my legs touches my bed. I lean back and lay myself down. The soft mattress against my back.

Asher is still discovering my skin with his lips. He travels down to the swell of my breast, and I sigh. This seems to be enough for him to remove the glitter top I'm wearing.

I wish I had chosen to wear a sexier pair of underwear. But Asher's eyes still widen as he sees my pink laced bra.

„I need to take this off," he breathes out, his hands already sneaking behind my back. I arch my back a bit to give him better access.

„Please," I whine out and wait for him to remove the material from my skin.

As soon as he throws it behind himself, his lips attack my breast. He harshly sucks on my nipple while his hand kneads the other breast. I couldn't hold back the moan that was escaping my lips.

I lift my hips against his hips, begging silently for more. I need more of him. Now. My hands are tucking at the material of his shirt. He is wearing way too many clothes right now.

He sits up for a second, sliding off the shirt. This is the damn first time that I have seen his naked chest, and damn he is beautiful. I bite my lip and reach my hand out to touch his abs.

He leans down again after my hands trail down his beautiful chest. But he doesn't lower above me. He moves down my body. I know his intentions right now, but we don't have time for this. I don't have the patience to let him do this. I stop him, grabbing his arms.

He looks at me, pretty confused, as if I told him to stop completely. But I pull him up to me, kissing his lips hard and demanding. God, I need him.

„I need you, now," I sigh into his mouth.

My heart is racing, and everything is longing for him to be inside me.

He looks at me for a second. His hands already pulling down my pants, along with my underwear. I wiggle my hips impatiently, trying to get rid of the clothes.

Next, I helped him to get rid of his jeans. I don't want to waste any time right now.

„Do you have a condom?" I breathe out as we admire each other completely naked. He quickly nods, leaning down to grab his wallet. He pulls out a condom, and luckily I am too drunk to question why he has one with him in his wallet.

Maybe all the rumors are true? I am thinking about it until I watch how he rolls it on for a second. The sight alone makes me moan out loud. The way he throws his head back as he pulls the condom on. His lips were slightly parted in lust.

This seems to encourage him because he looks up. Fire in his eyes, blown with lust. He pushes me into the mattress and kisses me hard. His lips are on mine, his tongue pushing itself into my mouth. He tastes so damn good. I'll never be able to forget the taste of him.

And then he pushes inside of me with one firm stroke. It happened so suddenly. A loud moan escapes my lips, and I automatically clench around him. God, this feels like heaven. This has to be heaven.

22

ASHER

I wake up as Sloane slowly moves around next to me. I hear her cusses, „Oh my god, no!" She groans.

„No, fucking way." And with that, she jumps out of bed, covering herself up. Even though I have already seen it all.

„Fuck, fuck, fuck!" She yells, and she quickly starts to get dressed. We were really drunk, apparently. God, we drank way too much yesterday. This wasn't supposed to happen. I don't even know how this happened, but I enjoyed every bit.

I can remember everything clearly. The way she screamed my name over and over again. How her nails scratched over my back and how I pounded into her repeatedly. Just thinking back to yesterday night gets me hard again.

„Get dressed! We have to leave! Irina is already waiting for us. I am sure she is pissed! We're too late," she cries out, and I quickly get out of bed.

I totally forgot about Irina and the rink. I forgot about ice skating for a second. We had the competition yesterday, and Flynn dragged us to the club. I told Sloane that she is fucking mine! Why did I do this? God, I don't want to know what she thinks right now.

I hate her. I hate skating with her, and I just need us to climb up the ranking. She is my ticket to the Olympics, nothing more. She is the ticket to my dreams.

I only have my outfit from last night with me. Luckily I still have some extra clothes inside my locker at the rink. I can change there. Irina is indeed already pissed.

„Okay, listen," Sloane turns toward me before she starts driving. I look at her curiously because of her serious tone. „Whatever happened between us was a mistake. We obviously had sex, but it was a mistake, and it can never happen again!" She tells me, and I nod.

„It was a big mistake," I agree, even though I know it felt too good to be a mistake. Sloane thinks the same. I can see it on her face. Well, her moans and screams were unmistakable yesterday night.

I quickly shake my head, trying to get rid of my thoughts. I can't think about her naked body underneath mine. Not now.

Sloane drives as fast as possible, and we run inside with big steps. It doesn't matter anymore. We're too late. Irina is already waiting for us, and she is pissed.

The first thing I do is go into the locker room and change into my training stuff there. I can hear Irina yell through the whole venue. She hates it when someone is late. She understood me the one time because I came here right after my shift at work. But this time, it is something completely different.

When I came back, she calmed down a bit. She is still grumpy, which leaves her telling us that we disappointed her yesterday at the competition. We weren't good enough. She wants to see us on top of the ranking.

We start with the training right away. The warm-up is weird already weird. Everyone is going to notice that something happened between Sloane and me.

Irina forces us to perform our choreography from the competition again. I can feel how distant Sloane is. She tries to avoid my touch whenever she can, making things even more awkward for me.

I don't know how to touch her anymore. It feels weird. She obviously doesn't want me to touch her at all.

Every element is weird, every position seems unnatural, and the magic from yesterday is gone.

This at least happened after the competition and not before.

„What happened to you?" Irina, her polish accent, is yelling at us.

„Nothing!" We both quickly say at the same time. We look at each other and quickly look away to avoid eye contact.

„Oh my god! I can't do this today. You both are killing me. We are going to have a break. The next competition is in two weeks. I have to come up with a new choreography anyway." Irina sighs, and she already grabs her stuff.

„Let's take a day off" she nods slowly, and with that, she leaves. And before I can think about it, Sloane leaves too.

23
SLOANE

A day off? I have never been so happy to leave this place. God, I need to get away from Asher.

My heart is pounding so heavily inside of my chest. What is wrong with me? I slept with my freaking skating partner?! And now I can't stop thinking about it.

As soon as the words left Irina her lips, I grabbed my stuff and left. I didn't want to say goodbye or anything else to Asher. I just need to leave.

I thought that driving home and lying down in my bed would make things easier. I thought I could escape everything. But looking at the mess in my room brings everything back into my head. The memories are still fresh, and I swear I can still feel his touch.

My skin was on fire where he touched me. His skin on mine was so heavenly. I never felt so good with someone else.

But I would never actually say this out loud. I hate Asher, and that's never going to change.

I leave my room and go back downstairs. Now I have to stay in the living room. I will stay here for a while until I sort my thoughts. I need to clear my head.

After hours I finally started cleaning my room. I destroy every evidence that Asher has ever been here. I try to remove the memories from my brain, but this is definitely not working.

How will I be able to skate with him ever again? I can't even look at him without thinking about him naked. All I had to think about it yesterday night. It starts with how we danced in the club, and he possessively told me that I was his. God, that was hot.

Everything he did was hot, and he surely knew what he was doing. This brings back the thought that all the rumors are true. Maybe he is a player? That would mean that I am just one of many girls who tingled between the sheets with him.

I am so freaking stupid! What am I going to do now? I risked my career as a skater when I invited him into my home. I just threw everything away.

I want to scream. I am angry at myself. How could I do this?

Irina told us that she couldn't do this anymore, and I mean, this will be awkward. I just can't forget that it happened. I can't undo it.

Whenever I feel his hands on my body, I have to think back to this night. And we have to touch each other a lot.

The next competition is in two weeks, and we have to get better. There is no way that we can stay like this. We are in the middle of the ranking, and to get into the next competition, we need to get higher. I want to stand on the winner podium again with a medal.

We're so far from experiencing this. We had been far from this, even before we had sex. But now, it seems to be even farther away.

I want to talk about this. No, I need to talk about this. But I can't tell anyone. Flynn would go crazy if I told him that I slept with Asher. I don't want him to say that it was a mistake and that I shouldn't enjoy it.

I know this already. So this is why I am not calling Flynn. He will be so mad at me when he somehow finds out. I have to make sure that he is never finding out about this.

And this will never happen again. There is nothing to talk about. I just have to pretend that it never happened.

When I am back at the rink tomorrow, I pretend that nothing will happen. We are going to skate just like we always did. It's not going to be that hard.

I sigh, knowing exactly how hard it is going to be. The worst thing is that I don't know who Asher really is. I just hopped into bed with him when I was utterly wasted. God, I was so drunk.

And he was drunk too. Maybe he doesn't remember anything from yesterday night.

This might make things a lot easier. Obviously, we had sex, but maybe he couldn't remember the details. That means he wouldn't look different at me at all. This would give me a better feeling.

I can ignore what I think about him. I can ignore the feeling in my stomach when he touches me.

I want this to happen again. I want Asher to touch me again. What is wrong with me? I bet that he is not even thinking about me. Maybe he is so proud of himself that I invited him to my bed.

Maybe he planned it all along. I'm so fucking stupid. This could literally ruin everything, and this is all my fault. How could I fucking do this?

No one will ever find out about this. No one is allowed to find out about this. Everyone will hate me as soon as they know. I always had a lot of self-control, and I never lost it. I don't know how this could happen.

It makes me so angry. When it comes to Asher, I seem to lose every bit of control. He makes me so mad that I hate him, but at the same time, I want him to fuck me again. I want him the same way I had him yesterday. I want to be close to him. And this is so wrong.

I know that I can't have him and that he doesn't want me the same way. It was a one-time thing.

I am sure that I don't want more. I just wanted to get laid. The last time was long ago, and maybe that's what I needed, right?

God, whatever this is, it has to stop right now! I am not allowed to even think about this anymore.

I need to remove this from my mind.

I should concentrate on winning again. Skating is the only thing that matters, and I don't want to lose it.

24

SLOANE

I was undecided when I drove to the ice rink. I still don't know what to do or how to behave around Asher. We're distant, and I know that Irina is biting back on her comments.

She is confused. Of course, she doesn't know what is going on and what happened.

Our next performance is Christmas-themed. The whole competition has some kind of Christmas charity thing going. Irina thought we should do something fun, with jazz Christmas music and a fast dance. I like this idea, and it gives me hope that I don't have to touch Asher this often. I don't want to be close to him.

„I thought you both were on good terms. I can feel the tension. There is nothing easy and happy about this performance. We will sink in the ranking if you perform like this," Irina sighs, and I slowly look at Asher.

God, this is terrible. I don't know how this is going to work out. We don't say anything. Instead, we're trying again. No matter how often we try again, it is not getting any better.

I wish this would be easier. But it seems to get even more complicated with every minute that we skate together.

A couple of weeks ago, there was a time when I would have done anything to get rid of Asher.

I wanted someone else as my partner. I thought it would be best if he would just quit.

Now, I don't want anyone else. I want Asher, and I want only him. There is no one else I ever want to skate with. I wish I could feel the same things on the ice as in bed with him.

But the feelings are not real. I was drunk, and I wanted to get laid. It was only sex and nothing more. There are definitely no feelings in here.

And that's why it is so tense between us. There are no feelings between us. It was only great sex.

„Maybe we should stop trying for today. We will talk about the costumes tomorrow over lunch and ditch training for the day. Maybe you both just need a minor break," Irina sighs.

It's frustrating to not satisfy her. There was a time when she never had to doubt me. Flynn and I were always the best. There wasn't another option and now look at us.

„I'll see you tomorrow," our coach sighs and turns around.

I hate to see her like this. She doesn't have any hope that we might win. It gets me angry. Angry enough for me to leave the ice behind. I grab my stuff and storm outside to my car. I need to get home and free my head.

I need to run. Running is the only thing that helps me next to skating, and right now, it is the only thing that doesn't remind me of Asher. I run to free my head and to stop thinking about him.

It works for a while, for as long as I am running. The minute I come back home, I start thinking about Asher again. My thoughts are always trailing back to him.

His hot body, the way he breathes out my name. Everything inside me is longing for his body against mine. It was pure perfection, and I wonder if this is just my needy side speaking.

Maybe I need to get laid again. Perhaps I need someone else, someone who is not Asher.

But here is the thing, I can't think about someone else. I don't want someone else. All I can think about is Asher. I couldn't sleep with someone else.

Something is deeply wrong with me. This is so not working.

And that's why I am running for longer than usual. I am pushing myself to run more. I push my body to keep going. I can't think about everything right now. I need a break.

God, this beautiful face of his is driving me absolutely crazy.

25

ASHER

We made everything worse. Neither of us is explaining why we're acting so weird. God, I don't want anyone to know that we had sex. This would make things even stranger.

But I don't know how to keep going. We're sitting at one table. Sloane is directly in front of me. Irina is talking about our costumes, but I don't actually care.

I don't care about the costumes at all. All I care about is Sloane. The way she hovers over the table to get a better look at the pictures on Irina's iPad.

Does she wear this top purposely to tease me? The neckline is deep enough for me to see the swell of her breast. She is wearing a red bra underneath, and god, I would do everything to see it. I want to rip off this top and have a look at her perfect body.

I try to look away. I try to think about something else, but Sloane is the only thing I can think of. I hate myself. I hate her for this.

Now I look back at Irina and nod as if I always paid attention to her.

The costume isn't that bad. I am wearing a black pair of pants, and a red silk shirt. My costume is nothing compared to Sloane's. She is wearing a fluffy red glitter dress. It has thick spaghetti straps, and the bottom hem is soft and white, just like Santa's hat.

Sloane has to wear gloves in the same color as her dress for the performance. We look silly anyway. Christmas costumes. I absolutely hate this theme. I hate Christmas more than anything. We never celebrated it. I don't celebrate anything because I have no one to celebrate with.

This is distracting me. Thinking about my asshole father and our family celebrations. When I was little, my mom tried to prepare something. It was never working as my mom wanted it to. My father destroyed everything. He destroyed her.

Now we don't even talk about it. I doubt that my father knows which date we have. He is always drunk. He is always in his own world. The gift I would want might be a day away from him. A day where he isn't hitting me. Usually, I'm his punching bag, and maybe I am lucky enough to escape this.

This is why I love skating that much. I love to drown myself in training and work. I love to be on the ice because I am not with my father every time I am there.

Now, I don't know if I like to be on the ice. Things have been more complicated since I slept with Sloane. It made things weirder, and I hate myself for that. We ruined everything.

We were on good terms before, and now all of this is gone. We ruined it.

„Everything okay?" Irina looks at me. Everyone is looking at me, and I quickly nod.

„Yeah…" I breathe out with a quick nod.

„You hate the costumes, right?" My coach asks me, and I quickly shake my head.

„No, it's okay," I reply casually. I don't want them to know what is going on in my head.

I can't stay here any longer. It's killing me to be with Sloane. It's killing me that she is sitting here, looking that damn good.

„Are we done here?" I ask them. I want to leave.

I need to leave now. Again everyone looks at me, surprised because we haven't eaten anything yet.

We are all waiting for our food, which might be the worst time to leave the table. I might be disrespectful doing this.

„I think yes…." Irina replies slowly, and with that, I stand up and leave.

I don't want to say anything else. I know they would hold me back from leaving, and I don't want this to happen.

I can't stay anymore. I'll be better tomorrow, for another day on the ice. I sort my thoughts, and I'll be good tomorrow.

26

ASHER

The next day wasn't better. I tried everything. I was working out to get rid of the tension. I went back to the rink and skated. Nothing worked.

And now we're back here, skating together. We still can't look at each other. We still don't know how to act. I can't touch Sloane because I know she doesn't want it.

There is only a week left until the competition and Irina is not happy with us. She thinks that we'll lose again. I think so too. We're worse than last time, and nothing can make us skate better. It's our own fault.

She is thinking the same thing. Otherwise, she wouldn't act like this. She is thinking about me too. We're both thinking about sex. Maybe we just need to get it out of our heads. I don't know how this is supposed the happen.

I'll tell myself that it'll get more manageable when I have her one more time. I'll forget about her, and maybe this makes me want to move on.

I need to see if she wants the same. This has to wait until the training is over, which takes way too long.

Irina wants us to perform again and again. She thinks that we might get better the more often we try it.

Nothing is the case. I even think it's getting worse with each time.

I am happy and relieved when Irina tells us that we're done for today. She is angry with us and glad herself to finally leave.

She grabs her stuff, and after a slight „Goodbye," she is gone. Sloane leaves the ice as well and walks off toward the dressing room. We're the last people here, it's late, and I think the rink will close after we leave.

I skate another round until I am finally leaving the ice myself. Sloane is still in the dressing room, so I remove my skates and see if she is okay.

It never took her long. Mostly she is not even going into the dressing room at all. She mainly drives home right away. But this time, she has been in there for quite some time.

I slowly and carefully open the door. I don't want to make a sound. I can hear the water running, and the room is filled with steam. She is taking a shower.

„It's not working, " I say aloud as I slowly come closer. Sloane doesn't reply, but I can hear her feet moving. The water is still running.

„What?" She finally breathes out.

„Trying to get rid of the tension," I reply and suck in a deep breath. She is still out of sight, and all I want right now is to see her. I want to feel her skin against mine and pull her close. God, I would give everything to be inside her again.

„Maybe we should do something against it…." I can hear how nervous she is. How quickly her heart must be pounding in that sweet chest of hers.

„There only seems to be one solution," she goes on, and I already know that we're thinking the same.

I slowly strip down my clothes. I let them fall to the ground and notice how my heart is pounding itself heavily.

„And what's that?" I ask her. This time I come around the corner.

I see her standing underneath the stream of the hot water. Her body glistened so perfectly.

I lick my lips. Sloane is perfect.

„You need to fuck me. I need you to fuck me" it sounds like she is begging me. Is she? Does she want this as bad as I do?

She turns around, facing me. She is staring right into my soul, and this next to her begging is enough for me.

I take giant steps toward her and smash my lips onto hers as soon as possible. I pull her closer to my body, pressing her against the tiled wall. The hot water is now soaking me thoroughly, the temperature burning on my skin.

Sloane is wrapping her legs around my hips, and I pull her up. My cock is already hard, begging to be inside her.

„Tell me, how bad do you want it?" I breathe against her lips.

Instead of an answer, I can feel her hips moving, her throbbing center against my erection. She is looking for some sort of friction.

„Please," she begs, her voice a low whine.

„So greedy," I sigh and finally thrust into her. She is lucky that I can't wait any longer myself. I finally want to feel her again.

And again, she feels like heaven. My personal heaven. I can feel her clench around me with every hard thrust into her.

Her moans and whines are music to my ears. She is so perfect.

I groan as she breathes out my name in the most delicate way. God, she is going to be the death of me.

She is like a drug. Now I know that I will never get enough of her. There is no chance that I can stop thinking of her ever again. This is not the last time we're doing this. I know that my need for her will never stop.

I reach between us to rub her throbbing bud. I can feel that she is close by the way she is clenching around me. I know that I won't last long myself.

God, this girl is killing me. We should have never started with this in the first place.

„When we're skating tomorrow, think about this. Think about my hands on your body, what they feel like when I am touching you like this." I whisper into her ear as my thumb brushes over her hard nipple.

This could be my worst idea or the best. There is only one way to find out. I know that she wants the same thing. She wants the same thing as I do.

Maybe the sexual tension leads to a better result. We could use this passion in our performance.

She holds onto me tightly, and my words seem to push her over the edge. She clenches even harder around me as she comes, which finally pushes me over the edge.

It takes us a while to catch our breaths, and this means we actually shower now and wash our bodies under the hot stream of water.

No one is saying another word. We have never really talked much, and this is just about the sex.

We don't have a connection. It's just sex, and this indeed was the last time. Even though I know that there is no chance that I will stop thinking about her.

„God, I hate you," she sighs as she turns off the water, grabs a towel, and starts drying her skin.

„I hate you too," I reply.

„This won't change anything."

„Not at all. We just satisfied our needs, nothing emotional. It's just sex to get rid of the tension," I reply, and she nods.

We're both getting dressed. And while Sloane is putting on her clothes, I watch her. She is perfect in every single way. Her body is perfect. I can never stop thinking about her. I can never stop wanting her and longing for her.

„It won't happen again, though," she quietly says, her voice so unsure that I don't know if she meant it.

„It won't," I agreed slowly.

27

SLOANE

I slept with Asher! Twice! And the sex in the shower was just as good as the night we spent together after the club. I am so ashamed of myself. This shouldn't have happened at all.

This is going to ruin everything. Now I can't skate with him. I can't act normal around him ever again. And I just hate him so much! I was so angry that he came after me into the bathroom. He wanted this to happen.

I wanted this to happen too! I wanted him so badly, and now I am sure I can't stop thinking about him.

I left him behind as soon as I got dressed. It's enough for me to know that I'll see him again tomorrow. I don't even want to see him again tomorrow.

Irina is going to kill us. She will kill us as soon as she finds out what is going on, and there is no way to keep this a secret. One of us will break and say something. It's always been like this.

I saw couples separate because they fell in love, and Irina always told us that this should never happen. She told us feelings can get in our way and ruin everything.

She was more than happy that Flynn was gay. She never had to worry about anything. The best thing was when he found a boyfriend. Gregg is the most supporting boyfriend existing.

And now we have a problem with Asher…

What am I even talking about? We absolutely don't have a problem with Asher! I don't feel anything for him. We hate each other! There is no problem, nothing Irina warned us about.

There are no feelings, at least nothing romantic. We absolutely hate each other.

It was hate that made him pound into me so intensely. And good god, it felt so good. I never want to be with anyone else. I know that no one is gonna be as good as Asher.

I really do have a problem, and this problem keeps me up all night. We have a competition in a week, and it's time to get back onto the podium. I can't be somewhere in the middle of the ranking again, or I'll lose my good reputation completely.

I am ruined if I can never climb back up, and it will destroy me. I need to win this. We need to be on the podium.

And this time, we have nothing passionate or sexy. We have a Christmas dance. We should only have a little bit of fun, something fun and easy. But we can't even do that.

So it's, of course, a massive surprise that the training is going so smoothly the next day. Irina is absolutely thrilled with us. She is constantly clapping her hands, and she even cheers at us.

We performed the dance three times, and each time it was fun and easy. We are smiling as we skate, and everything seems different. What happened to us?

It definitely can't be the thing in the shower. We're cursed! I know I am super dramatic, but this can't be normal. This is my post-orgasmic euphoria or something, and I am sure this won't last until the competition.

But today is so easy. We're having fun, dancing to the music. The ice feels like home again, and it's the first time in a while that I don't worry.

„I was scared that we would lose again, but this gives me some hope! Whatever you did, it worked! I am so happy that you could finally get over it and act professional" Irina smile at us and nods.

If she only knew. I avoid her eyes because I know that I would definitely tell her something by just looking into her eyes.

She would be so mad if she knew that Asher and I had sex more than once.

No one is saying another word. „Well, anyway. You both perform again," Irina instructs, and we nod.

It's as good as the other three times. Maybe we're lucky, and this time it's actually working out. I can already see us on the podium.

This actually gives me hope, and it makes me even happier. My dream might come true after all, and this is the only thing I should focus on.

If I think hard enough about it, I might forget everything else. I might forget about Asher. And he isn't always going to be my partner. I might get a new one in one of the higher competitions. Someone qualified for the Olympics as well. Even though Asher is a great candidate for the Olympics. Not that I want to skate there with him.

„Please, stay like this until next week. You both just have to be like this at the competition. This isn't too much to ask, right?" Irina asks us after we're done.

„I shouldn't tell you this, but I think you need a little more motivation. We can't lose again," Irina starts, catching both of our attention. I look at her, curious about what she will say now.

„The first three couple of this competition are going to Toronto. I'll kick your ass if this happens because the Toronto competition is even more important, and it's highly important to win it." She tells us, and I squeal excitingly.

Flynn and I won the competition in Toronto once before. It's an honor to get invited.

„This is not the only thing. Roman Balas is throwing a dinner for some selected couples," Irina tells us, and I gasp.

„I need to go to that dinner! I need to see Roman Balas!" I yell at her, and she nods.

„You have to really try your best. We need to win. If Roman sees potential in you two, he might invite you. But for that, you need to do good in Toronto," she sighs, and I know that she barely has hope for us to go there.

„We will do it!" I tell her more sure than anything.

Roman Balas is one of the most famous skaters right now. He and his partner were at the Olympics. It would be a tremendous honor to be at his dinner.

28
SLOANE

I think we never trained as hard. And our training made me forget all about Asher. I never thought about what happened between us. Maybe this is a good sign. It could at least be the beginning of something good. It would be a big step for us to go to Toronto.

I look at Asher as we're waiting for our turn. He nods slowly, and we step onto the ice together.

Now I would really say that we're a team. And for the first time, everyone can see it. We accept each other as a team, and I don't want anyone else. I learned that it can actually be fun with Asher. It at least was fun last week.

Even though hating him entirely was a lot easier. It was easier to deny absolutely everything when it came to him.

But now our Christmas song starts playing, and I forget about everything around us. We smile so widely and begin with our performance. It is fun for everyone else to watch, as it should be. Every spin looks so smooth and easy. The lifts are perfect, and we even included some more complex lifting elements this time.

We are way better than the last time, and the judges have to see it. They know that we're good today. There is always something we could do better, and the theme is shitty, but we're doing great so far.

We totally deserve it to go to Toronto. I want nothing more than to be there.

But now we have to wait a long while until they announce the winners and show the ranking to us. We were the second couple who performed today. There are tons of other couples after us.

I change back into my regular shoes. I don't need my skates anymore. And as soon as I wear regular shoes, I check out the buffet to get myself a hot coffee.

I haven't eaten anything so far because I was way too nervous, and I still can't eat anything. So coffee is actually a good idea. I need something to fill my stomach.

As I pay for my coffee Asher appears behind me. „We actually did well today," he tells me, and I shrug my shoulders.

„I don't really know. I mean, yeah… but maybe it wasn't enough for Toronto," I sigh and look at him.

„Relax, it'll be fine," Asher tells me with this sweet smile. I quickly look down into my cup. I need to avoid eye contact with him.

„Yeah, sure," I reply and try to leave, but he holds me back. His grip on my arms is firm, and his look is concerning.

„Everything is good between us, right?"

„What do you mean? We hate each other, remember?" I tell him, and a slight laugh escapes my lips.

Am I asking him that, or am I asking myself?

„Yeah, sure," he replies this time. It seems like he is disappointed. But he finally turns away from me and lets me leave. We hate each other. We always had.

We did well that week, and we made it without actually fighting or bitching at each other. But this is because we're now behaving maturely. There is no different reason behind it.

I don't even like him. I don't know him well enough to actually like him.

He is avoiding me after our conversation. At least I can't find him, and I can't spot him whenever I talk to someone else.

For a while, I was scared that he had left. But he is right next to me again as everyone is gathering their seats, ready for the announcement.

It takes an eternity until they finally reveal the ranking. My heart is pounding heavily inside my chest.

I am nervous to see where we are in this ranking. With every name that pops up, my heart skips a beat. It's not us. The higher the scale gets, the more nervous I get. This is an excellent sign. We have already climbed higher than before. We're not in the same position, which gave me hope.

We're not sixth or fifth… fourth… and I finally see our name. We made it to third place. We are on the podium.

We made it!

I cheered the minute I realized what that meant. „We made it!" I yell and happily hug Asher. I hug him so tightly.

But as quickly as I throw my arms around him, as quickly and awkwardly, I remove them again.

This has been the weirdest hug ever, and he sure doesn't look like he enjoyed it. We quickly parted and stood next to each other, pretty awkwardly. No one is saying a word, Irina is cheering, and she isn't noticing anything right now.

She is happy. Of course, this is our first victory. We achieved something today. We should be satisfied, but Asher is giving me some weird vibes.

I glance at him every now and then. He was smiling, but he never looked at me, not even once. Not even when we're standing on the podium taking out medals and the Toronto invitation.

Something feels so odd. Something seems to be wrong. I won't ask Asher. We're not friends, so it shouldn't bother me.

We talked to a bunch of people after the victors got their medals. Some people tell me that they are happy to see me back on the ice, even without Flynn. Flynn, who is still beside me, even now. He is always there, nodding and smiling at everyone. He tells everyone how proud he is and that he can't imagine anyone better besides me than Asher.

It took us way too long to figure out how to skate with each other. And it still feels like we're not trying out best. We could be so much better. We still have a lot to figure out.

I wish we could just act normal around each other. Maybe we could try to be friends.

But on our way home, no one is talking. Asher is listening to music with his headphones on. I listen to Flynn his story, and Irina is driving in silence.

Asher doesn't say goodbye when he leaves the car. He doesn't even look back as he walks home. This is where he lives.

I had never seen his house, and Irina stopped right in front of it, which bothered him.

It's a small neighborhood with tiny houses. Most of the homes are somehow broken and dirty. The yard is chaotic, and it seems like no one really cares about gardening or anything else.

Asher's house is not pretty either. It is small and dirty, the lawn is mowed, but the bushes are growing wildly in every direction possible.

The walls could use fresh paint, and the roof needs a hole fixed. I am a bit shocked to see how Asher is living. I never expected something like that. I knew he didn't have much, but this was far worse than I thought.

I know that we all might think the same right now, but no one says anything. No one dares to comment on it.

I for sure also know that no one will say something to Asher. I don't want him to feel uncomfortable with this.

29
ASHER

I hate that they know where I live. Irina knew it as she came to see my dad. But I never wanted anyone else to see it. I don't want anyone to meet my dad, ever.

And this is not the only thing bothering me right now. After Sloane and my conversation yesterday, I realized something.

Maybe it is better to keep this on a professional level. Sloane told me that she still hates me. I want to hate her. I would lie by saying that I hate her because I don't. There is something else when I look at her. I can't tell what it is, but it isn't hate.

Maybe it is just the desire to sleep with her again. I hope it is nothing emotional, only a desire toward her body. But I highly doubt this.

I can't have sex with her when she tells me that it was a mistake. It isn't a mistake for me. I wanted this to happen. I even want it to happen again.

Right now, I can stop whatever is inside of me. I can stop before it gets too much. This is about my passion, and I should focus on skating with Sloane. Nothing emotional or personal should stand between me and my sport.

We're handling this completely wrong, and continuing like this would separate us further.

This is why I am early today. I know that Sloane is always early. She loves to skate a few rounds by herself.

I look around, trying to find her. The first person I spot is Flynn with his boyfriend, Gregg. I walk over to them because they are also on my usual spot. I need to put on my skates anyway.

„Asher! You're early!" Flynn greets me with a smile. He is hiding his red hair underneath a beanie today. But his smile is as bright as usual. His brown eyes are sparkling happily as he looks at me and then back to Sloane on the ice.

I nod slowly, „Yeah, I need to talk to Sloane before starting the training session," I tell him.

He doesn't reply anymore, and I realize way too late that it sounded harsher than I wanted it to. Maybe he thinks that I have some bad news.

I don't tell him otherwise. He might be Sloane's best friend and her former partner, but this is nothing that he needs to know about. I am not even sure if Sloane told him about what happened.

I quickly tie my shoes and then already step onto the ice. Right when I enter the ice, Sloane comes closer. She smiles at Flynn or me. I am not sure about that right now.

„We need to talk," I tell her right away, and she nods.

„Go ahead," she tells me, and I quickly look to Flynn and Gregg. „Alone."

„Well, we don't have a secret, right?" She replies, and her voice sounds so unnatural that I am confused for a second.

Does she expect me not to say anything about us?

„If you say so… We need to set some boundaries," I start, and she looks at me, confused now.

It seems like she forgot about what happened. Is she playing with me, or is she serious?

„Like?" She asked me so I could tell her what I was thinking about.

„No more sex. It's not working for me. I want to keep it professional and fully concentrate on my career," I tell her.

Her eyes widen, and I know we're close enough for Flynn to hear it.

She wasn't expecting this. Maybe she thought this was something different, but I told her that I would rather talk to her privately.

„Fine. I told you it was a mistake and won't happen again. I am more than happy to fulfill this wish. It's strictly professional from now on," she nods, and before anyone else can say something, Irina greets us.

I haven't even noticed her coming closer. I look at Sloane. She is darting some looks to Flynn, who indeed heard our conversation. Based on his facial expression right now, I would say that he didn't know about us. She hasn't told her best friend. She must really hate me.

I look at her while Irina explains the plan for the upcoming weeks. We have two weeks to prepare ourselves for Toronto. We will be in Toronto for four days, and hopefully, we'll come back as victors.

„I want you to perform the second choreography you learned! With more passion and love," our coach announced.

We both look at her, totally shocked and, for a second, even speechless. The first performance we had was terrible.

„No way! It was terrible!" Sloane complains.

Irina is sure that this is the proper performance. She thinks that we can win everything with it.

And she might be right if we wouldn't be that damn stupid. It is a good choreography with a good song. A couple with good chemistry would rock this. But for us?

We are terrible. There is no way that we can score with this performance.

„Let's try it, and you better give your best!" Irina tells us, and I nod. The choreography is still in my head. I know what to do, and it seems like Sloane knows it well.

We skate to the middle of the ice, and as the song starts, we start with our choreography. This time it feels a lot easier than the last time.

I am not scared to touch her anymore, and it seems like she is a lot more comfortable with it.

I can't explain it, but somehow we're doing a pretty good job. After our first try, Irina wants us to try something different. She is changing a couple of elements, switching them with some harder ones.

We have to be the best at the competition in Toronto. There is no way that we're leaving without a medal.

We have to work hard for it, try our best, and maybe we finally have some excellent chances. Perhaps I can think about the Olympics again.

The first time I heard that I would skate with Sloane, I felt hope. There was nothing else but hope. Skating is my dream, and it is the only thing I want to do. But it is hard to find the right partner.

It's hard to have a good coach. It's hard when you don't have the money to buy the world. Irina wanted me because I am a good skater. She wanted me, and I never had to pay anything for this. It's the best I could ever get.

We had a rough start, but this gives me real hope for the first time. We're both trying our best right now.

I know that Sloane wants to go to this dinner, and I want to win. I want everyone to see that we're a good team, that we can win.

30
SLOANE

God, I was so happy to see Irina, and I am even more delighted that she started our session right away.

I can't escape Flynn. I have to talk to him at some point. I never expected Asher to say something like this. I thought he would say something harmless. But he brought up the two times we had sex. I thought it would be clear that it would never happen again.

Well, I said that the second time wouldn't happen, and it did. I may enjoy it a bit too much as well.

I don't know what is going on with me. I long for Asher. Everything inside me screams for him, yet I am here denying it all. I tell him that I hate him, and I swear a part of me does.

I can't tell what it is inside me. But I shouldn't concentrate on that anyway. We're here to skate, and we're here to be a good team. Nothing else matters. It's all about skating.

I want to be at the top again. I need to be the best again. So I concentrate on skating. I focus on the performance.

Irina is a great coach, and I trust her. The performance is good, and with the new elements she told us to do, it's even better.

But somehow, training is over so quickly today. I wish we could just stay here a little bit longer. But there is no need to exercise more. We have two weeks on our hands, and this indeed is enough. We already know the choreography. Now we only have to perform perfectly and learn some new elements.

Asher is the first one leaving the ice. It seems like he needs to get home as quickly as possible. He doesn't turn around, and he doesn't say goodbye. It's strictly professional.

We're not friends. We're co-workers, partners, or however you wanna call this.

Flynn is already waiting for me. He needs to talk to me, and I know I messed up. I should have told him.

He is my best friend. I would have told him if I had sex with someone else. But it was Asher, which made things weird and complicated.

„I'm sorry," I tell him quickly before he can say anything else.

„You had sex with Asher?!" He tries to keep quiet. Not everyone has to know about this, and there are definitely too many people around us.

Irina is standing close to us, and she cannot know about this. She would surely kill us.

„Yeah, it just happened. A total mistake, " I reply quickly, and I try to just simply stop talking about it.

It makes me feel uncomfortable. I know what Flynn thinks about it, about me. I know what is going on inside his head now. He indeed hates me for this.

„When did it happen?"

„When we were in the club and a couple of days later again," I reply, avoiding his eyes. I can't look into his face, and I sure don't want to know what he is thinking right now.

„It happened twice?" He asks me, even more, shocked.

I slowly nod, not saying anything else. I feel bad it happened, and I feel worse that I haven't told Flynn about it.

„Oh god, Sloane, you know what will happen when Irina finds out," he tells me slowly.

This is the first time I look up right into his eyes.

„Irina won't find out! She can't. You heard Asher, it's not going to happen again. We're fine, and we're finally good skating together." I quickly tell him.

I don't want a new partner. I know that Irina will get me a new partner if she finds out.

She always told me that it was the worst thing that could happen. And there is not even something between Asher and me. She doesn't have to worry about anything.

„Just be careful," my best friend sighs, and then he turns around and walks away.

„Flynn, please don't be mad!" I yell after him, and he stops. He turns around and looks at me one more time.

„I am furious! I thought we were best friends, and you were not even talking to me. I just found out by accident today!" He tells me, and I sigh. I really messed up.

„I know! I am sorry! I wanted to tell you…."

„But? You couldn't trust me? What did you think?" He asks me, and I shrug my shoulders.

„I thought you would judge or hate me." I reply.

I know what he thinks about me right now, so I haven't told him. I don't want to hear what he has to tell me now.

„Oh, I partly do judge you! But I can also understand you," he smiles at me. Now I am confused. I thought he would hate me for sleeping with Asher.

„He is hot. I would sleep with him too!" He laughs, and I quickly join him. It feels good to hear a joke about it.

„But I am still a bit mad. You know what Irina always told us about a relationship between partners. And I thought you take this seriously here," he tells me slowly.

„I do take it seriously! I don't know why it happened. I was drunk at the club, totally wasted, and it just happened."

I really don't know why it happened. I would have never done it when I had been sober. But I can't go back in time.

„It happened twice… so there has to be a reason for it… it doesn't just simply happen twice," he replies, raising an eyebrow at me.

„As you said, he is hot, and it was a moment of weakness. I just want to forget about it and continue with my life. Skating is important to me, you know that."

I would never risk my skating career for something so stupid. Asher and I are partners, we have to work together, and I surely know that there is nothing between us.

We're not even friends. It is professional between us.

„Oh, Sloane, just be careful you're skating on thin ice," my best friend replies as he lays his arm around me.

He leads me outside into the night. I know that he is right. I crossed a line with Asher, and I can't go back anymore.

31
SLOANE

All I can think about is the Toronto competition. We have to win it! I can't take another loss. The first place is the only thing I want. And we try our best with more complex elements in our performance. I try to put all my passion into it. It's even a bit of acting. We're telling a story, and it seems perfect this time.

Our performance is at least better than the last time. Irina recorded us to show us the difference and what we could improve.

We have to see the details and make sure that there isn't a single mistake.

„So here is the plan for Toronto…." Irina starts as we're taking a break. Toronto is now two days away.

„We have two days to practice there, to get a feeling for the stadium you're skating in. I want you to skate there, and I want you to have a look at the competition. But we're only doing something easy as a rehearsal. It would be best to keep our choreography a secret," Irina tells us, and we nod in understanding.

It's nothing new for me. We always did it. No one could copy us or ever actually see how good we are.

„And we're getting the costumes as soon as we land there. I have a friend in Toronto, and he was kind enough to design something for you. Hopefully, it'll fit when you both try it, " she adds.

It surprises me. I had never heard of a friend in Toronto, even though we had been there before.

We always brought our costumes from here, even the last time we were in Toronto. It makes me anxious to get the outfits that late.

I don't know what happens if they don't fit. We might have a huge problem then. We only have two days there before the competition. I try to ignore the fear inside of me. I always trusted Irina, and this time is no different. She knows what she is doing, and I fully trust her. She would never do anything to harm us or our career.

„I don't know when we're returning back home. If we're going to this dinner, we're staying for a bit longer." She tells us, and I nod. My heart already skipping a beat.

I need to go to this dinner. I always wanted to meet Roman. This is my reason to try even harder. We need to impress him.

And this is why our breaks end here. We have to get through our performance again, and we have to practice the new elements again.

Everything needs to be perfect and smooth.

The good thing is that we're always. We are always in sync as if we were being remotely controlled. It looks perfect. And they say that synchronized ice skating is the most difficult. Asher and I somehow managed this perfectly from the beginning.

At least something was working from the beginning on. Even though we're better in general now. Maybe we fixed your problems. Perhaps now we have an excellent start to our skating career. We have to win back a lot of lost points.

Maybe it will work between us, and one day we're at the Olympics together. Right now, I think that everything is possible. We're both in a better place right now.

Everything will be fine as long as we keep our hands to ourselves and concentrate on skating.

Irina praises us for our excellent work today. I know that she is pleased with us. Even Irina has some hope now. This is a good sign.

She ends the training today. We're both sitting down to get out of our skates. It's a relief to finally take off the skates. After a while, they even hurt. Your feet hurt. I am used to the bruises on my feet, but the pain is always the same.

As soon as Asher is done, he stands up and leaves. We're still not friends. He is still not saying goodbye to me.

Something is bothering me. I wish Asher would talk a bit more with me. I don't know why I want him to, but I want to hear his voice. I want to know more about him, but he just wants to keep his distance.

32
ASHER

Our last day of training is here. Tomorrow we're sitting on a plane on our way to Toronto. It's my first time flying. It's my first time traveling.

I am nervous because I don't know what will happen, but I am more than ready. We're doing a good job lately, and this gives me a bit of hope. I am also confident that we're going to win this competition.

Today we're starting with off-ice practices in the training room. We're trying the lifts on solid ground. Today seems more relaxed than the other days. The competition is getting closer now, and everyone is more than nervous.

I look at Sloane. She is very good at keeping a straight face. I never know what she is actually thinking about. I don't know if she is nervous or if she is scared.

She smiles widely at Flynn as he talks to her. He is joking around, and it seems like they got closer again. I have never seen them like this before.

Flynn won't be there in Toronto. It's the first time he won't be there at a competition. But the costs are only covered for Irina, Sloane and me. A part of me is happy that he won't be there, but another part also understands that he wants to be there.

He was once in my position, and he is Sloane's best friend. But he makes me nervous, and I don't want him to steal my spotlight.

Everyone still sees him as Sloane's partner. I know they had been good and that everyone loved them. But now I am her new partner, and people need to accept this.

We can be as good, if not even better. I see a huge potential now. It'll be good if we keep up the way we skate now.

I look at Sloane, her blue eyes looking back at me. She looks at me most innocently right now, and it kills me. God, this girl is going to be the death of me.

Everything inside me screams that I am stupid. Sloane can't know who I really am. We can't even be friends because I would long for more. It's not possible because we're partners. We are dependent on each other. We need to skate together. Skating should be our priority. We should concentrate on that alone.

But good god, my heart skips a beat most delicately whenever I look at her, whenever our eyes meet.

It might just be the desire for her body, that I want her in a way no one else can have her. I know that I want to feel her wrapped around me again. But there is also something else. I can't quite tell what it is, but I know it is forbidden as partners.

The only thing I can do is keep my distance from her. We just have to be professional toward each other. We have to be good at what we're doing, and everything will be okay.

And right now, I would say that we're pretty good at doing our job. There is no need to get distracted right now.

We're not even talking to each other. I can get attached to someone I don't really know. Sloane is a stranger to me. I don't know her enough to befriend her. It's that simple.

Irina pulls me out of my thoughts. She tells us to go onto the ice now. We are going to rehearse our performance.

I think that we can now do it with our eyes closed, in our sleep.

We put our skates on and skate some rounds to warm up until we start our work.

We stand with our backs to each other in the middle of the ice. This is our starting position, and I have to stay in that position longer.

The song starts, and Sloane is skating around me. Her hand touched my shoulders. Then she takes my hand, and we both start sliding forward.

We first need to gain some speed. Our first element is a couple spin, which leads into a lift. The lift we once struggled with. It is now the easiest one in this performance.

I let her down as soon as the element was done. We're one with the music as if we're an ideally moving part of it.

Next, we skate in sync, with small skating elements combined with jumps. We have to be on time, doing everything as if we're one. It looks smooth, which might be the best part of this performance. It's our kind of magic.

Every single lift, spin, or jump is absolutely perfect. We are ready for this competition, and I honestly can't wait. It feels good to be on the ice now. It felt good before, but this here is quite different.

It feels like magic. It feels so right.

For this one song, the world stops spinning. Everything stands still. It's a moment that just belongs to us. Every pair of eyes is on us, and everyone is so focused on us that they forget the time. Everyone is so busy watching us doing our magic that the world stops spinning for them.

33

ASHER

Today I am traveling for the first time. I had a hard time packing my bags, but I somehow did it. My dad threatened to lock my door and let me starve to death. He doesn't want me to go. He doesn't want me to skate at all.

I had to tell him that I'd be gone for a couple of days. I actually told him this morning. I explained that I had left some money for him to buy himself some food.

I know that he won't do it. He probably spends this money on alcohol, but I can't leave him without anything. I can't let him starve because he won't cook for sure. I don't even know if he can still cook something. He never cooked anything for us.

I leave the house, escaping him. I thought he would come after me for a second, but the door never opened again.

I wait for Irina to pick me up, and I hope she is coming without Sloane. I am not embarrassed that she sees how I live, but I am scared my father is coming outside.

Irina's car is coming closer, and as she stops in front of my driveway, I see that Sloane is sitting next to her.

I quickly get into the car, greeting them both. Irina doesn't waste any time. She starts the engine right away and leaves.

„Do you have everything you need? We might need something more formal?" Irina asks me with a look at my bag.

I have one bag with me, and one is more than enough. I have everything I need.

„Yes, I have a dress shirt in there and dress pants. This is hopefully enough?" I reply.

I don't own something like a suite. It has always been too expensive.

„Sure. I just thought that this is a tiny bag," Irina replies, and I nod.

„Nope, I don't need much for that short time."

I only need a few clothes and my hygienic articles. I can't think of anything else that might be important.

My skates are in an extra bag. They always had their own case. We don't have our show outfit now, so there is nothing else I need to pack.

The ride to the airport is quiet. No one is saying a word, and it makes me feel anxious. I have never been to an airport, and I have absolutely no clue what will happen.

I just follow the other two like a lost puppy and hope no one notices my strange behavior. The last thing I need is their pity because I had never flown in my entire life.

We give up our luggage and get our tickets in exchange. I have a bizarre feeling in my stomach right now, and I don't really know if I am ready for this.

Everything is new to me, the security check, the gates… I am amazed at how many people know exactly where to go or what to do. It seems like some people are traveling more often. For me, it might be a luxury to do so, but for some, it's part of their daily life.

We sit down and wait for our boarding to start. Irina starts talking about our time in Toronto and the competition. We have some spare time on our hands when we're there.

Our tight schedule starts tomorrow, the competition is in three days. We don't know what will happen after the competition, but the best thing that could happen is that we get invited to that dinner party.

I want to stay away from home for as long as possible. Coming back home is going to be the hardest thing. I don't want to be back home. My dad is going to hate me the day I come back. He will be so mad that I left in the first place.

„Is everything okay?" Sloane asks me, and now I notice that she looks at me the whole time.

I slowly nod, not replying to her. It's best if she doesn't know how I feel right now. I don't want her to know what is happening inside me.

So I just look at her for a moment, and before she can say anything else, they open the boarding for our flight. We slowly stand up, the tickets and our passports in our hands. My heart is pounding inside my chest. I have never been so scared in my life.

But no one notices how I am feeling right now, which is good for me. I don't want anyone to know that I am too poor to travel. I don't want them to find out that this is a new situation.

The aircraft seems enormous to me. It's a massive machine, and it makes absolutely no sense that such a heavy thing can fly at all. The inside is small to fit tons of people in here. It's always three seats next to each other. Irina has a window seat, while Sloane sits in the middle, and I am outside the aisle.

We take a seat and wait for the aircraft to fill up with all the other passengers. It's a strange feeling to know that we will be in the sky in just a couple of minutes.

Sloane is buckling her seatbelt, and I do the same. Irina already has a book in her hands. She seems already lost in her story. Sloane takes out her phone and earphones to listen to her downloaded music.

I am totally not prepared for now because I have nothing to do. There is nothing that can keep me occupied now. Instead of that, I get more nervous with every second.

I don't know what will happen now, and I feel totally alone in this situation.

Everyone else is busy with themselves, and I am here alone.

Sloane, her hand, pulls me out of my thoughts.

„This is your first flight?" She asks me quietly.

I just nod. Again I am not replying. I wonder how Sloane knows it? I am trying to keep a straight face, but I am not good at it.

„It's not that bad. You'll see," Sloane smiles softly and offers me one side of her earphones. She wants to share her music with me.

It takes a while for me to take it because I am unsure if I should do it. I wanted to keep my distance from Sloane. Being close to her is dangerous for me, and this is not helping.

It would be a lot easier if she hated me. It would make things easier if she kept her distance from me. But now I am sitting here, listening to her music.

She is listening to classical music. I never expected her to listen to classical music, but it seems to calm her as she listens to the piano piece right now.

I look at her for a while. She seems so calm right now. She closes her eyes for a second and enjoys her music to the fullest. I have never seen her that relaxed. I know her as someone who is always stressed about something. Someone who always got something on her mind. Now she seems comfortable. She even closes her eyes for a bit, and I try to calm down.

34
SLOANE

The flight to Toronto was short. But now that we're here, I am even more excited.

Asher and I have separate rooms. His is down the hall. While Irina is a floor above us. She will spend the day at the spa and asked me to come with her. But I declined politely. I have something else in my mind, and this is why I knock on Asher his door as soon as I am ready.

„Get your skates and come with me," I say as soon as he opens the door. I don't even let him time to think.

He looks at me for a second, unsure of what to do now. But then he grabs the bag with the skates and comes with me. He closes the door to his room and looks at me.

„I hope you're not tired! I have to show you something amazing," I tell him with a smile.

I lead the way and walk straight out of the hotel. I ordered an Uber for our little trip now. I remember a place from the last time I have been here. Today I want to see it again.

Being here comes with many memories, and I want to have new ones to remember. I can't go back to the time before, Flynn is not my partner anymore, and I have to leave behind the time we had with each other.

This is why I bring Asher with me. He is not talking for the entire ride. He is not even asking where we're going.

Maybe he thought that we would check out the venue. But now we're too far from the city. And he is still not asking a question.

I wonder if he wants to be here. Maybe he regrets coming with me. But now it is definitely too late. We're too far from the city. The second I see the mountains and the trees, I know we're close to our destination.

I look at him for a second. I don't know what he thinks or what he feels right now. I can't tell what is going on inside of him.

As we arrived at our destination, I paid the Uber driver. He leaves as soon as we're out of his car. And here we are, in the middle of nowhere.

„What are we doing here?" Asher asks me, and it seems like he is pretty much annoyed.

It bothers me that he isn't open to being here with me. I thought he might be happy to go on a trip with me.

So instead of saying something, I lead him closer into the woods. We have to walk a bit to reach our final destination. And while we're walking, no one is talking.

I hate that he is so quiet. He is not even trying to get to know me. He doesn't want us to be friends.

I remember the one time I have been here with Flynn. We laughed the entire way that we walked.

After a small hill, we're there. In the middle of nature, the mountains in the background and a massive lake in front of us. A very frozen lake, which allows us to skate on the ice. Some people are already here, but the area is big enough. We're still alone, far away from everyone else.

„It's beautiful," Asher breathes out as he looks around. I already kneel down to change my shoes into my skates.

„It's perfect." I reply with a smile.

He doesn't hesitate and changes his shoes as well. He smiles so sweetly at me. As he is done, he reaches out his hand for me.

He pulls me onto the ice. It feels like a dream. It's even better than I remember. The nature around us is breathtaking. Asher fits perfectly into the picture.

It seems like a fairytale to me, which might be the first time he looks pleased. He is smiling so brightly, showing small dimples around his eyes as he does.

It seems like he doesn't worry about anything right now. We skate right next to each other, not saying anything.

„I have a good feeling about the competition," I tell him after a while. I want to talk to him. I can't bear the silence anymore.

„Me, too. I can feel that it will be good," Asher smiles as he skates backward to face me.

„I never thought we could actually do it," I tell him slowly. We were in such a bad place when we started skating. It's only been a couple of weeks, but we made quite a progress.

This might be the first time now that we're talking for real. This is the first real conversation that we have had.

„Me, neither. Honestly, I think it is still good if we're keeping our distance from each other," Asher tells me.

I feel rejected the minute he says this. He is against building something between us, even a friendship. For a second, I just look at him.

„We could be friends… just friends," I reply slowly. I am scared of his reply. I don't know what is going on inside of him.

„I don't think that this is a good idea. I'm not a good friend. It's better if you keep your distance from me. We're keeping it professional, remember?" He replies.

I am disappointed, and something inside of me hurts. I never expected Asher to have no interest at all. And somehow, it breaks my heart.

„Okay, it's all about winning anyway," I try to reply neutrally. I don't want Asher to know that I am disappointed about it.

We fall back into silence again. No one is talking, and we're just skating.

He grabs my hands as we spin. It feels too good to skate with him. Especially after what he just told me. His actions are speaking against his words. This is at least what it feels like right now.

It feels too good to skate with him right here. Something gives me the perfect feeling.

I try to shake this feeling off. We're being professional, not friends. It's all about success and winning.

This is what I wanted. From the beginning on, I just wanted to win. I never cared about being friends or getting to know him. I just wanted to be the best again.

Now something changed, and I don't know what, but Asher seems to see it differently. He wants a strictly professional relationship. I have to accept this.

Maybe this is going to make things even more accessible. We won't get close to each other, which means that we definitely don't think about sex with each other. Even though it is tough to forget.

I skate alone for a while and keep my distance from him. I need to clear my head before doing something that I might regret.

A part of me thinks that this might be easier if we're friends. Maybe the more I know about him, the more I dislike him.

35

ASHER

God, Sloane makes it so hard for me to stay away from her. Even though we weren't talking much, I know her better now. It's hard to hate her, and I am sure I absolutely don't hate her. She is incredible, a perfect skater, and a good person with a big heart. Even if she is not showing it, I know that she cares about others. There is so much within her that I don't know yet. But I want to know it. I want to get to know her better and be closer to her.

But this is not possible. Sloane doesn't know who I am. She would hate me or pity me if she found out the truth. Maybe Sloane would run away. I can understand if she doesn't want me if she knows everything. Lots of people ran, and I saw them all leaving me behind.

But this is nothing I should worry about right now. Since we returned from our little trip, Sloane has kept her distance. I think my words hurt her a bit. I feel sorry, but I know it was the right thing to do.

She barely looks at me during our costume fitting. Even though I can't take my eyes off of her. I'm just wearing a regular white dress shirt and a black pair of pants. Nothing special, but it's perfect for our performance.

I bet that every pair of eyes is on Sloane. She looks stunning. Irina says that her hair is going to be in a messy ponytail. She is wearing small crystal earrings framing her face.

But the prettiest thing is the dress. It's a short seam ending at her upper thighs. The burgundy-colored dress has spaghetti straps, and the chest part is embroidered with lace.

God, she looks too good in it. It's absolutely perfect. So I try not to look at her, even though it is hard.

I can feel that this performance is going to be something different. We could really win this. I want to win this for Sloane. I don't even want this for myself anymore, even though I always wanted it. I want this for her. I know how much Sloane intends to win this. I want to make this happen.

I know that we can be the best as well. Maybe we're even better than her and Flynn before. I don't know why I am setting this as my goal, but I want to be better than Flynn at her side.

„Maybe you should use the chance today to rehearse the performance again. You can't do it tomorrow in front of everyone." Irina tells us after we changed back into our regular clothes.

„You could drive to the farthest away rink," she adds the suggestions.

We look at her, and then we look at each other. We indeed haven't planned on spending some time alone together. Yesterday was enough for the both of us, I think.

Now I look at Sloane. She seems unsure at first, yet she nods. „Okay, I think I know a place," she tells Irina.

I wonder if she wants to return to the lake. It's pretty far, and I don't know if it's worth it to just rehearse our performance.

But I don't say anything. I just look at Sloane and nod. I will do whatever she wants to.

Irina is not coming with us, which I think is weird. She should see us skate and give us one last good feeling about the performance. But she won't come with us and watch us rehearse.

„Isn't it stupid to go without Irina?" I asked Sloane as soon as we left the store.

Irina is gone by now. I think she went back to the hotel. I wish she would be there. That would also mean that Sloane and I are not alone. Not entirely, at least.

„No, I think she just wants us to feel good and comfortable with the performance. We might feel it differently when no one is watching, you know?" Sloane replies, and I nod.

We should perform like no one is watching. Of course, we skate differently when we're alone. But I don't think that we're actually better then.

We're not going back to the lake. Sloane chooses a rink outside the city. „I think the rink is closing in an hour." She tells me, and I nod. I don't know what we're supposed to do with this information, but I just get along with it.

It seems like she exactly has a plan. She knows what to do because now she confidently walks to the front desk. I look around while she is talking to the lady there. She is even showing her competition passport to her. The woman nods, and Sloane turns around with a massive smile on her lips.

„Okay, the rink closes in an hour, but we can stay here and practice. We have two hours until we have to leave," Sloane tells me, and I nod. So that was her plan the whole time.

It's good, but I don't want to be alone with her. No one else is going to be here, not even strangers.

„I would say that we wait here," she tells me and points to a bench to sit down on.

We're already changing our shoes, and then we just sit there and wait. We're not doing anything else. We're just sitting here waiting.

„So, why did you start skating?" She asks me with a smile. It comes so suddenly that I first stare at her.

„My mom took me skating when I was younger, and I just fell in love with it. I couldn't stop, always wanting to come back and skate. What about you?" I ask her.

„I don't really know. I skate since I can think of it. I loved it since the first time I stepped onto the ice, and thanks to my parents, I got a trainer and started doing competitions." She shrugs her shoulders, and I nod.

Yeah, doing a sport is so much easier with tons of money.

„Your mom was into skating as well?" Sloane looks at me. She is trying to find out more about me.

I shake my head slowly.

„No, not really," I tell her. There is a reason why she took me to the rink that day, but I'll never tell anyone.

I can't tell her that my mom wanted to escape my dad and get out of the house for a couple of hours. My dad wasn't a bad person back then, but sometimes they fought. My mom always took me to the rink whenever they did.

„Is one of your parents skating?" I ask her back, and she shakes her hand as well.

„No, they would never," she laughs softly. „They love to work, and I think this is sometimes the only thing on their mind."

„But your parents seem to be lovely," I tell her.

When I was younger, a family like hers was everything I ever wanted, next to going to the Olympics. I always wished for a better dad and a still alive mom.

My family couldn't be more broken, but I learned to get used to it. I won't ever get anything better. I can't choose my family.

I let Sloane tell me stories about her skating history with Flynn for the rest of the time. She is talking with so much love and passion about it that I could listen to her for hours.

Her eyes are sparkling as she tells me about the time she had with Flynn. She smiles so widely, and I think that she doesn't even notice it.

She stops talking when she first notices how most people are leaving. It's time for us to go onto the ice. And while some are still skating, we could use the time to warm up.

We do this individually. We stretch our muscles and skate some rounds on our own.

As soon as everyone is gone, Sloane sets down her phone and turns on the music. It is not as loud as it should be, but it's enough.

We skate to the middle, and the light gets turned off as soon as the song starts.

We look up to the ceiling. Well, the light is not entirely switched off. There is still a dim light shining above the ice. Enough for us to skate.

It's setting a different mood, to be honest. Something that makes me feel nervous right now. I look at Sloane as she starts skating around me, her hand touching my shoulder. She starts leading me, and we both skate to gain speed.

Everything feels a lot more intensive right now. Every touch seems to be electric and somehow on fire. Now, I am delighted that Irina isn't here with us. No one should see us like this.

It feels intimate somehow, and I guess this is how we should perform in two days.

We should share something intimate with the judges and the people watching us. This is the kind of magic they want to see us doing.

We're lost in the moment. The world stops once again, but this time differently. There is tension, something I had never experienced before.

Now, I feel it clearly. As the performance is over, I can feel Sloane breathing, her chest heaving up and down. My lips are so close to her chest that I could just press a soft kiss on her delicate skin. But I am not doing it, of course. I can't destroy this special moment with something so small yet stupid. I can't risk the competition tomorrow, not after telling her that we shouldn't even be friends.

I have to control myself, which I am doing right now. I move away from Sloane. She avoids my eyes, and then she smiles at me for a moment.

„That felt good. I think we're doing well," the blonde says, still out of breath.

I just nod, not sure of what to say now. I know that we both feel the same right now. Sloane felt whatever I was feeling, and we can't deny it.

36
SLOANE

It's only one day until the competition. Today we're meeting the others, our competitors. I bet they are all so good! It is going to be hard to win against them. But after our rehearsal yesterday, I feel pretty confident.

I look at Asher as we change into our skates. Some of the others are already on the ice, practicing some elements of their performance. Asher and I won't do anything. They should better think that we won't be a competition at all.

Most of them might know us. I know that some skaters are watching the performances of the others. There is not much to see when it comes to Asher and me. We weren't that good before. The last competition was our best one, and we only got third place.

I take a look around. I know a couple of them. Hopefully, they won't talk to me. I really don't want to talk to anyone right now.

The other skaters seem to be so good. Of course, everyone is showing off what they can do. Some are really practicing their performance for tomorrow.

We're not doing such things. We're just standing there for a while. I am unsure of what to do now. I don't want to move a bone in my body. It feels like I am not able to move right now.

Asher is taking my hand as he slowly pulls me onto the ice. We are moving forward slowly because we're mostly watching the others.

„We are not skating synchronously. That's our biggest strength" Asher smiles at me.

I slowly nod. Well, I don't think that we're doing anything at all.

„If this isn't Sloane Griffin, I honestly wasn't expecting you here," a high-pitched voice says behind us.

I turn around to face a young Asian girl. She is standing there all alone. I know her from the competitions I had before. She is a good skater, and she might be our biggest competitor today.

„Well, as if I am missing a season. Plus, I can't let you win," I reply confidently. On the inside, I am praying that I am damn right with this. I hope that we're winning tomorrow.

„Good luck with that! I saw you skating before, and I don't have to worry about anything at all. Maybe it's my time to shine now," she replies mockingly.

Her eyes are darting to Asher. She looks at him in a way I immediately understand. A lot of girls are doing this. They know that Asher is attractive, and sometimes I think they might make a move toward him.

„Good luck tomorrow," I say before she skates away. Then I look at Asher and smile.

„She likes you," I giggle. Somehow I think that it is funny.

„She doesn't know me," Asher replies, not having a clue.

„No, she doesn't need to. She thinks you're hot," I try to clarify it to him.

„Too bad she isn't my type" he shrugs his shoulders and turns away from me.

I want to say something, but I don't. What comes into my head is mean, and I don't want to ruin the good mood. It's working so well for a while now, and I don't want to destroy that.

I hope that Asher opens up to me. He shouldn't be scared to talk to me. For now, we're making slow steps in the right direction.

„So, are we gonna skate now?" He asks me after a while. He reaches out his hand for mine.

We should skate a bit. We should get a feeling for the rink. Tomorrow everything here will be filled with people. There might also be someone from the media. Roman Balas will be underneath all these people. He will watch us skate.

My heart already pounds faster when I think about it. I am a little nervous but mostly excited. I feel prepared and ready for this competition. Now that I talked to the girl, I am even more eager to win it.

37

SLOANE

The morning of the competition, I woke up early. I have never been that nervous before. I couldn't sit still and had the urge to go for a run. I couldn't even eat breakfast. Asher ate more than usual. I guess that he ate more because he was nervous too. Irina is the same as always.

Thankfully, she understands our nervous behavior, but she isn't commenting on it. I just stare at my empty plate. Out of nowhere, doubts are filling my head. I don't know where it is coming from, but suddenly, I am asking myself what would happen if we were not winning.

I would completely give up probably. We have been working so hard, and I have always been a person who reached her goals. I can't believe that this shouldn't happen anymore.

I secretly look at Asher. He is the only hope I have. He is the best skater in my small town. I will have to move if this isn't working out with him. I would have to find a new partner, and I don't want to have a new partner.

It was easy with Flynn. Irina has trained out since we started being partners. We grew up together, and everything we learned, we learned together. It was easy because I never knew the difference.

„We have to leave in an hour. Get ready!" Irina orders as she is done.

I never ate something, and Asher is done as well. Now it's getting serious. I can't wait for this to be over.

One part of me wants to enjoy it, while the other wants it to be over. I need to find out how it ends. I want to know the ending now as if I want to prepare myself.

I go back to my room and put on my costume. I wear my tracksuit over my costume again. Today is a momentous day, and we can't mess this up.

We're quiet. No one is saying a word. Not even when we arrived at the skater's lounge. We sat there in silence, watching everything. Our hearts are pounding as fast as possible. It feels like it wants to jump right out of my chest.

We're somewhere in the middle with our performance. There is enough time to watch the others before getting ready. My eyes are gliding over the crowd. I already spotted Roman Balas. He sits next to the judges with the best view on the ice.

He watches everything intensely. God, he looks even better in person. His dark locks are perfectly styled. He is wearing a black suit, and even from afar, I can see that he is tall and muscular. His eyes are bright blue, his jawline sharp. He is a skating god.

I bet that every girl is feeling a little extra nervous today. I am feeling a bit extra jumpy. I really want to get invited to his dinner.

And his dinner is next to the victory, everything I can think of right now. Even when we're warming up, even when we're stepping onto the ice to start our performance.

But then I look at Asher, and I look right into his eyes. The green of the deepest forest pulls me in, and suddenly I calm down. I stop thinking about the dinner and the competition at all.

I go back to the evening we rehearsed our performance for the last time. The song was playing somewhere in the background, the light was dimmed, and we were alone.

This is how I feel right now. I forget everything around me. I pretend that we're entirely alone right now. It works.

The song starts playing. Everything else is quiet and calm. It feels like some people are holding their breath as we start performing. I can even hear ourselves breathing. I touch his skin, and once again, it feels electrified.

I feel only the beat of the music and his touch. This is how we wanted to perform it. We wanted to share an intimate performance, and this is what we're doing right now. Everything is on point, nearly perfect. Every lift, every spin, or every jump. Everything seems to finally work out.

The song ends, and the performance is over. Asher's head is lying on my chest, the both of us heavily breathing. I swear for a second that I could feel how Asher pressed his lips on my neck. A soft but barely there kiss.

We wave to the crowd one last time, a huge smile plastered on our faces before leaving the ice. Our performance is over. Now we can lean back and wait for the results. This time I have an excellent feeling. We did great, and I bet that the judges saw it.

We sit down, watching the others perform. We have to wait for quite a time now. That's why I like higher competitions a lot more. They show the ranking at all times. We can see the points we receive and where we're right now. But now we have to wait until the very end.

It's hard to watch the others. They are good, but not as good as our performance felt. Irina is ensuring us that we are way better. Even she thinks that we're going to win.

So we're sitting next to each other. Waiting for the announcement to start. They want to build up the tension, of course. First, they introduce Roman, who is now taking over with his dark voice. He is announcing the ranking and the winners.

My heart is pounding so quickly that it feels like I can't breathe anymore. I can see how Asher is rolling his eyes. I thought he liked Roman or that he could be his role model. He is someone who skates for the Olympics. But yet he is sitting here looking pretty annoyed.

I listen to every word the star skater is saying now. He first talks about his skating experience and how much he loves being here with everyone else.

Then he starts announcing the ranking. Every couple is shown on the board, everyone except the first three places. It takes me a while to go through the names.

And it takes even longer for me to realize that our names are not in the ranking. Asher takes my hand, and our fingers intertwine.

We're underneath the first three. I can't believe that we're on the podium once again.

We're definitely climbing the ladder. Slowly Roman is announcing third place. It's not us.

We look at each other, our faces full of hope. Maybe we really did it. Perhaps, we finally made it.

Irina is taking my other hand. Now she is nervous as well. We're now waiting for him to tell us who the first place is.

It better be us. It better be us. It better be us.

I silently pray on the inside. One massive part of me gave up hope a long time ago. I thought I might never get this feeling again. And I thought that I might never win again. Here we are, and I would say that this is a pretty huge deal for us.

„It's a huge honor to announce the first place, with by far the best score of today. Sloane Griffin and Asher Williams!"

Roman Balas his voice is a blur. I can barely understand what he is saying. All I can hear are our names.

Everyone is cheering. Even Irina seems to scream out of happiness. Asher throws his arms around me and pulls me into the tightest hug. We did it!

 I can feel his lips against my cheek as he presses a kiss on it. But I couldn't care less. I would even kiss him on the lips right now.

While the ranking reveals the first three, and everyone is still cheering, the podium gets set up. We have to go back on the ice and climb up first. There we'll receive the medals.

Roman Balas is hanging them around our necks himself. I couldn't be happier about that as well. It's such an honor.

Pride is filling me as he puts the medals around my neck. His smile is enough to sweep me off my feet. He is way too old for me, but he is the closest I have to a celebrity crush.

I had a crush on him for as long as I can remember. I watched every step of his career until he finally skated at the Olympic Games.

We stay on the podium for some pictures. Then we climb back down and take some more pictures. My personal highlight is a picture with the celebrity Roman Balas.

Roman stays after the photographer leaves. „You did really well on the ice. I am impressed by your skating skills," he compliments Asher and me.

„Thank you so much, Mr. Balas" I smile sweetly.

„Oh please, it's Roman." He tells me with a charming smile. A girlish giggle escapes my lips.

„I would love to invite you two to my dinner party tomorrow night. A skating couple like you two deserves to celebrate your victory," he smiles. And this is how it happened. We're now invited to his party. I am already dying on the inside.

38

ASHER

Sloane couldn't be more excited about this stupid party. I haven't seen her all day. She went shopping to find the right outfit for tonight, I guess.

All I do is starring at my medal. We won the competition yesterday, and I want nothing more than to celebrate with Sloane.

All she is thinking about is this asshole Roman Balas and his stupid party. I can't even tell why I am so annoyed. I don't know him. I know that he is a great skater, and I could take him as my role model. But something about him is just so sketchy.

I'll never forget the way Sloane looked at him yesterday. She was so happy as he put the medal around her neck. She was talking about his party all night but never mentioned the victory.

We won the competition. We never talked about the feeling we had during the performance. I know that Sloane felt the same. I know that she had the same feeling.

I know that there might come a point where we can't hide whatever is between us. So we should at least talk about it, just to make sure that there'll never be anything between us.

I need her for my career. I need her to be successful.

I stand up and leave the bed with a groan. It's also time for me to get ready. I only have these black dress pants and my white button-up shirt for the party. This has to be enough.

I take a shower, which takes me longer than usual. I let the hot water stream down my body.

I sigh. Sloane is stuck in my head. She is all I can think about right now. I can't help it.

I won't go to this party if she isn't coming with me. If she stayed here in the hotel, I would be here.

But now I am getting ready to accompany her tonight. I style my hair. I at least try to tame my toffee-colored curls. I spray on some perfume and leave the first buttons of my shirt open. It looks less formal but formal enough, I guess.

I take one last look into the mirror as I hear a knock on my door. This has to be Sloane. It's time for us to leave. So I grab my jacket and my phone. I walk toward the door with significant steps and open it just to reveal the most stunning girl I ever laid eyes on.

Sloane always cares about her appearance, and she always looks good. But this right now is something different.

Her blonde hair is curled, and it's falling over her shoulders. She is wearing a black short silk dress. God, she looks too fucking perfect. And I bet that she knows it. She has to know that she looks like a fucking goddess.

„Are you ready to go?" She asks me, noticing how I stare at her.

I nod, I usually compliment her, but I am not doing it now. I didn't compliment her because I told her that we couldn't even be friends. I close the door behind me, and she leads the way toward the elevator. She walks in front of me, her hips swaying, and her legs seem even longer in those heels. I notice that she is dressing up like this for another guy. She is dressing like this for Roman, the douchebag, and I absolutely don't like it.

It makes me hate him even more that she wants his attention. Irina is staying behind. Only we're invited, and even if she got invited too, she wouldn't go, I think.

She told us to use this chance wisely. We are meeting tons of important people there. But this isn't business. They are there because they want to have fun.

It's a party, not a place to meet influential people.

We're not talking. Again no one is saying a word. I thought we would stay together at the party, but Sloane disappears in the opposite direction as soon as we're there.

I feel a bit lost. This party isn't important to me.

„Asher Williams, it's nice that you made it! Where is your beautiful partner?" Roman Balas asks me. He greets me with a broad smile on his lips, but I know that it is fake. Roman isn't happy to see me. Why would he?

„Thanks for the invite! She is somewhere here," I reply politely, and he nods.

„Well, make yourself at home," he replies and walks past me. Maybe he is now looking for Sloane. The thought alone is enough for me.

I walk into the kitchen. Every little spot here is filled with people. I don't know the people who don't even look at me when I pass them. I bet that no one really has an interest in talking to me.

So I grab a beer bottle and just walk around. Roman has a lovely home. Everything looks luxurious and expensive. A bit cold, in my opinion, there is nothing personal in this apartment. Nothing that shows to who it could belong.

I lean against the counter, which separates the kitchen and living area.

„I was hoping to see you here," a familiar voice comes closer. I look to the side and see the Asian girl from the competition standing next to me.

She smiles sweetly as she looks at me. Innocently she looks up to meet my eyes. Sloane might be right about her.

„Why?" I ask her.

„I wanted to congratulate you on your victory. I loved your performance,"

„Thank you," I reply with a smile.

„So, Asher, right?" She asks, and I nod as a reply. „Where is your partner?"

And with that, I take a look around. I haven't seen Sloane in a while now. But as I scan the room with my eyes, I see her standing on the opposite side.

I point at her. „There"

She looks gorgeous, laughing at something the asshole in front of her says. Roman found her, and now he is clearly flirting with her. But I think that he is at least ten years older than Sloane.

I look back at the girl next to me, she knows my name, and I feel bad that I can't remember hers.

She is actually pretty. Her long black hair is in a tight ponytail. Her dark brown eyes are outlined with black eyeshadow to make them look even more prominent. She is a good skater, I saw her performance, and I knew she might be our biggest competitor. She got second place with her partner, yet I still don't remember her name.

If I weren't so distracted, I would give her more attention. Maybe I would even flirt with her. But I am not really interested. My eyes are constantly darting back to Sloane, who is still laughing.

The girl next to me is now talking about something. I don't know what it is because I never actually listened. I sip my beer as I watch my blonde skating partner.

Roman is reaching out, touching her shoulder softly. He strokes back her hair, and this simply is enough for me. I can't watch this any longer. I put my beer aside and walked over to her.

39

SLOANE

Roman is flirting with me. If someone told me this, I wouldn't believe them. I was crushing on him for such a long time, and now he really is flirting with me.

He handed me a drink as soon as he found me. He even gave me a tour of his beautiful apartment. This tour ended in the living room, where we're just talking right now.

I have a perfect view of Asher, whom I haven't seen the whole night. But he seems to be in the best company. He looks at the girl intently, and I know the look on his face too well. The fuck me look. God, why do I even care.

I turn back to Roman, who tells me about his successful career. He climbed up the ladder with nothing at the beginning. Now he is a trainer.

„I would love to train you. I see a lot of potential in you. Some are still undiscovered" he smiles at me. He touches my shoulder swiftly, his broad hand brushing away my hair. He reveals my neck, and he stares down at the exposed skin.

My heart is pounding, but not in a positive way. Something feels strange about this. The flirting was nice, but I wouldn't jump into bed with him. He is much older than me, and somehow it feels highly inappropriate.

I bet he isn't even really interested in me. He saw me skating once. This can't really make an impression on someone. Not like this.

But suddenly, someone grabs my hand. I pulled away, thinking it was Roman.

„We have to leave. Irina wants us back at the hotel," Asher interrupts. He doesn't smile. He loses his polite tone.

He looks at me, and I think something might have happened for a second. I quickly nod and hand Roman my drink.

„Thank you so much, but we have to leave," I tell him with a sweet smile. He shouldn't be pissed at me. He is still a prominent personality in the skating world.

„Sure, I totally understand. Call me. Maybe you're free one night before you leave town," and he hands me a piece of paper with his number on it.

I take it, unsure of what to do with it. I don't really want to have Roman's number. I won't give him a call, even if we would stay here for longer.

Asher pulls me away right into the hallway. There is already an Uber waiting to bring us back to the hotel. We slip right onto the backseat. I have a look at Asher. He seems pissed somehow, even though there isn't a reason for him to be pissed. I don't know what is going on inside his head. Maybe something terrible happened.

I paid for the Uber as we arrived at the hotel. Outside, the cold night air is stinging my skin. I adjust my dress quickly.

Asher is leading the way inside. As soon as we're in the elevator, I finally look at him.

„What the hell is your problem? And what happened?" It was burning on my tongue the whole time. I just want to know what happened and why we had to leave.

„Nothing happened. I just couldn't bear it anymore. How could you even go to this party looking like this?" He spits out. His eyes seem darker as he looks at me.

„What?" I breathe out. My voice suddenly seems so small.

„Did you dress up for him? Did you want to leave an impression so he would fuck you?" Asher asks me. My eyes widen at his choice of words.

„Maybe I wanted someone to notice. A girl has needs," I reply.

He pisses me off. First, Asher told me that we can't even be friends, and now he acts like this. It seems like he can't make up his fucking mind.

„Believe me, I noticed. I noticed the second I opened the door." He breathes out, coming instantly closer.

„And yet you only had eyes for that bitch" I reply.

„What? I can't even remember her name because all I can think of is you," Asher replies.

He pulls me out of the elevator. My breathing had already gotten heavier. Did he just say that he can't stop thinking about me? Nothing makes sense anymore.

„God, Sloane," he breathes out. When he pulls me into this room, he smashes his lips onto mine. My arms are automatically flying around his neck. I wanted to kiss him for so long. Now that it's finally happening again, a fire starts in me. I want more. I want all of him.

He presses me against the wall. His hands are grabbing my thighs, lifting me up. I wrap my legs around him. My shoulder lifts the picture next to me on the wall, only for it to fall onto the ground.

It doesn't bother us. We don't even notice. Asher pulls away from my mouth. His lips are exploring my skin eagerly. He pulls down the straps of my dress, revealing that I am not wearing a bra underneath.

„Oh, Sloane," he sighs so sweetly that I swear I am in heaven. And right then, he licks my skin, he kisses the skin now exposed to him. He knows exactly where to kiss, lick or suck. He knows my body too well, as if he paid attention to every detail every time we got intimate.

I throw my head back as he sucks on my left nipple, his fingers playing with the right one.

„Fuck me," I beg him.

I don't want to wait anymore. I need Asher now.

„Not before I finally tasted you," he replies, his voice full of lust. The wall behind my back disappears. Asher is carrying me to the bed quickly. The soft mattress of his bed hits my back.

It seems like he doesn't waste any time right now. He pulls the dress off, kissing the newly exposed skin. A sigh escapes my lips as the dress finally lays on the floor, and he plays with the waistband of my underwear. I wait for him to finally pull them off. I even lift my hips to help him.

I can hear him chuckle at my impatient behavior, even though it is nothing new to him. It seems to work because he is slowly peeling off the last piece of material on my body. I sigh as the cold air hits my core.

Asher is grabbing my thighs, spreading my legs for him. „Mhm, so wet, already? And I haven't even started," he sighs, and before I could reply, he dives right in.

One hand grabs the sheets while the other is grabbing his hair. I closed my eyes as I couldn't hold back the moan. God, he is good at that. He knows exactly where to lick or suck. As I look down at him, his mouth buried in my pussy, he stares back up. And the look in his eyes alone has the power to make me come undone.

His arms are caging me, holding me in position as he eats me out like I am his last meal. It isn't a surprise that I come quickly. I throw my head back, moaning out loud as the first wave of my orgasms hits me. I can feel how Asher is looking at me intensely.

„God, you're so beautiful when you come," he sighs as he moves up. I pull him down to me and kiss his lips. I'm sliding off his shirt first, freeing him from the material he worse before. He is wearing way too many clothes. So I next pull down his pants. His erection is just waiting to get freed. He moans out in the most beautiful when I pump him a couple of times.

„Stop, or I won't last long enough," he sighs, grabbing my hand, and forcing me to stop.

He stands up to get a condom. He looks like a freaking god, standing there all naked, his hair already messy. I long for him. It even seems like the desire is growing even more with every second.

He quickly comes back. I snap the condom out of his hand to help him. I don't want to waste any time now. I open the package and roll it on, pumping him again.

He is quickly pushing me back into the mattress. I spread my legs, wrapping them around his hips.

He thrust into me with one hard stroke, which has me screaming out loud. God, he feels like heaven. So perfect that I might think we're made for each other.

He doesn't wait and starts pushing into me hard. He groans. Our sounds fill the room, along with skin slapping onto the skin. His hands caress my breasts as he looks me into the eyes.

Why did I ever say that having sex with him was a mistake? This feels more than right to me. Damn, it is addicting. I know that I will long for more now every time I look at him.

40

SLOANE

I wake up, not remembering that I fell asleep in the first place. I open my eyes and take a look around the room. I am still in Asher's bed. I never went back to my hotel room, and I think it never mattered in the first place. It was already early in the morning when I must've fallen asleep. I look to the side. Asher is still sound asleep.

He looks so peaceful. His curls are a mess, and his long lashes are touching his cheeks. He doesn't snore. I can see his chest slowly moving up and down, sleeping deeply.

His naked body is halfway hidden underneath the blanket. I slowly sit up, trying not to wake him up. His hotel room is a mess, which only takes me back to our night together. Pillows are all over the floor, and the picture fell off the wall. Everything that was on the small table is now on the ground.

I fish my purse from the ground to grab my phone. I see that it's nearly time to leave the hotel with a look at the screen. We're flying back home today.

„Oh shit!" I say out loud and jump off the bed. I grab my stuff and immediately get dressed.

„Asher, wake up! We need to pack our stuff. We're leaving in an hour," there is no need to wake him up because he has already opened his eyes.

It seems to take a minute for him to realize what I am doing here. I put on my dress as quickly as possible and grabbed my shoes and purse.

„What time is it?" Asher asks me, his voice raspy and still sleepy.

„It's nearly eleven," I reply and sigh. He needs to get up and pack his stuff. Irina will be pissed if we're not down in time, worse if we miss our flight.

„I'll see you in the lobby," I say and turn around. Luckily my room isn't that far from his. I open the door at the end of the aisle.

It's neat, and my stuff is still in my suitcase. There might still be some time for a quick shower, so I grab my stuff and run into the bathroom. I don't waste any time washing my hair and my body. But while I am in the shower, I finally have the time to think about what happened last night.

Actually, a lot happened, and I have no idea what this means. Asher and I had sex again! Multiple times!

He just told me days ago that we can't even be friends. He told me that he wanted to keep his distance, and then the exact opposite thing happened. I remember how he said that he was thinking about me. All the things he said are still in my head.

Do I like him? I think I do. Otherwise, I wouldn't have done this multiple times. I hate myself because of this. This could put my skating career in danger. Irina might tell me that she has to separate us. Couples are not supposed to skate with each other.

You don't mix your private emotional life with work. Separating this makes everything more manageable, and I messed up. I messed up real bad.

I quickly put on something comfortable, my hair is still wet, but I don't care about it. I pack my stuff and go back down into the lobby. Irina is already waiting for us.

She is sitting in one of the armchairs and drinking a coffee. She quickly looks up as I hand her my room key. She has to check us out as soon as Asher is here.

Asher comes down with damp hair as well. He took a shower, as it seemed. His smile fades as he reaches us. He is avoiding my eyes instead.

Asher quickly hands Irina the room card. Our coach stands up to check us out.

„Sloane?" Asher begins. I look up, right into his green eyes.

„About last night… let's forget about it. It was clearly a mistake, and it will never happen again," he starts, thinking that I might want to hear this.

I look at him as my eyes widen. I stare at him in pure shock. It was a mistake? This can't be true. He started it yesterday, and this is on him.

„What? Are you out of your mind?" I try not to yell at him. I would slap him if I could. I am so furious right now. „Don't tell me this didn't mean anything to you? Was it just a meaningless fuck?"

„It doesn't matter, you're my partner, and this is not allowed to happen again. We crossed our boundaries, and if this happens again, I tell Irina that I'm quitting. I won't risk my career over something so stupid," his voice sounds so cooly that it breaks my heart right away.

Over something so stupid? So it meant nothing at all? Did he just think I looked good yesterday or that he is the better choice than someone else?

I try to hold back my tears. Asher doesn't deserve to know that I will cry over this. He shouldn't see that he hurt me right now. Instead, I nod quickly.

„You're right. It's idiotic. Skating is more important, so we have a deal," I reply. I turn around, my back now facing him.

I quickly wiped the tear away that escaped. Irina is already coming back, and I don't want to explain what happened.

I hope that we have separate seats on the plane. Maybe I get some privacy to cry in silence. I am not sure if I can control myself until I am at home.

Right now, I need Flynn. I wish he would be here with me. He would tell me how stupid I was. He would tell me that Asher is not worthing it. Skating is more important. Skating has always been my priority.

That should never change. It is still my first priority, but I care more about Asher than I thought.

41
ASHER

I broke my own heart saying this. I never wanted to hurt Sloane, but it was the best thing I could do.

First, we shouldn't risk our skating careers. It should be our first priority. I know Sloane doesn't want me as much as I want her. I like her. I like her more than I would ever say out loud.

And this is the problem because, second, I am not capable of a real relationship. I can't even be really successful in skating. My father is a terrible person, and no one can ever find out about my life. No one is allowed to know the truth. And I may be as awful as him.

I don't want anyone to live with this. If I turn out as terrible as my father, I don't want a girl or a kid. I want to be on my own because that's the only thing I know and deserve.

Today is going to be one of the most challenging days. I don't know what will happen when I walk inside the door.

My father might want to kill me. He indeed is angry at me. I left him even though he told me not to.

But this isn't as bad as sitting next to Sloane, who is crying. She tries to hide it, probably because I am sitting next to her. But I can hear her sniffles. I can see how she wipes away a tear every now and then.

Her eyes are red and swollen when we leave the plane. She doesn't talk, and Irina isn't asking about her behavior.

My heart breaks over and over when I see her like this. I never wanted to hurt her.

It's only for her own good, even if she doesn't know it. She gets over it quickly. We're practically strangers. She doesn't know me, and she can't like or even love someone she doesn't know. If she knew it, she would surely hate me.

They drop me off first. I quickly say goodbye and hop out of the car. I take a deep breath, fumbling around with my keys to find the right one. My heart is pounding heavily inside my chest, and my breathing gets heavy. I don't want to go inside. I don't want to go back.

This weekend was too good. I slept through the night for the first time in an eternity. Sleeping is easier when I have Sloane by my side. I had never slept that deep and heavy in ages, but next to her, I just felt so comfortable. I don't know what will happen now, but I know it can't be good.

My father already hears the door open. He is waiting for me right at the door when I step inside. I look at him, unsure of what to say.

„Took you long enough," he barks. His scent hints that he already drank something today. I can't tell when he is sober or if he is ever sober. I don't think I ever saw him sober in the past years.

„I'm sorry. We stayed a day longer, but I am here now. And I'll do the groceries now. Do you need anything?" I try to keep him calm.

Of course, it is not working. My father is already pissed. He is always angry. There isn't a single day he isn't mad at me and the world.

42
SLOANE

The minute I arrive home, I run up into my room and call Flynn. I miss my red-haired best friend, and I need him right now. My parents are still at work, so I have to talk to them later. I am sure they want to know everything about our victory and the competition.

I call Flynn and ask him to come over. He luckily agrees quickly. While I am waiting for him, I unpack my stuff. I hang the medal to the others and have a good look at it. It was a great weekend. At least, I thought it was great until today. Somehow Asher ruined everything. What he said really did something to me.

Flynn has a key, so I don't have to worry about opening the door. He is straight coming up to my room, opening the door after he knocked once. I sit on my bed, staring holes into the wall.

„Oh my god! What happened? Shouldn't you be celebrating? You finally did it!" Flynn looks at me. He carefully sits down next to me. I know I should be celebrating right now, dancing through my room with some happy music in the background. This is all I ever wanted. I wanted to win so badly.

But now it's not about winning anymore. It's about so much more.

„Something happened...." I started and looked at him. I know that I don't have to say it.

„What?" He asks, and then he looks at me. His eyes widen in realization. „Oh... again?"

„Yeah….“ I whisper and let my head hang.

„But it was so confusing. To be honest, the whole weekend was, “ I tell him and sigh.

„I took him to the lake on the first day because I wanted to know him better. It didn't really work out that well. He told me that we couldn't be friends and wanted to keep his distance from me. That already hurt. I thought that we could at least be friends…..“ I start telling my best friend about the weekend.

„The next day, we got our costumes, and everything was fine. Irina told us to rehearse our performance once more. We were on the ice, utterly alone in the complete building. The light was dimmed, and I swear that we both felt the same when we skated together.“ I sigh and look at him. I bet he saw our performance, and it was the same there.

„Let's just say that you both had incredible energy at the competition. It was great like there is something deeper between you,“ Flynn replies, and I nod.

„Well, we were at Roman Balas party. I looked hella good, by the way… and Roman seemed to like it. He was flirting with me, and Asher disliked it. He got so mad, I also think jealous. He dragged me back to the hotel, and there it happened…. Quite often,“ I sigh.

„Okay, I see it's confusing. What exactly happened afterward?“ My best friend asks me.

„I thought that everything was fine, but apparently it wasn't. Asher told me that it was a mistake and never wanted it to happen again. That we shouldn't risk our careers for something so stupid. Even though we both know that it isn't just sex anymore,“ the tears are rolling down my cheek.

A guy that I never wanted to know broke my heart. I never thought that I would even like him at all. And he broke my heart in the worst way possible.

Flynn is thinking about my words, and I think a part of him is unsure of what to say next. I understand that we crossed a line. Everything would be easier if we would just be friends or partners. Irina always told us that a relationship between partners is not working. She knows tons who lost a good partner because of it. Maybe they missed the most excellent chance in their career. I don't want this to happen to me.

„Do you like him?" My best friend asks me carefully.

I wasn't expecting this question. I thought Flynn might ask something different.

„I don't really know," I reply, shrugging my shoulders.

„So, yes," Flynn replies for me, and I sigh. I might like him, but I also don't really know.

„It's a challenging situation. You could tell him that you like him, but you have to be clear about what you want. It's him or your career for now. Both might not work out," Flynn tells me.

I groan, letting myself fall back. He knows that I am going to choose skating. I would never choose anything over skating ever. It's important to me.

„It's unfair. But well, Asher doesn't like me anyway."

„He does like you. He wouldn't have sex with you if he wouldn't like you. And I think it is pretty obvious in the way he looks at you," Flynn tells me, and I shake my head.

He doesn't look at me very often, and if he does, it is not telling anything positive.

„Keep on dreaming. I don't know why Asher wanted to sleep with me again, but I am pretty sure that it doesn't have anything to do with his feelings for me. Simply because they are non-existent," I reply.

I have to live with this. There won't be a chance for Asher and me. If we decide to try it, we would be separated as partners. I can't lose him as my partner. He is the only chance I have.

„I am scared that I might want to do it again. I don't want to screw this up."

I could cry forever right now. There is no end in sight.

„You won't mess up. You have always been a very rational person. Just shut your emotions out, like you always did," my best friend tells me.

He is right. I have never been really emotional. It's the first time right now that I am emotional about everything.

There are things inside of my head that I worry about. I would have never thought about it before. I want Asher to like me, and I want him to talk to me.

There is something within him. He has a secret. He doesn't want to talk to me because there is something that I am not supposed to know. I want to find out what it is.

It feels wrong. I would have never done such things before I met Asher. I couldn't care less about another human being. It sounds selfish, but I only cared about myself and my career. But this was the reason why I climbed so high so quickly.

Now I fell so quickly and so deep. It's harder to climb back up. It's because I am not only focussing on myself. I don't only care about my career anymore.

I hate myself for this. And I have to change this.

„Do you want to go on a trip?" I ask Flynn out of a sudden.

I have some free time on my hand. Irina told us to come back next week. The next competition is a few weeks away.

„Sure, I'm in," the redhead replies. I nod.

„You could ask Gregg if he wants to come with us, " I tell him with a smile.

„Can I also ask another friend? I know someone who could need some time off, " Flynn says.

I shrug my shoulders and nod slowly, „Sure, why not"

„Great! Where are we going?" he asks me curiously.

„I thought we could stay at my parent's cottage in the mountains. The lake is frozen and perfect for skating on. Even you could skate a bit, nothing special, of course, but you could skate. And I don't know if Gregg likes snowboarding" I shrug my shoulders.

But it would be a lot of fun. We have a hot tub there, a sauna, and many opportunities to get our heads free.

I would also love to spend more time with my best friend. It feels like I neglected him the past couple of weeks.

43

SLOANE

The trip is quickly planned. It took us a day. I asked my parents the minute they came home. They agreed, thinking it might be the perfect opportunity to celebrate my victory.

They think I might climb back to my original position. They believe I will skate for the Olympics one day. I highly doubt that right now.

I volunteered to drive, which means I have to pick up the others. Flynn told me to just come to his house. Everyone will be there.

It makes me nervous that he is bringing two of his friends, and I am not bringing a single one. The worst thing is that I don't really have a friend except for Flynn.

Maybe I'll like the second guy. I bet that he is gay as well, which is nothing bad. I just hoped it would be someone for me. Flynn knows tons of nice guys. I like Gregg, too. We never really spend time together, but this will change in the next couple of days. We might stay there for four or five days, and I couldn't be more excited.

I look around, checking if I have everything that I need. My bag is packed, and my skates are in their bag. Everything is good to go.

Now I need to carry everything to my car. I'm already taking my keys and everything else down with me. The minute I am done, I'll leave.

I am sure that Flynn is already waiting for me, and I can't wait for our trip to start.

I know that it is going to be so much fun!

I sing out loud to the songs on my radio, happy about the fun we're about to have. There is nothing that could ruin my mood right now.

I park my car in the driveway of Flynn's house. He is already waiting outside, waving with a big smile.

„Hello there! Are you excited?" He asks me.

I nod eagerly. Flynn knows how happy I am about this trip.

„Well, then promise me that you won't be mad. No matter what will happen now," he quickly tells me.

He is talking so fast that I am slightly confused and worried. I don't understand what he means. Why should I be mad at him?

„Please, promise," he begs again. I slowly nod.

But before I can say anything, I see what he means. Asher is leaving the house together with Gregg.

„Asher is the second friend?!" I keep my voice low. But if my look could kill, Flynn would already lie on the ground.

„I knew that if I told you, you would have never agreed to it" he shrugs his shoulders.

Flynn knows well enough that there is no going back for me now. I can't tell Asher that he has to stay home.

„I hate you " is the only thing I can say right now. I don't want to spend my time with Asher. This is supposed to be a getaway from Asher weekend.

„Maybe this is going to be more than helpful for you. You get to know Asher better, and you might lose your feelings. Also, you have to see this as some kind of partner bonding thing. You two need to solve your issues," Flynn explains, for which he earns a groan from me.

I don't think it is good for him to come with us. I thought I would spend this time without Asher.

„Thanks for inviting me, Sloane! This is going to be amazing!" Gregg smiles as he hugs me. At least one person is more than excited about this trip.

My excitement is now gone. I just want it to be over already.

Before Asher can say anything, I turn away and hop into my car. The others are putting their bags into the trunks. It takes a while until everyone is in the car and ready to go.

It will be a long drive, even longer for me now that Asher is here too. Flynn takes over the radio and plays some fun music. He and Gregg are singing along to the songs, and both are so happy.

I am already annoyed, simply because Asher is here with us. He is looking out of the window, not saying anything. He isn't even smiling.

I don't know why he agreed to come with us. Asher and Flynn weren't even talking. I never knew they were actually friends. Right now, it doesn't really seem like it.

„Do you like snowboarding?" I ask Gregg. I want to start a conversation with someone in this car, and he seems to be the best choice.

„Not really, but I like snow, and maybe I will learn a bit about ice skating," he replies politely.

I nod slowly. Gregg is not the biggest fan of skating. I remember the last time Flynn forced him to skate a bit. He couldn't hold his balance and fell more often than sliding forwards.

He tried because he loves Flynn, but I know he never wanted to do it again. „The lake is beautiful! I bet it's incredible to skate there" I smile at him.

And with that, the conversation is already dying. We're listening to the Christmas songs playing on the radio. Flynn is humming along.

I don't know how he can be in such a good mood. He knows what he did by inviting Asher.

We're still not talking an hour later, the Christmas songs got calmer, and Asher fell asleep. The closer we get to the mountain cabin, the more snow there is. I hate driving during this weather, but it could be more.

We'll arrive in the late afternoon, maybe we'll cook something for dinner, and try to enjoy our first evening together. It's nothing special, but we're here to relax.

Tomorrow I want to go and skate on the lake, alone, to free my head. I want to use this time here, even if Asher is here with us. I want to come back stronger and better.

44

ASHER

I don't know what I am doing here. Sloane seems to be pissed to see me. Of course, I hurt her. Flynn thought it would be a great idea to help us. I am not sure about that, but I would do anything to escape my father.

No one was talking to me in the car, and after a while, I fell asleep. Sloane woke me up the minute we got there. It was the only time she actually talked to me. Sloane avoided me for the rest of the night. She wasn't even eating dinner with us.

I am happy that Flynn and Gregg do not hate me. I know that Sloane must have told Flynn about what happened. He is way too nice to me.

I excuse myself to go to bed a while later. It's peaceful here, another escape from my daily life. Even if I think that it was a mistake to come here. Sloane wanted to come here to have an excellent time. I ruined it. I know that she wanted to spend some time apart from me.

The following day I first take a look around the cabin. I thought the others might still be asleep, but Flynn was already standing in the kitchen. He is brewing some coffee.

„Good morning," he greets me with a smile. I quickly learned that Flynn is always in a good mood. He is the total opposite of Sloane.

„Morning," I reply.

„Coffee?"

I nod, and Flynn instantly hands me a cup. It's hot, and the smell is fantastic. I carefully take a sip, not wanting to burn myself.

„Listen, I am sorry that you might feel unwelcome by Sloane. I didn't tell her I invited you," Flynn starts slowly.

„She really hates me....." I reply quietly. I understand that he didn't tell her. She would have said no, and he thought it might be a good idea.

„No, I wouldn't say that. Sloane is hurt, but don't worry, she'll get over it eventually" he smiles at me, trying to encourage me. It's not working. I don't think that she'll get over it.

I am an asshole for doing this to her. It is all my fault. I started it that night, I wanted to sleep with her, and I made a move.

„I'll get ready and head down to the lake. Don't wait for me," I tell Flynn and return to my room.

I get ready quickly. Maybe it is easier for Sloane if I am not close to her. I need to get my head free anyway, and the ice is the only thing helping me with that.

My life got so messy the last couple of months. Skating with Sloane was the best thing that happened to me. But it also made everything so much more complicated.

I'm in a massive conflict with myself, what I want, and what I might need. Everything is so complicated that I can't even explain it to myself.

I grab my skates and leave the cabin behind as quickly as possible. The lake is already visible. Not a single human being is here. Perfect for me to skate all by myself.

As soon as I reach the ice, I put on my skates, and I don't waste another second stepping onto the ice. I quickly lose the feeling of time, not knowing how long I have already skated.

Everything around me is blurred. It's just me and the ice right now. I feel free, and there is nothing to worry about for the first time. My head is empty. There is nothing I need to think of. I can shut everything off right now, enjoying the moment thoroughly.

„You stole my spot," someone says behind me.

She is pulling me away from my trance. I stop skating, catching my breath as I look at Sloane.

She is standing in front of me on the ice, wearing her skates. She is probably here to free her head as well.

I don't really know what to say because I don't know if she is still mad at me. Her voice was neutral, so I couldn't tell if she wanted me to leave.

„I always skated here when I was a little kid. We came here every now and then during the winter. My parents love to ski, and I always loved to skate here," she tells me with a soft smile on her lips.

„It's stunning here." I reply with a nod. She starts to skate around me. It seems like she isn't mad at me anymore. But I still don't trust it. For a second, I was even scared she would yell at me. I deserve it. I want her to be mad at me.

„Flynn thinks that we should have a game night later," she tells me, shaking her head as if it is a bad idea.

„And you don't like that idea?" I ask her.

„Depends. Are you good in charades?" Sloane asked me, and her question surprised me.

„I don't really know. I never played it before," I reply, shrugging my shoulders. I am not an idiot. I know the game. I had never played before. We never played any games at home, and I never had friends to play with.

„What? I can't believe that I now have a teammate who has never played before! Ugh, we're so going to lose," she sighs.

„Flynn and Gregg are the perfect team. It's impossible to win against them," she explains, and I nod.

She is so chatty today, and she seems to be in a good mood. I am slightly confused.

„This is weird, but can we skate together?"

This question surprises me even more. I don't know why Sloane wants to skate with me. Yesterday she didn't even want to talk to me.

„You sure?" I ask her again, and she nods.

"Yes, please"

She hands me one of her AirPods. I can hear the same music now. A song I heard before, but not a song we ever performed to. I look at her. We're now standing directly in front of each other.

We need a moment before we actually start to skate. There is no choreography. We're not talking. We're just skating, communicating through our moves on the ice. I don't know how we're doing it. I might never understand it.

We're dancing a dance we don't even know, but it is working. Our moves are smooth as always. It feels like we have known each other forever. It feels like we're one and the same.

At least it feels like this on the ice because as soon as we have solid ground underneath our feet, it's different.

But today is a good day. Sloane is laughing. She is chatting and joking with everyone. She is different, but it's good to see her like this.

45

ASHER

Flynn really holds on to his plan. The game night is a sure thing now; no one can miss this. Everything starts with a stupid round of monopoly. This already takes an eternity.

But then the actual game night starts, charade.

As Sloane said, Flynn and Gregg are really good at this. They understand each other without saying much. It seems like they're sharing the same thoughts.

„I never played it before, be nice," I warn Sloane as she stands up. It's our turn now. My heart is racing. I am nervous because I don't want to mess up. I know how eager she is to win. I want her to win. I want to see that beautiful smile on her face.

She picks a stack of cards and looks at the first one. The game is pretty straightforward, but it's also a lot of teamwork. I try to guess whatever comes into my head first. She pretends to skate, „Ice skating!"

Her face lights up. I guessed right. Climbing mountains, delivering the mail, flipping pancakes… the game isn't challenging. The first round was pretty easy. I think they wanted to go easy on me because I had never played before.

Now, Flynn picks another category. Movies and tv-shows. My knowledge when it comes to it is zero.

I watch the other team perform perfectly. I understand what Sloane means when she says it's impossible to win against them. I think that Flynn must know this game by heart. Otherwise, it is impossible to be as fast as them.

It's our turn now. I have to act out the names on the cards, and Sloane has to guess. This is going to be a mess.

I pick the stack and have a look at the first card. I show Sloane that it is one word she has to guess, an easy movie. I try my best and hope that she knows this movie. I think that everyone knows it.

I point out my fingers as if I am throwing spiderwebs, just like the character does.

„Spiderman!" Sloane quickly yells. I take the next card and have a look at it.

Next, I try to make my best interpretation of the Grinch, Harry Potter, and Dracula. Sloane is guessing everything in a couple of seconds. We are not as bad as I thought.

We're laughing at our interpretations. We fool around, making jokes about everything. It's fun. My first game night with friends. It's my first trip with friends as well. I just realized that I have never been away like this.

My fear and my family were always holding me back. But this here feels more than perfect, and I am more than happy to be here.

Maybe there is still a chance for me to make everything right between Sloane and me. Even if I can't get closer to her, we can't be friends, but we can try our best when it comes to skating and being partners.

We clean everything as we're done. The lights are shut off, and everyone goes into their rooms after saying *Goodnight*. Everyone except Sloane. She stays behind in the kitchen. The dim light is showing her at the counter.

„Is everything okay?" I ask her as I decide to check on her.

„Yeah, I just want a hot chocolate before I go to bed. Do you want one too?" She asks me with a smile.

I nod slowly. Unsure if I should really stay here right now. I don't know if this might be a good idea.

But I sit down at the counter, watching her as she prepares everything for the hot chocolate.

She seems so relaxed and happy here.

„You stayed here often?" I ask her quietly.

She looks at me for a while and then nods, „Yeah, mostly Flynn was with us. But that was before my parents were workaholics."

„Does it bother you that they're working that much?" I ask her carefully.

I don't really know if I am crossing a line here. I would love to have workaholics as parents. Everything is better than the father I have now.

„Sometimes… They are gone most of the time. They miss important things like my coming home after winning the Toronto competition with my partner. But I understand that I grew up and that they can't always be there," Sloane tells me.

She slides the cup over the counter. I take it with a smile on my face. „Thank you"

„What about you?" She slowly drops the question. I can see that she is unsure to ask me something.

„What?" I want to know precisely what she means.

„There is something you don't want to talk about. You have secrets…."

„Everyone has secrets," I tell her with a small laugh.

Some secrets are not as bad as others. My secrets are bad. I don't want anyone to ever find out about my life. It's better if people don't know me that well.

„Yeah, but you keep your distance because of that. You push me away. It can't be that bad," she starts.

I shake my head. We're not doing this now. She had such a good day. I don't want that to be ruined.

„You don't know me, Sloane. You don't want to know me."

„Why don't you leave that choice up to me? I do know you, and I know that you're a wonderful person. I know that you sacrifice everything for the people you love, you're passionate, and obviously, you're terrible at handling emotions" she smiles at me.

Why is she smiling?

I know that now I will say something to hurt her. I keep pushing her away. This is the best for her. She should stay away from me. But she doesn't understand that.

„But that's not me. You don't know me at all," I say again.

This time she shakes her head, reaching out her hand for mine.

„I am pretty sure that this is who you are. Nothing could make me run away," her voice is so soft. I nearly believe her.

But this is something I don't want to risk. Sloane doesn't know what she is talking about. She doesn't know who I am or what it means to be part of my life.

„No, you're wrong. You have no idea who I really am," I tell her harsher than I wanted to.

„Why don't you try it and let me decide?"

„I am not going to risk our partnership! I need you as my partner because if I lose this, I'll lose everything in my life!" I try not to yell at her. I try not to get angry.

Why am I so angry about it? I can just tell her that my father is abusive and hitting me. He hit my mom before she died. He is always drunk, and he can't keep the money I earn to pay our bills. He is wasting it on alcohol and gambling.

Skating is the only thing that brings me joy. The only thing that I really love. I can't lose that.

Maybe she is going to think that I might become my father. Perhaps it's in my genes to be an asshole.

„We already crossed a line. There is no going back, you know that. You know that there is already something between us, something we can't take back," Sloane whispers. Her voice is so quiet but still calm.

Of course, I know that. There has been something between us since the first time we had sex.

„I still think it's best to forget about it. We could ruin everything…."

„So you basically tell me that we don't feel the same?"

„Even if we feel the same, it won't change a thing," I reply, sounding as neutral as possible.

All I want right now is to be close to her, to press my lips against hers. There is this huge desire. Everything is longing for her.

But there is so much that could go wrong. Sloane doesn't know me. She knows nothing about my life.

And I never want her to find out about it.

46

ASHER

I avoided Sloane the following day by staying inside my room. I only came out to eat. It seems to be acceptable for the three of them. I heard they went on a walk and had tons of fun during the day.

I don't feel good spending time with them after the conversation with Sloane. I know everything has to go back to normal again when we're back home. We continue with our training schedule. The next competition is coming closer.

I wait until everyone is asleep. The cabin is getting quiet, and I finally leave my room. I grab a towel, wearing my swimming trunks. There is no way I'll miss the hot tub while we're here. I need to at least hop in once.

The water feels hot on my skin, which is a massive contrast to the cold air around me. I take a look around the darkness. There is nothing but snow around me. The cabin is still pitch black. No light is on. Our bedrooms are on the other side of the house, but I can be sure that everyone is asleep now.

I close my eyes for a second, leaning back. I enjoy the water I am sitting in. It's been too long since I sat in a hot tub the last time. I can't even remember it.

„I thought you were already asleep," I hear a familiar voice at the door. I can't see Sloane, but I know she is standing there.

„I could say the same to you," I reply calmly, looking to where I think she might be.

„Too bad, I really wanted to use the hot tub," she sighs as if she wouldn't come and join me. Something in her voice sounds playful, as if she came out on purpose.

„I can leave."

„No, no. It's fine. You have been in your room all day, avoiding me. You deserve this," she replies.

Sloane is not coming any closer, but she isn't moving away either. She is standing there, waiting for something. I can't tell what she is waiting for, though.

„What are you doing here? Are you waiting for an invitation?"

„No, I'm just taking a deep breath before heading back inside," and I swear I can hear her dramatically sigh. I know she wants to join me or use the hot tub.

I could still leave after she got in. Or we just sit here in silence. No one has to talk. I could close my eyes and pretend that I was alone.

„Come and hop in. There is enough space" I finally breathe out.

Now I am waiting for her to move. First, she seems to be unsure about it. She is still waiting. But then I can hear her small steps through the snow. Sloane comes closer, finally stepping into the light of the hot tub. It's a dim light, but it is enough to see her.

The blonde girl is wearing a pink bathrobe, her hair up in a bun on her head. She is quickly undoing the knot, then she lets the robe drop.

My eyes widen as I realize that she is not wearing anything underneath. I stare at her in complete shock, not being able to look away. „What are you doing?"

„What? There is nothing you have never seen before," she shrugs her shoulders, lowering herself into the water. On her lips is laying a satisfied smirk. Sloane surely planned this.

„Why are you doing this?" I look away, moving farther away from her.

„What? I'm not doing anything," she shrugs her shoulders, playing dumb. But Sloane knows precisely what she is doing.

„Yes, you are! Is this why you came outside?" I ask her hoping to get an honest answer from her.

I doubt that she is going to talk about it. She is sitting right there naked. I don't know what she expects me to do.

„I forgot my swimwear at home. Why are you making such a drama right now?"

She is still acting dumb, playing along with her story. I sigh, looking at her. I try to keep my eyes up to her face, which is hard. I have to admit that I love her body. She looks stunning. Seeing her naked in front of me makes me want to touch her again.

I'm happy that it is so dark outside. Otherwise, Sloane would see the growing bulge in my pants now.

„You know why, and that's why you're doing it. Stop playing games with me," my voice is darker, filled with lust.

God, if she would only know how much I want her. There is not a single second that I don't think about her. Sloane seems to feel the same. She slowly comes closer to me.

„You sure? I should stop playing?" Her voice sounds so innocent as she sits herself down on my lap. I take in a deep breath, looking up into the black sky. The stars are clearly visible tonight.

„You know this is wrong, " I whisper, still not looking at her.

She seems to forget about the consequences. There is so much we could lose. Sloane doesn't care about anything right now.

I can feel her hand moving over my stomach, I know what she is up to, and I stop her. My hand grabs her wrist, keeping her hands away from my body.

„We can't do this," I whisper, looking right into her blue eyes this time.

I swear that I can see the pain of rejection in her eyes. I know that Sloane hates to hear this. I know that she wants me. Maybe Sloane even has feelings for me. For the person, she thinks I am.

But we can't do this. Skating is important to me, and I'll be the one who is losing everything.

„Yes, we can. We can't stay away from each other. The only way to stay away from each other is to not see each other again, you know that," her voice sounds like the sweetest curse.

It's something I can't resist, just like Eve couldn't resist eating the apple.

„We can still skate. I think that we're even better when we're letting everything out. It's just sex. No friendship, no emotions. It's just sex, simply because we can't keep our hands to ourselves," so seductive, how could I resist? She is looking at me, pure lust in her eyes. There is no way I'll be able to stay away from her.

I think about it. There is no way that this is going to work. Something has to go wrong; if it goes wrong, we'll lose everything. But she is already correct. Sloane has a point because we can't stay away from each other.

I have the choice now, but pushing her away might do more damage than anything else. And I don't want to push her away. I want to be close to her.

It's not working without any emotions. They are already involved. Sloane knows this, but I am sure that we can still ignore it. We are not talking about it. I think we never will.

I look at her for a moment. She is still waiting for my answer. With every second it takes, the disappointment in her eyes grows. My hands are touching her sides, moving up her body.

I pull her closer, finally kissing her. God, I could never stay away from her. I want her, probably more than it is possible.

„We're not going to have sex in the hot tub," I pant as soon as we part. I don't want to get caught by Gregg or Flynn.

„Then let's go inside," she whispers, removing herself from me. Sloane stands up, reaching out her hand for me.

„So eager, huh?" I smirk, taking her hand. We grab our stuff, quickly disappearing inside. God, she drives me crazy.

47

SLOANE

I'm going to crack his shell. I know that one day I earned his trust. He is scared to share whatever he hides, but he doesn't need to feel like this with me. I would never run away. I'll be there for him.

He wasn't staying over that night. He left as soon as I fell asleep. And the following day, we acted like nothing happened. I'll tell Flynn about it when we're back home. There are no secrets between us. Besides that, I already think they know what happened. I am sure they heard us.

They are looking at us the following day, surprised that we're coming out of separate rooms. I know they expected something else. But no one is saying something about it.

We take another walk outside. After that, we're all grabbing our skates. Gregg is trying his luck on the ice again. Flynn is holding his hands, pulling him over the ice.

We're laughing, joking around. It's fun. It's the first time I have had fun for a long while now. I know there is so much more to come in the future and more to worry about. So I want to enjoy this even more.

We have to prepare ourselves for the next competition quickly. We climb higher, and the competitions are getting harder. Maybe we'll really make it to the Olympics.

I have my hopes up now. But honestly, everything is working a bit too well right now. This trip feels like a dream to me.

Maybe we'll get back, and everything gets terrible as soon as we're settled in our daily lives.

So it is hard to pack my bags. I don't want to leave the cabin behind. I am scared that everything is getting worse again. I enjoyed this time here. We all have to continue living our lives, and we can't stay here forever. But a bit longer would be nice.

Now, we're going back to training tomorrow. And it'll be more complex. We have to give more. We have to try our best. Asher and I even have to try to be better than before. There are no mistakes allowed.

My heart is racing, thinking about the following competitions. We have new competitors now. We have to skate against new people, against outstanding ones too.

No one will be easy on us, and we had a bad start. No one else had it, and everyone knows how we messed up.

No one is talking on our way back, possibly because we're all sad. It is over. It really was too good to be true.

48
SLOANE

I unpacked my bag as soon as I arrived home. I cleaned everything and took a long, needed shower. It's a weird feeling to be home now. The house is empty as usual. My parents are at work still. They indeed come home way too late.

But right when I sit down in my sleepwear, I hear the door downstairs. Someone is coming up the stairs, and no one is talking. I am confused because this person is coming right toward my bedroom. It can't be my parents. They would never come straight up to my room. They also first yell through the house, ensuring I know they're home.

I look at my door, waiting for the guest to come inside. I see his red hair first. Flynn stretches his head inside, a smile on his face as usual.

„Hello there. I thought it's time you update me," Flynn says, sitting down beside me.

He is already waiting for my explanation. I know very well what Flynn wants to hear right now.

„Well, I think I had sex with Asher again," I spit it out immediately.

„I already know that. Can we just skip to the part you explain to me why? I mean, okay, I get it. It was a bad idea to bring him along. I'm sorry for that," Flynn looks at me quite confused.

I am confused too. I don't really understand what my heart wanted or why I stood naked in the hot tub.

I wanted Asher's attention and thought sex was better than nothing. My plan worked out perfectly. I hope that I can crack his shell like this. It sounds stupid because I should accept that he doesn't want to talk, but something inside me doesn't want to give up.

„We're just dealing with our emotions. I think sex is the only thing we know when it comes to it. I mean, this might be a good step in the right direction," I try to explain. I won't tell Flynn everything.

„That is the most idiotic thing I ever heard. Irina will kill you two, and you'll lose your best chance. You won't skate together anymore, and honestly, you can't start from the beginning again. A new partner, and you'll lose everything."

Flynn is honest. Mostly he is doing it sweetly. Flynn is someone who doesn't want to hurt his opponent. But right now, he was honest, even when it might be hard saying it that way.

He is right. I could lose everything. Irina would separate us.

„It sounds so stupid, but I made the right decision. Something inside of me tells me that this is right. I know that Asher is worthing it, even though I'm risking my career now," I tell him.

I am sure that Asher is worthing this. My feeling is strong regarding this, even though I don't control whenever Asher is around. It seems like my body is betraying me, even my mind is betraying me, but this must be a sign.

„Well, if someone as career-driven as you is saying this, there has to be something true," Flynn says slowly.

He is entirely correct. I would have never risked my skating career for anything. I was always very career-driven, only thinking about myself. I missed periods in school to go skating. I missed prom. I never cared about any of that. There was nothing more important than skating.

„I'm absolutely crazy, maybe stupid, right?" I ask my best friend. Hoping he would tell me that I was doing the right thing. That the heart is never lying.

„Love makes you do crazy things. I would do the same for Gregg, I think" Flynn shrugs his shoulders.

Love. Is this really love?

„You and Gregg are different. He is your first boyfriend. I honestly think that you both are meant for each other. You can't compare that," I reply slowly.

My best friend shrugs his shoulders. It takes a moment for him to reply like he is searching for the right words.

„I'm just keeping whatever I think to myself. You're not ready to hear it, but I believe that there is something special between you and Asher," Flynn says.

I don't really know what he doesn't want to tell me right now. He thinks that there is something special between Asher and me? We're a good skating team, but other than that, we never brought anything but chaos.

„I've never met someone who has such good chemistry, especially when it comes to skating. I hate to say this, but we never had been like this. Not even in our dreams," Flynn explains as I don't reply to him.

„What are you talking about?" I laugh. I ask him this question even though I know what he means. Asher and I have perfect chemistry on the ice. I guess it is something special, something others might dream of. We can put on a show and cast a spell over people. It's our magic, knowing that people love it.

„You know exactly what I mean. And I hate to say it, but Asher is a better skater than me. He is the best thing that could ever happen to your career. First, it really hurt me realizing it, but I'm okay with it now." Flynn is talking absolute none sense. He has always been the best one.

I don't know why he is saying he wasn't the best or that Asher is my better partner.

„You're talking nonsense. We had amazing chemistry. We would have made it to the Olympics. I know that we had a massive chance of winning it." I reply, shaking my head at his words.

„Maybe. But be honest with yourself. We were harmonic. We had nothing special. Of course, we were great, and we never made a mistake. But this is it! There is nothing special, no story that we could tell. We didn't have the fire. But you and Asher...." He smiles at me, „There are so many emotions between the two of you, and it shows in your performance. This is a good thing. You have a story to tell, and people love it."

I hate to say that he is right. This is why I am not replying anymore. I don't say a word about this. Flynn and I have skated since we were little kids. I never knew anything other than skating with him together.

I still love skating with him, and I miss it deeply. But at some point, I stopped being sad about him not being my partner anymore.

Maybe I know that Asher is a better fit for me. It might be chaotic sometimes, but something between us when we skate is special. Flynn is right.

„Please don't ruin what you have with him," my best friend says. His voice is a low whisper. As if I am destroying everything right now.

My heart is pounding. Now that we talked about skating, I realize how bad my situation is.

„It is already too late, I think. I can't change anything. I took the risk. There is no going back," I reply.

„I know, just be careful. And maybe talk to Irina. I am sure that she won't be mad when she finds out about it that way. Perhaps she even let you stay together, " he suggests, but we both know this is not true. She would never let us stay together.

„I'm not going to tell Irina. There is nothing to tell her. We're not in love with each other" nothing I am saying is making sense, and I know that. It's simply because nothing inside my head or heart is making sense.

I don't know how to feel or what to think. I don't know what is going on inside of Asher. Maybe he hates me. Perhaps he is just using me for sex.

Telling Irina will cause more drama, and we're still skating usually together. There is nothing to be worried about. We're even better now than before.

„You'll start with the training tomorrow. Are you ready?" Flynn tries to switch the topic.

„I am more than ready. Can't wait to see what Irina thought of. And I am sure we'll also win the next competition," I smile widely.

I want to stay optimistic. I am sure that we can climb the latter to the top. One day we'll stand on the ice skating for the Olympics. I know that we can do this.

It has always been my goal, and now it isn't that unrealistic.

49

ASHER

Going on this trip wasn't really my best idea. My father was already against the Toronto trip. He was even angrier when I came back yesterday. He was drunk again. I filled the fridge and cleaned the house. Even though there was not much to clean. I am not allowed to touch my father's things anyway. The living room is his. I avoid it at all costs. I wouldn't go in there and try to clean his mess.

The television is switched on the whole day. Mostly he sits there watching something he doesn't actually care about. All he cares about is the bottle of liquor on the table.

He spent every dollar I left him. With a glimpse, I could see fresh bottles on his table, two of them already emptied.

Sometimes I wish I could return them, but then I would surely die. I took another shift at my job just to escape my father. I am doing everything to not be home anymore.

I can't just move out. I could never actually pay for my own apartment. There are many things I need to buy. I would need to pay tons of bills, excluding that I'll ever live alone soon. Right now, I am paying only a small amount of bills. The house is my father's.

I wish I could just run away. I wish I could leave it all behind. But this home is also everything I have left of my mother. I have nothing left of her except the memories in this house. The memories might not always be good, but I can see her clearly.

Sometimes I miss her, even though I know she isn't in pain. She was sick. And next to all of this, my asshole father hit her. She is better now. This is what I am telling myself.

The night I returned from work, I felt my father's anger. It's been long since he laid a hand against me. It's a ticking time bomb. There will always be a time he'll explode.

This time it was yesterday. I sensed that something was wrong when I opened the door. My father was already waiting for me, he was so furious. There doesn't have to be a reason for that.

I tried to save myself, moving into my room. I locked the door behind me, sliding down at the wall. I just sit there on the floor of my bedroom, waiting for his banging to stop. I wait for him to stop banging on my door. Once he stopped yelling and kicking against my door, I relaxed. A breath of relief comes over me, and I move for the first time in a while.

I won't leave my room tonight, so I grab my phone and check my face with the camera. I'll always make sure that my face is safe. There shouldn't be a scratch or mark visible. No one can tell what happened behind closed doors if nothing happens to my face.

I don't want anyone to know. If someone knew, I would have no home anymore. I have nothing left then. I don't earn enough money to live alone.

I quickly change out of my clothes and lay down on my bed. I should try to sleep. Tomorrow is a big day. Training starts tomorrow. I need to be in the best shape for this.

50

ASHER

The following day I woke up with pain in my abdomen. I lift the blanket to have a look at my stomach. It's bruised, and it hurts.

I groan, sitting up. I have to act like everything is okay. This shouldn't be a problem. It's the first training day, and we probably won't do anything complex. Maybe I am lucky, and Irina is only explaining some things.

I am sure that by tomorrow everything will be okay again. And Sloane is light as a feather. I am sure I won't even have a problem lifting her up.

I quickly get ready, but I check if my father is still asleep before opening the door. It is still early. He mostly sleeps till noon. The alcohol in his system let him pass out for several hours.

I can hear his snoring from the living room. My father passed out in his armchair again. I first slowly sneak into the bathroom.

I learned to be very quick with getting ready. I don't need to do much anyway. I quickly brush my teeth, wash my face, and take a quick shower. Afterward, I get dressed, grab my stuff, and leave immediately.

I don't have a car, so I'll always go by bus. The rink, luckily, isn't that far from my home. I'm early today. But I don't think that I'll skate on my own. My stomach hurts. The bruise is darker than I thought. I think it is better to keep a slow pace today. It needs to heal. I can't go and see a doctor about it.

When I arrive at the rink parking area, I see that Sloane is already here. Her car is parked at the front. I know that she loves it to be early. She is always skating a couple of rounds on her own.

I slowly walk inside, looking around. I wave at Flynn, who is sitting on the bench. He is watching his best friend on the ice. It seems like Gregg isn't here today.

„Hey there," I greet him with a smile. I like him now that I know him a bit better. He looks at me with a huge smile plastered on his face.

I am surprised that he is always so kind to me. I know that Sloane is talking to him. They are best friends. I bet they share everything with each other. And yet, he is treating me neutrally as if he doesn't know anything.

„Oh good, you're already here" I turn around to face Irina. She is early, and she is smiling. She is rarely smiling, and I have to admit it looks kind of weird.

Sloane is coming closer in just seconds. It seems like we're starting early today.

The first hours are basically what I thought they would be like. Irina is explaining what she thought of for the next competition. She explains what we have to do and what she expects from us. She also has a new choreography for us to learn.

This time she wants something sexy and full of desire. Less dramatic. She wants a hot and breathtaking show.

She shows us some new elements which we have to learn. For now, we have started learning the choreography. The easy things, at least.

We have some new lifting elements, and we must first try them on solid ground. This is the first thing we do tomorrow.

I have to make sure that I'll be better tomorrow. I can feel every small move on the ice now. Everything hurts a bit.

My dad really hit the damn right spot this time. It happened before, of course, but it never mattered that much. I never cared because I never had to do anything like this. I never had anything that important.

Sloane looks at me quite confused as I have difficulty getting up from my spin fast enough.

„Asher, what is going on with you?" Irina sighs. She shakes her head in disappointment.

„I couldn't sleep. I promise tomorrow will be better," I reply, entirely out of breath.

„I hope it is for you. We don't have the time for mistakes anymore. We don't have time to waste. You have to be in the best shape," Irina warns me. This time she'll let me pass with it. But tomorrow, she won't go easy on me.

I have to find a solution. I know that this won't be gone tomorrow. I might have to get some painkillers. They'll help for the next couple of days. I can use them until the bruises are gone.

„Is everything good?" Sloane asks me as soon as we're back in the middle of the ice. We have to start from the beginning.

„Yeah, I'm fine," I reply, and right when she opens her mouth to say something, we have to start skating, luckily.

She is suspicious. I know that she wants to know everything about my life. Sloane wants to know this secret, and now she senses something is off.

There is no way that she is going to find out what happened. I take a deep breath and try not to think about my injury. Maybe it'll hurt less when I am not thinking about it.

I even distract myself by looking at Sloane. She looks gorgeous today. The tight training pants are hugging her peachy ass perfectly. Her hair is in a ponytail. Sloane is wearing a black thigh sweater, and good god, it's perfect.

But watching her is distracting me a bit too much. My movements are not as smooth as I want them to be. I miss most of the elements, and we're not on time anymore.

I can hear Irina yell. Her voice is filling the building. She is getting angrier with every second. I know that she is going to end today's session.

I hate to be a disappointment today. I am angry at myself that I didn't take painkillers this morning. I am sure that it would have been a lot easier then. But it's too late for that now.

„You're done for today," Irina sighs as we skate toward her. She looks at me with her killer stare.

„I warn you, boy, tomorrow you're in best shape again. Or we'll have a problem. There is much to learn. We don't have that much time," Irina storms off with that.

God, I never saw her so pissed before. She was always easy on us, mainly because we started from the beginning.

„Chill, she is getting nervous. It's because she is scared to lose." Sloane tries to calm me down.

I don't want to hear her soothing words now. So I quickly change back into my regular shoes. I don't talk. I don't even look at the others. I grab my stuff and leave without saying anything as soon as I am done.

51

SLOANE

I can't believe that Irina ended this session so quickly. But I have to admit that Asher wasn't doing his best today.

Something was off. I just couldn't tell what it was.

„Everything okay?" Flynn asks me as I sit there looking at Asher, who is now leaving. He isn't even looking back as he disappears through the door.

„He was weird today. Something is wrong," I tell my best friend. I just don't know what exactly it is.

Flynn looks at me, shrugging his shoulders. I don't know if he noticed anything, but he is not telling me if he did.

„Do you want to skate a while with me?" I ask him. I still wear my skates, and I don't want to leave yet.

He nods, „Wait here. I'll get the skates."

Flynn still has his locker here. There he is, keeping his skates and some other things. He can't do figure skating anymore, but he can just skate a couple of rounds with me. No spins, no lifts, and no jumps. Just some skating.

I wait for him to come back. And when he does, I am still sitting in the same position, staring against the wall.

„You're really worried?" He asks me as he changes into his skates. I slowly nod. Something makes me feel concerned.

„Yeah, it seemed like he was struggling to move quickly enough. Something was holding him back."

„And what should that be?"

„I don't know. Maybe he is in pain" I shrug my shoulders. This is the first thing coming into my head. I don't know much about Asher. He is a mystery, and an injury seems the most logical thing right now.

Flynn shakes his head. He seems to have a different opinion. „Asher is candid when it comes to this. He would have told us. He knows that he can't train injured. It would make things worse."

Flynn might be right about this. Asher is a person who would have told us. Or he would at least tell Irina that something is wrong. Irina also knew about his second job the whole time. He is always honest with her. But today, she didn't know a single thing.

It has to be something else then.

„Maybe it really was the lack of sleep. We'll see tomorrow," I smile at my best friend. I shouldn't worry too much about my partner. We're adults, and I am sure that we're acting honest and mature.

Flynn is reaching his hand out, and I take it. Both of us are stepping onto the ice.

I miss skating with him. It was always something putting us together. Sometimes I am scared that skating is the only thing keeping us together. We spent our whole lives together, but there is nothing we bonded over except figure skating.

Our whole life was about skating, but he changed. He is still coming here every day, but this will change as soon as he starts going to college.

I still don't know anything about that. I'm scared to ask because I am scared that he might be leaving me. I don't want him to go. I need him at my side.

„Do you have any plans for the future by now?" I finally dropped the question after a while. I need to ask him. Simply because I care about him and want to know what is on his mind.

„I think I'll go to university close to the city. It's the easiest thing to do. I have never been a person who wanted to move away. I have everything I need here," he tells me with a smile.

I am relieved about this. „Well, Gregg is also there, right? You at least won't be alone on campus" I smile at him.

This might be a sensitive topic for him. I know how much he wanted to be a professional skater. His dream isn't possible anymore. This minor accident took everything from him.

One part of him may still hurt, while the other accepts it. He has no other choice than to accept it.

„And I surely don't want to miss your competitions and every step you'll take in your career. Seeing you living the dream is like living it on my own," Flynn tells me with a smile.

„You're my lucky charm. I won't allow you to miss something," I joke. I need Flynn near me. There is no way that I'll let him go anywhere else.

We keep skating. Now everything is about Flynn. I ask him everything about his life. There is actually a lot he has to update me about. I am happy to hear about everything he thinks about and how much he loves Gregg.

He also wants to find a new hobby that keeps him busy. He can't do most sports, so he must find something else.

„Maybe you are good at doing arts? Or music?" I suggest with a giggle.

„We both know that it is not music." He laughs. I join him, even though I think that he might be able to learn an instrument. He is undoubtedly not the best singer, but he doesn't have to sing.

„But maybe I should try pottery. It seems so interesting, and I can totally imagine doing it!" Flynn smiles as he tells me everything about the pottery class he found online.

„You have to try it! It sounds absolutely amazing! I am sure you'll love it there."

Now that he is talking about it, I can totally imagine it. Flynn is very patient, loves details, and takes his time to make things perfect. I am sure he could sit there for hours, creating his own art.

I never saw him doing anything artistic. Flynn never painted or drew. He never built anything.

But there is always a good time to start and learn something new. He is right about finding a new hobby. It keeps him busy, and maybe he'll be less sad that he can't skate anymore.

52

SLOANE

I'm nervous and excited to see what the next day brings. We're practicing new lifting elements today. I can't wait to try them. Irina showed us what she was thinking, and it looked promising. It's very complex, and we might need some time to practice, but I am sure it will be perfect.

We're going to win every competition with choreography like this. Irina is a genius when it comes to this. She has good taste. Her choreographies and song choices are perfect.

I'm early as always. Just in case, I have my skates with me. We don't need them today, but maybe I want to skate afterward. Or maybe we're good, and we might already try the elements on the ice.

I trust Asher. This time is different from others. I know that he would never let me fall. He keeps care of me.

I take a look around. It seems like no one is here. Flynn has his first pottery class today, so he couldn't come. I walk into our training room and drop my stuff to the ground.

While waiting for everyone to come, I already used the time to warm up. I stretch my muscles carefully. I take a deep breath every now and then.

I am nervous, but I try to shake it off. There is nothing to be anxious about. I just hope that Asher is doing better now. He has to be in his best shape.

Irina was already tense when she arrived. She has an eye on Asher, ensuring he is still doing well.

He is smiling, but there is something behind his smile. I can see it in the way he moves. Asher, his movements are way slower. He sucks in a breath every now and then.

„Let's begin," Irina says to us. She shows us the first element. Irina explains quickly how we start and the ending position. Everything has to be perfect.

I stand in front of Asher, looking at him quite concerned. „You okay?" I ask him, still concerned. He should just lift me. We're starting off easy, nothing special.

Asher nods. His hands are grabbing my hips, slowly and hesitant. I trust him. This is why I take a good jump off the ground.

The lift is shaky, and it is unsure. It feels like I am going to fall any second. I grab Asher's wrists tighter, holding on for dear life. I know that he would never let me fall. I know that he would never let anything happen to me.

Just a second later, I am back on the ground. Irina is shaking her head eagerly. She is not happy with the lift. It looked way worse than it felt.

„Again. This time, I want perfection," Irina tells us.

„You sure everything is good?" I ask Asher again. My voice is a faint whisper, only for him to hear. I don't want Irina to notice that something might be wrong. She isn't in a good mood today.

Asher nods, putting his hands on my hips again. I don't think everything is fine, but he has to know better.

When he nods, pointing out that he is ready, I jump. I don't know what is happening now, but we're definitely not doing the lift. His hands disappear for a second. I thought I was going to fall.

I hear the sounds he makes. He is in pain.

I catch myself. The solid ground underneath my feet again. I look at Asher, who is holding his stomach in pain. I knew something was wrong, and now he is standing here clearly hurt.

„Oh my god! Asher!" I look at him in pure shock. How did this happen? I don't understand how he could get injured.

He was fine when we were on this trip. It was only two days ago. Asher was already hurt like this yesterday. I don't understand what happened.

„I'm fine." He presses out, standing up straight.

He tries not to show any emotion. „We can continue now, " he tells us. Irina is shaking her head.

I can't tell if she is mad at him or worried.

„Are you injured?" She asks him neutrally. I look at him quite concerned.

Asher shakes his head, „I am fine," he replies. I can see how his hand is quickly ghosting over his shirt. He is injured. Nothing can tell me otherwise. I don't know why he doesn't want to show it. But I can't let anything wrong happen to him.

„You're lying," I reply, reaching out my hand to lift his shirt. He, of course, steps away from my touch. Asher doesn't want me to lift his shirt. He even pushes away my hands.

„You have to be honest to us," I beg him. He has to see the fear in my eyes. Something is deeply wrong, and he is not helping with his secret-keeping.

„Please, let me have a look," I beg Asher.

I took him deep in the eyes, hoping he would let me have a look at his stomach. It takes a while, but he relaxes a bit. I take another step forward as I grasp the hem of his shirt. I carefully lift the material and have a look at his stomach. A gasp escapes as I see the bruises. They look pretty bad.

„Oh my god! What happened?" I ask him, my voice full of worry. We indeed have to stop our training for a couple of days. This has to heal before Asher can do anything. It could get worse if he continues like this.

„Yeah, that's it. You'll see a doctor. He'll tell you if you can still train," Irina sighs.

„No, no! I can't see a doctor," Asher replies, shaking his head eagerly. I don't understand what is going on right now.

„I don't care. You'll do it if you want to skate with Sloane and stay as her partner! You should have told me first," our coach is mad.

I can see in her face what she is thinking right now. She thinks that Asher was in a fight. But I am pretty sure that he wasn't.

Nothing makes sense right now. I know that Asher is not the aggressive type of person.

„This session is over," Irina tells us and turns away.

She had never had to deal with an injury before. Well, at least nothing we kept a secret. Most of our injuries happened on ice or during the training sessions.

A lot changed, and if she knew everything, she would surely kill us. Asher is grabbing his stuff now. He is mad, and I can't tell if he will see a doctor or if he is going to quit. Asher leaves the room without saying anything else. I run after him, stopping him before he can leave. I need to know what is going on. The bruises are dark and undoubtedly deep.

„Are you in danger?" I ask him. Even though I know that I won't receive a reply. I need to try. I want to help him.

„No," Asher replies, but this is a lie. He doesn't look at me. He looks away, down to his feet. If he told the truth, he would look me in the eyes.

„Let me help you," I whisper.

„You can't help me" Asher is still not looking at me. I swear I can see the pain in his eyes. Not the physical pain but his emotional pain. My heart cracks seeing him like this.

It clicks in my head. He doesn't really go outside, except for here and work. We were on a trip, and I dropped him off when it was nearly evening. He wasn't working on that day. He never left the house after I dropped him off. Yesterday he already came here injured.

„Does your father hurt you?" I ask him, knowing I cross a line.

It's stupid to ask this question, but this is the only thing popping into my head. I don't know much about his family. I don't know what is going on or what he is going through.

I only know that his mom died a long while ago. It's just him and his day. He doesn't have any siblings.

But now Asher is shaking his head. „You don't know anything about me. And it's best to keep it that way. Leave me alone," and with that, he walks past me.

I grab his wrist, holding him back. I can't let him leave. That means he is going back to his father. And now I am sure that his father did this to him.

„I won't leave you alone," I tell him. Now I am not sure what to do. He is an adult and doesn't have to live with his dad anymore. I don't know why he is still doing it.

Nothing makes sense, actually. Asher could just leave if he wants to. But I am not in this situation. I don't know why he isn't helping himself.

„You can't go back," I whisper. It's loud enough for Asher to hear it. And it makes him turn around to face me. I can't tell if there is anger visible now. Surely frustration.

„It's my home. Where else should I go? I don't have anywhere else to go," Asher replies, and this time he looks at me. He looks straight into my eyes. This is breaking my heart more than anything else.

I try to think of something. I try to think of a solution. My reply is taking too long for Asher. He frees his hand, and with a nod, he turns back to leave. I see him walking through the door.

I can't let him walk away. There is no way that he can go back there. My legs are moving by themselves, running after him. „Asher, stop!" I beg him.

He doesn't, but luckily he isn't running away from me. I look at him as I stand in front of him. I try to catch my breath.

„You can stay with me," I suggest.

It's a stupid suggestion, a foolish idea. But this is the only thing I can think of.

„No."

„Yes, you can. We have a guest room. My parents are barely home. They won't ask questions, even if we can lie to them. I can lie to everyone, even Irina. No one has to know what you're going through. But you can't go back there, " I tell him.

He has to come with me. I won't bother him when we're in the same house. I just need to know that he is safe.

„This is stupid."

„It's not. It's safe."

„And how do you think it's supposed to work?" He asks me, rolling his eyes at me.

„We'll tell everyone that your dad is out of town. You don't want to stay alone, so I offered you our guest bedroom. No one has something against that. I am sure that everyone thinks I am just being nice to you. And no one has to know the truth. I won't bother you. You can use my bathroom, the kitchen and other rooms in this house. You can make yourself feel at home until you earn enough money. And then eventually you can find our own apartment and have your first own safe home," I explain.

I need to make him stay with me. I can't live with the thought of him going back there. I don't know his dad, but the bruises tell me everything.

53
ASHER

She is offering me a home. Somewhere I can escape my father. But yet, it feels so wrong to say yes. I can't leave my father behind. He is still my father.

But the thought of not being scared to come home or sleep with an unlocked door wants me to say yes. Deep inside, I want to escape.

I could feel the peace I felt during our trips every single day. I could have this feeling every single day of my life. If I had enough money, I would have already moved out. I am sure about that.

Now I look at the blonde girl in front of me. She is not going to accept a no. „Okay, only for a couple of days. Just until my bruises are healed," I reply.

This is a compromise. I can't stay with Sloane for longer than that. It feels like I am taking advantage of her.

„Okay," Sloane smiles softly at me. „So here is the plan for now. I want to keep you as my partner, so after you grab your stuff, we'll go to see a doctor."

„We're not going to do such things." I reply, shaking my head. I don't go to a doctor. He is going to notice that the bruises are from my father. They see when someone gets abused. This is not the first time I have had bruises.

„He won't know anything. I'll tell him a story. Everything will be fine. No one will know anything. But we have to do it. Otherwise, Irina will kick you out," the blonde girl says as she unlocks her car.

She is so sure about Irina that it scares me. Our coach was pretty mad today, and I still feel sorry for that.

I look at Sloane and not. „Okay, I trust you," I nod slowly.

She starts the engine as soon as we sit in the car, and she doesn't waste any time. Our first stop is my home. I have to get my stuff now.

But it is hard as I look at the house. I can't leave my dad without anything here. He has nothing, no money. Maybe I'll just throw something in the mailbox every week.

„I'm coming with you," she tells me, already unbuckling her seatbelt. I'm quick to stop her. She is out of her mind, and I won't let her come with me.

„No, you're not getting yourself in danger."

„Nothing is going to happen. We'll just get some of your stuff. You can't carry it anyway," Sloane looks at me. She is right. Heaving a heavy bag might hurt. But this is a risk I am going to take. There is no way that she is going inside there.

„You wait here. I'll do this alone. He is going to be pissed," I tell her slowly.

He won't be happy that I am leaving, and I don't want her to be in the middle of this. I wait for her to say something. But she just nods, showing me that she understood.

So I leave the car, grab my keys and open the door. Sounds pretty easy, but my hands are shaking so badly that it takes me a minute until I get the key inside the lock. My heart is pounding so heavily inside my chest that I think it will jump right out of it.

„Son, is that you?" I can hear my father's voice. He wasn't expecting me that early. And I was hoping he would still be asleep.

The door opens and closes again behind me. I turn around to see Sloane standing there. Hearing the door again makes my father move. He looks at me as he appears at the door.

„What's going on?" My father asks in his usual drunk behavior. I can't even remember him sober.

I try to swallow the heavy lump down my throat.

„Nothing, I just need something for training today. I'll be gone again in a minute," I try to keep my father as calm as possible.

He nods slowly, unsure of what he should do now. He just stays there, and then my father sees Sloane. A smile appears on his face, this stupid bastard.

„Who is your little friend there?" He asks.

„No one you should care about," and I pull Sloane into my room. I quickly grabbed a bag and threw everything I could find inside. Everything I might need for the next couple of days.

My father followed us. He is now standing there looking at us. Of course, he notices that we pack a lot of stuff together.

„What are you doing?"

„Nothing," I reply, quickly zipping my bag.

I look at Sloane, pushing her forward toward the door. I want her to leave as soon as possible. We don't have to waste any time here. But my father seems to think differently. He moves quickly, grabbing Sloane and pressing her against the wall.

„You think you can leave? You want to leave me alone here?" He asks me. My heart is pounding even faster if this is possible.

„Is it because of her? Is this your new whore?" My father growls.

I can feel how fear is running through my body. I don't know what to do. I can't stand up against my father. I had never done it before. But as I look at Sloane, I can see the fear in her face. She never thought my father would do anything.

I don't want her to feel like this. I don't want her to feel the way I did the whole time.

„Let her go!" I push my father away, so he stumbles back, and lets go of Sloane. She is already lurching toward the door, opening it.

„You stupid bastard, do you think you can live alone? You're getting nowhere with that silly whore!" He yells. Anger is raging through him.

„Don't you dare talk like that about her! And don't you dare ever touch her, or I'll kill you." And with that, I push Sloane outside.

She looks at me in pure shock, walking to her car. She doesn't waste any time getting inside. But I am unsure now.

„I understand if you don't want me to come with you anymore," I look at her. I stand there, waiting for her answer.

The door is opened, but I am unsure if I should hop into the car.

„Are you insane? I am not going to let you stay here.“

And with that, I move into the car. She doesn't say anything about my father or about what just happened.

Sloane didn't talk, even after arriving at the doctor's office. She is doing all the talking there. She explains to the woman at the front desk what happened.

It's a lie, of course, but it works. The nurse lets us through right away. The doctor should be here any minute now. This is going to be another bill I can't pay. I am not going to the doctor, no matter what I have. It was expensive. I don't have insurance.

„What do we have here?“ The doctor asked with a smile as he entered the room. Sloane smiles politely at him as she starts talking.

„I think my partner is hurt pretty badly. We just won a figure skating competition and went to a club afterward. He got into a fight, protecting me from some strangers. But now the bruises look so bad,“ she tells him.

I try hard not to react, especially not to look surprised. I wasn't expecting a story like this. It makes me sound so noble, something that I am definitely not.

„Okay, let me have a look at it“ the doctor smiles, and I lift my shirt to show him my stomach area.

54
SLOANE

Asher will be fine in a couple of days. I texted Irina to tell her that we won't have training for the next few days. We have to give our best when we're back on track. Otherwise, we won't make it.

I look at Asher as he looks around the guest room. „I know it is pretty simple, but if you need anything, we could get it, " I tell him with a smile.

I hope that he likes it here. I want him to feel comfortable and happy. The shock is still in my bones, and I can't believe he has lived like this for his whole life. I don't want to know the amount of fear he feels.

„I'm so sorry," he sits down on the bed. He doesn't look at me. Instead of that, he looks to the floor. I sit next to him, not knowing what he means.

„For what?"

„For what happened today. I told you to stay outside."

„I am happy I did not. Otherwise, it would have been you. You went through enough," I tell him slowly. My hand reaches out for him, but I am unsure if this is not entirely inappropriate.

„I never wanted you to see this." Asher shakes his head slowly.

„I might be just as terrible as him. And I don't want you to be close to me because I don't want anything happening to you," he whispers. This is enough for me.

My hand lays itself on his cheek. I could cry when I saw how broken he was right now.

„Don't say that. You're nothing like your father, and you'll never be. You are a wonderful person Asher. You are kind, and you protected me just minutes ago. You care about people. You would never be like him," I softly tell him.

He shouldn't have thoughts like this. He is a fantastic person. I love him for who he is, and I know the person he really is, even though he thinks differently. And he isn't terrible or aggressive at all.

„I'm terrible," he whispers.

„You're not," I reply automatically. I pull him closer to me. My arms are sneaking around his body. Asher is burying his head in my neck. I hug him, trying to comfort him.

My heart is burning for him. Everything inside me is burning for him. And it breaks me to see him like this.

He lifts his head just a little bit, and a second later, he lays his lips on mine. It is gentle and loving. Different from every single time before.

My hand is driving through his soft hair. My body presses itself further into him, if possible. I can feel his hands on my body, roaming up and down my sides. He touches me so softly and gently. This might be the negative aspect of living in the same house.

How can I keep my hands to myself, knowing he is in the next room? I can't even stop now. I long for him.

He pushes me back so that I lay underneath him. We're slowly getting rid of our clothes. Everything is happening at a much slower pace than the times before. We're kissing each other, touching each other most gently. This here is filled with love, not only lust and desire. This isn't anything physical. This is purely on an emotional basis.

I can feel his lips at the swell of my breast. My head is pressing itself into the mattress as he starts to swirl his tongue around my nipple. He knows my body so well by now. He knows exactly which spots I like best.

My hands are softly touching the soft skin of his muscular chest. I am carefully avoiding the huge bruises. This time it shouldn't be about bringing me pleasure.

So I am quick to switch our position. Pressing Asher into the mattress, straddling him. I quickly peel down his pants, along with his underwear.

I never gave a boy a head before. I never wanted to. But I have to say that I am, in general, not the most experienced person. But now I want to do it. I want to touch and satisfy Asher.

He groans as I lay my lips around him. His eyes roll to the back of his head as he presses his head into the mattress. Every moan and every sound I pull out of him motivates me.

It isn't as bad as I imagine it to be. It even turns me on as I see how I affect Asher.

„God, Slo, don't look at me like that," he sighs as he pulls me away from his dick. He pulls me up, switching my position underneath him again.

„You make me absolutely crazy," and with that, he kisses me. God, if he only knew how I feel right now. How my heart is only beating for him.

This time when he entered me, he went slow. His touches are tender. Our fingers are intertwined. This time we don't just have sex. It's different. It makes my heart burst from love.

55

ASHER

I thought that living with Sloane would be a lot different. And I thought that her parents would kick me out. But I quickly learned that they welcomed me with open arms.

I had never felt so good in my life. I am happy, even though I feel guilty most of the time because I take advantage of everything, but I feel safe here.

It's the first time we're having dinner tonight with her parents. They have always been away because of business.

„What if they hate me, and they kick me out?" I ask her, slightly worried. I even thought about dressing up, but Sloane assures me that this isn't anything special. She will wear her sweatpants.

„Stop worrying. My parents already like you. It's just a regular family dinner, and I think my mom counts you as part of our family now, that you're living underneath her roof" Sloane smiles at me.

Her family is lovely. It's something I always wanted to have.

This is a perfect dream, but it has eventually come to an end. One day I will wake up, just like you have to wake up every time you fall asleep and dream.

But for now, I am really enjoying it. I appreciate it to be here with Sloane. I sit at a table with her and her parents.

Her mom cooked, and I had never seen something that looked so good. At a restaurant, maybe, but not homemade.

„Go on and fill your plate, Asher," she smiles at me. Everything is set. I am the first one who gets to fill his plate.

„It looks absolutely delicious, Mrs. Griffin, " I praise her cooking, already shoving the first fork into my mouth.

„Thank you, and please call me Samantha," she tells me again.

She told me that a million times by now. I just can't call her by her first name. They are doing so much for me. It just feels inappropriate to me.

For a while, no one is really talking. Sloane's father is telling us about his new business in Chicago. He has to leave again in a couple of days, and her mother is going with him. We'll be alone, even though we are busy too. Irina already warned us that we'll train every free second of the day.

„I am happy that Sloane isn't alone anymore." Her mother smiles at me. But if she only knew what we mostly do whenever we're alone.

Maybe they would hate me if they knew that I love their daughter. I am sure that they're hoping for someone better. Someone who truly deserves her, someone who isn't broken at all.

I can understand if they tell her that she can't be with me. I am not even sure if she wants it. As she said, it is just sex.

I don't even know if I can be in a normal relationship. Nothing around me is healthy. I haven't seen a healthy relationship before, so how can I be in one?

„Asher?" Her dad pulls me out of my thoughts. I look at him quickly, smiling.

„Sorry, I wasn't paying attention. Could you repeat that?" I ask him politely. Sloane burst into laughter before her father could reply to me.

Everyone is looking at her as she laughs at me. „Oh my god, stop being so stiff and polite," she tells me.

Her mom is now laughing as well. Her parents are making me nervous. She might not understand why but surely can't change that.

„Sorry, I'm just so scared," I tell her slowly.

„There is no reason to be nervous. We love to have you as our guest, " her mother assures me, and I nod slowly.

„I just don't want to take advantage of your kindness."

„You are not! Don't think something like this. We really love to have you here. Honestly, I loved to cook for one more person," her mother smiles.

She could say this over and over again. I don't know if I should believe that. Part of me still feels different.

The conversation died after that. Sloane starts talking about the next competition after a while. And when everyone finished, we cleared the table together.

I help them clean the kitchen. It's the least I can do.

„I think I'll head to bed now," I tell everyone with a smile as we're done. It's time for me to sleep. I want to be in the best shape tomorrow.

My bruises are nearly gone and painless by now. It's time for us to start training again. This time there is no going easy. I want to show Irina that I deserve a good chance. She doesn't have to doubt me.

I get ready for bed and even lay down. But this time, I just can't find sleep.

I am sleeplessly twisting and turning around in my bed. I don't know what it is, but something keeps me awake. It's bothering me.

I'm sweating as if I just had a terrible dream. And to cool down, I decide to get a glass of cold water.

It's already late, and the house is quiet, so I think everyone is asleep. I slowly leave my room, wearing only my pajama pants. I just want to get a glass of water really quickly.

Everything is dark. As I move into the kitchen, I switch on a small light. I move around the kitchen as quietly as possible, filling a glass with cold water.

„Ah, I thought I heard something," a voice says behind me.

I turn around to see Sloane's mother leaning against the doorframe. Her blonde hair is in a braid, and she is wearing a bathrobe to hide her sleepwear.

„Sorry, I never meant to wake you," I apologize quickly, thinking it is my fault that she is awake.

„Nothing to be sorry about. I woke up because I had the same needs," she tells me, pointing to the glass.

I quickly fill one for her too and hand it to her. „Thank you," she smiles at me.

„So, since when are you and my daughter together?" She asks me after a while. This question hits me with surprise. I don't know why she is asking this, but I am sure Sloane and I are not together.

„What?"

„Oh, I thought something was going on between the two of you. I thought you wanted to keep it a secret from us because you're skating together. I know my daughter, and I saw how you look at each other," she tells me slowly.

This isn't a moment to lie about anything. It isn't the moment to not tell the truth. I don't want to fuck up when it comes to her parents.

„I really like your daughter, but we're not together."

„Too bad. You're a perfect guy, and you're always welcomed here. I mean, if it is too hard at home."

I am shocked at her words. Sloane promised me not to tell anyone. She told me that no one has to know about it. But it seems like she told her mother.

„She told you?"

„Who told me what?" Her mother asks, quite confused.

„Sloane told you why I am staying here?" I don't want to say it out loud. Just in case she doesn't know the truth.

„She lied to me about it. I know when my daughter lies. I know that your father is not on a trip. I don't know what happened to you or if your father is involved in it, but this is a safe place, and you can stay here however long you want to." She tells me.

I am surprised that she knows her daughter lies. It isn't that obvious, and everyone else believed it.

At least, I think that everyone else believed her. No one knows my family or who I am. So they can't know that my father isn't on a trip.

„Thank you," I whisper. Unsure if I should say anything else. But it seems like there is no need to say more. Her mother turns away, wishing me a good night. She walks back into her room, and I do the same.

56
SLOANE

I could really get used to all of this. Driving to training with Asher together. Living in the same house with him is fun.

We're laughing the whole way to the rink. Singing along to the songs on the radio. Our relationship got better. Now I would consider us friends (with benefits), but we're still ignoring this. Whenever we have sex, we act like nothing happened after that. We just continue our lives like before.

Irina also seems to be in a better mood when we see her. She smiles at us. But soon, we learn that she isn't going easy on us. We have to learn the elements straight on the ice. We're not going to do the dry practice.

It's difficult. I honestly don't see it working now. We have two weeks left.

But it is fun. Asher and I are smiling at each other. We even laugh at learning the choreography.

„What happened to them?" Irina asks Flynn. Both are watching us intensely. He shrugs his shoulders, pretending to not know something. Flynn knows everything. I told him that Asher was staying with me. I told him the lie, though. He will not find out the real reason, but he knows that Asher and I share a deeper bond.

He hates us for having sex with each other. Flynn thinks it's a bad idea. Flynn believes that we're damaging our career with it.

„I don't know," Flynn replies, shrugging his shoulders. His eyes are fixated on us. He avoids Irina's eyes, knowing that eye contact with her would give him away. They're both watching us as we're dancing over the ice.

This might be the first time that training actually feels good. We're laughing, joking around, and having fun. Even Irina is lighting up a little bit.

Today feels different, and this might be the start of something outstanding. I often had this thought, and we somehow messed up every time. I am scared that something will happen, that we won't skate together in the future.

What if Irina finds out that something is going on between us? She would surely kick our asses and tear us apart.

But everything is working so well now. We became a great team. It couldn't get any better.

„Amazing! Bravo! Bravo!" Irina claps her hands as we're getting off the ice.

„If you keep going like this, we won't get a single problem! You're doing fantastic, learning quickly, especially after your break," she smiles at us.

I nod quickly. We don't have that much time left. The competition is coming closer.

„I can already see you at the Olympics," Flynn smiles brightly at us. The Olympics might take some years. We have to join many competitions and win them. We have to go national and then international.

„Maybe I can get you into the competition in Paris. It would be a big step," Irina starts thinking.

„This season?" I ask her, skeptical. I don't know if this is a good idea.

„Of course! The sooner, the better. I think that the both of you are definitely ready!" Our coach nods.

I still don't know if this is a great idea. Asher and I are just started to be good. And we only won once.

I look at him, but he is clearly avoiding my eyes. I want to know what he thinks of the whole situation.

„You always wanted to go international," Irina sighs as if I just told her no.

„Yeah, but I don't know if this might be a bit too early," I tell her slowly.

She shakes her head. I know that no one can change her opinion. She is our coach, and she does whatever she wants to.

We have to obey. Irina always made the right decisions, because of her we won our last competition.

Our training session ended late today. It's quiet as I am driving home with Asher. He is not saying a single word to me.

„Is everything alright?" I ask him slowly.

„Yeah… Irina just surprised me," he replies honestly to me, and I nod.

„Me too. But I love the thought of us in Paris." I reply with a sweet smile on my lips.

My heart is skipping as I think of Asher and me in front of the Eiffel Tower. I have been to Paris before, but it would be different with Asher by my side.

But now I look at him. He is avoiding my gaze once again. Now he is having a look outside the window. It's quiet again, and he doesn't reply. My heart breaks a little when he is not responding.

I thought he would like it. I get excited thinking about flying to Paris with him. We could see so many things there, and the competition was significant.

I never thought that I would cross a line with that. I never meant to. But Asher isn't eating dinner with me, and I think I might have done something wrong.

I lightly knocked at his door after I finished dinner. I just want to check on him.

„Asher?" I ask slowly before entering.

He is lying on his bed, his phone in his hands. He doesn't look up as I enter.

„I'm sorry if I said something wrong," I apologize slowly. I slowly walk closer to him. He finally looks up.

He lays his phone aside, „I don't want you to have the wrong picture of me."

His deep voice is low. I can barely understand him. And I surely don't know what he means.

„What?"

„I don't do relationships. I don't want you to have feelings for me. Because it genuinely sounded like it," he replies. He is avoiding my eyes.

„What? No! I thought as a team. Skating in an international competition is a huge thing!" I tell him slowly.

I can hear him breathe out in relief. He looks up at me and nods slowly. „Okay, then I'll be happy to go to Paris with you," he smiles.

57

ASHER

Why did I say this? *I don't do relationships.* I instantly regretted my words after Sloane left. I know that I hurt her.

She is disappointed now. I even hurt myself with it. I want her. I want her more than anything else. Maybe even more than skating.

When I think about Paris, I think about going there with her. God, I have never been the romantic type of guy. But I can only think of kissing her in front of the Eiffel Tower. I am sure this is what every girl dreams of.

But now I told her I didn't want her as more than a friend. Simply because I am too scared, I might be exactly like my father. And I am afraid that I'll hurt someone. I don't want to hurt anyone, especially not her.

I don't want anyone to go through what I had to endure. I don't know what the future is going to look like.

Thinking about Sloane, I couldn't find any sleep tonight. I turned and twisted, trying to find a good position.

The following morning when I wake up, I am more than tired. I don't feel good or relaxed. Sloane isn't talking to me. The good mood from yesterday is gone.

Our training session is more severe today. It's less fun than yesterday.

There is no way that someone is noticing a change between us. We want to try our best.

I want to go to Paris or Europe in general. It's essential and a huge step for us.

But before we can think about going international, we have to win the competition in a couple of days. We have to work hard and win this one as well. From now on, we're only allowed to get the first place.

Our choreography is perfect. We're doing perfectly. Even though I can feel that Sloane is keeping her distance from me, I can't take back the words I said. And I know that she shouldn't hope for too much. I can't make her happy and give her what she wants and needs in life.

„I think we're done for today!" Irina calls it a wrap. She has already packed her stuff together. She never wastes any time when it comes to leaving. And a couple of seconds later, Irina is gone.

I look over to Sloane. She is laughing about something Flynn said to her. Now, I am waiting for her to be ready to leave.

While she is still talking to Flynn, I try to think of something else. I wonder if I should go home and talk to my dad. I should at least check on him.

I have never been happier since I am not with him anymore. But I feel like I am responsible for him. He can't care for himself, and I am not there anymore.

„Are you ready to leave?" Sloane asked me, and I never noticed that she was waiting for me now.

I quickly stand up and nod. „Yeah."

We're not talking much anymore. This time I am not missing dinner with Sloane. Her parents are gone again, and I don't want her to eat alone again.

We're sitting in front of each other. No one is saying anything.

It feels a bit weird, but it could be worse. We return to our rooms as soon as we're done and everything is cleaned up.

It's hard to find some sleep this night. I am rolling around again, trying to find some peace. Every position is uncomfortable.

And then I finally fall asleep. But my dream is even worse than being awake.

I am in my old home again. I can hear my father yell. I know what is going to happen now. I went through this way too often. All I can do is wait right now.

My heart is racing. It's hot, and I know I started sweating. I want this to be over. I thought I could escape it, but there actually is no escape. I thought my father was gone. But here I am, sitting against my door, trying to keep him away. I close my eyes, pressing them together as if everything would disappear like this.

And when I open my eyes again, I am back in a dark room. I quickly looked around, scared and filled with fear.

It takes a second to realize that I am in my room at Sloane's house. I breathe out, relieved that everything is fine. I just had a nightmare.

„Asher?" Sloane, her voice, let my eyes dart toward the door. She is standing there, wearing the oversized shirt she sleeps in.

„Yeah?" I reply quietly. She isn't moving. I am scared that I might have made a sound. Maybe she heard me.

„I can't sleep. Can I stay with you?" She whispers. Something in her voice is off. Maybe she had a nightmare as well.

„Sure," I reply, not sure if I really want this.

58
SLOANE

I heard him. I heard him scream, and then I ran into his room. I tried to be as quick as possible.

I opened the door slowly, unsure of what to expect now. Asher is already awake. I can hear him panting, trying to catch his breath. His breathing is heavy.

„Asher?" I breathe out, hoping that he can hear me.

„Yeah?" He replies surprisingly calmly.

„I can't sleep. Can I stay with you?" I whisper back, hoping that he will let me stay. I wanted to check on him, but I thought he wouldn't actually talk to me about his nightmare.

„Sure," he replies, surprising me a little bit.

I slowly walk closer, regretting that I am only wearing a damn shirt. I hurried over without thinking about what I was wearing.

Now it is too late to change. I carefully slide underneath the covers. I am unsure if I should slide closer to Asher or keep my distance.

„You heard me, right?" He asks after a while.

„I didn't want you to feel uncomfortable, but yes," I reply quietly.

„I'm sorry."

„For what?" I am confused. He has nothing to be sorry for. Yet he is apologizing to me.

„For waking you up."

„Do you have them often?"

„Sometimes," he replies.

I hate that he has nightmares that often. I can imagine why he has them, but I wish I could make them disappear. I want to help him. He is safe now, and I would never make him go back.

„I'm sorry," now I am the one apologizing to him.

He doesn't reply anymore. I am sure that he doesn't know what to say now.

So I look at him, even though I can't see him. It's too dark in his bedroom.

„You know, you shouldn't be here," he whispers. My heart cracks again. He pushes me away again, making me regret that I am here. Maybe I should just leave.

„Why are you pushing me away?" I ask him slowly.

„Because I am not good for you. I am not better than my father, and I don't want to hurt you. I want you to be safe and sound. I am not the right person for that," he replies, which is clearly not what I expected.

I absolutely don't know what to say right now. Asher is nothing like his father. I wish he could see it. Asher is a beautiful human being from the inside and the outside. It's a shame that he thinks that he is like his father.

„But bad people don't have thoughts like this. It makes you a good person that you worry." I reply. And now I move a little closer.

„You are amazing! A fantastic friend. You are kind. You care about others. And I don't think you could ever do what your father did. Not even in the slightest. You are very different from him. Don't you dare think that you are a terrible person," my hand lays on his cheek, softly against his skin.

„This is still not allowed. We might make a mistake," Asher whispers. Irina said that she wouldn't allow it. I don't know why. But it is generally not forbidden.

„Does it feel like a mistake?" I ask him slowly.

For me, the answer is no. With Asher, everything feels so right. I don't care what Irina is telling us. The closer we get, the better we skate.

It is a win-win situation.

„You know it doesn't feel wrong," Asher whispers.

„Then let's give in. Don't you think everything is easier when we stop fighting against it?" I ask him.

„But that would destroy our career. You know that Irina isn't okay with that. She would tear us apart," he replies slowly. I know that he is right. Irina would disapprove of this.

„We don't have to rush into anything. It doesn't mean we're together from now on, right?" I am confused. Does it mean we're together?

„We kinda are?"

„Yeah, but we're still trying to figure our feelings out," I reply slowly, and this actually doesn't sound that bad.

We don't really know what is going on. We don't understand everything. There is still some stuff that we need to figure out.

„Right," he replies.

We kept on talking about everything. We talked for so long that I can't even remember that we fell asleep.

59

ASHER

I open my eyes slowly. Right now, I am trying to remember what happened last night. Sloane came in here, and we talked. God, I think I love her. She told me that we should try to give in to our feelings. She feels that everything is easier if we try to be a couple.

I never had a healthy relationship. I don't know what a healthy relationship looks like, and this scared the heck out of me.

How do I know what is right and what is wrong? How do I know how to treat her correctly?

It takes a while for me to realize that her head is bedded on my arm. Well, partly on my arm and partly on my chest. I watch her. She is still sleeping and looks so damn beautiful and peaceful right now.

My heart is racing inside of my chest. Sloane thinks I am a good person, but I am still terrified that the bad genes of my father are inside of me. I don't want to hurt her.

„Why are you so nervous?" She murmurs, half asleep.

„I'm not," I reply.

„I can feel your heart racing in here," she tells me, tapping onto my chest. I sigh.

„Maybe I am freaking out a bit. I am scared that I'm messing this up. I mean, you can't mess up sex, but this is so much more now, " I tell her. At least I try to be honest with her.

„You can't mess up. I promise you that you can't. Just be yourself because this is who I fell in love with," she tells me.

Now her eyes are open, and she looks at me with a soft smile on her lips. God, she is gorgeous. I don't deserve her.

I don't deserve something so pure and perfect like her. My life has always been bad. Only negative things have been in my life as far as I can remember. I wasn't even good with my partner. We never made it that far in the ranking.

Then I met Sloane. She changed everything. She changed everything for the better.

I don't deserve that she is kissing me now. Her lips are so soft, moving ideally against mine. Like they're made for me.

„God, I wish we could stay in bed today," I groan. Somehow I am so not ready for training.

I have a weird feeling, mainly because of what we talked about yesterday. How are we going to act in front of others?

Is something going to change?

„Are you crazy? I absolutely can't wait for training!" She smiles. Now she seems to be wide awake. She already jumps out of bed, happily about today.

This makes me even more nervous. But we can't stay in bed anyway. We only have a couple of days left. The competition is getting closer.

„I think tomorrow we're getting our new costumes. I can't wait to see them. The performance is kinda sexy, so the costumes might be sexy as well," Sloane exclaims excitedly as she storms around the house.

She is already getting ready for the day while I lie in bed. I don't need that much time. I'll be done in no time, then we're all ready to go.

And there is actually nothing I have to worry about. Sloane is acting just like always, pretending like everything is normal. Irina can't find out the truth about us anyway. She would kick me out, indeed.

But the mood is better now that we have talked about everything. It's easier to skate.

I think the others are noticing the change as well. We're more relaxed, and it is easier to have fun.

Irina is in a good mood. She is talking about Europe again. She tries her best to get us in if we win this competition. There are still tons of other matches here. We have to win every single one of them.

I can feel the pressure building inside me. It's getting a lot more serious. We're climbing higher than ever before in the ranking. Every single time we're reaching for a new goal. We're hungry for a more significant win.

We want to climb as high as possible.

This is something that I could've never dreamed of. I never thought that I would actually make it. But I guess that with Sloane, everything is possible. Even if this sounds super cheesy.

I hold her close for the finishing position. Our breathing is heavy. We look at each other for a while until we stand up and skate back to Irina and the others.

„This is amazing!" Irina claps her hands together. She is still happy with us and our performance.

„Tomorrow, we'll have a fitting for the costumes! We're done for today!" Irina smiles at us.

We nod slowly, getting ready to leave. Right now, everything is perfect. Training is complex, and the days are long. But it's all worthing it. We might win the next competition as well.

Everything is a bit easier with Sloane now. We're laughing on our way home, making jokes. She is talking excitedly about the costume fitting tomorrow and the competition in a couple of days.

I love to listen to her. She is talking with so much passion and love. She doesn't even stop during dinner. She is so excited and happy. Now she is talking about Paris again, and I welcome this conversation.

„Do you want to see the Louvre? I have already been there, but it's beautiful!" She tells me with a huge smile plastered on her lips.

„I bet it is. I have never left this town. Well, except for the Toronto trip and the cottage trip," I tell her slowly.

I never had the luxury of traveling.

„Oh, you will love it! I am sure of that! I can show you around the city."

„I would love that. I am sure you're the best guide" I smile at her. I don't really care about sightseeing, but I would do everything for her. If I had to go and do some sightseeing just to see her beautiful smile, I would surely do that.

We're cleaning everything as soon as we're done eating. We have to get up early again tomorrow. Maybe we'll go skating again after we have the fitting.

We both walk upstairs, and I honestly have no idea what will happen. Is Sloane coming with me? Or do I have to follow her into her room?

Before I can waste another thought on that, she is pressing her lips onto mine. She surprises me with that kiss, but I welcome it. I wrap my arms around her, pulling her closer to me.

„Good night, Asher," she whispers against my lips.

„Good night, Slo," I reply with a soft smile.

And then she frees herself and disappears into her room.

60

ASHER

Sloane woke me up the following morning. She is too excited about the costume fitting, which makes me a bit nervous. We don't know what Irina is thinking. It has to suit the choreography.

We arrive at the usual store right in time. Sloane and I are looking at each other, and then we enter.

Irina is already waiting for us. She stands at the checkout, talking to the shop owner.

„There you are! I can't wait to see the two of you in the costumes! They are absolutely amazing!" Irina raves about the costumes.

She doesn't waste any time. She leads us to the back toward the dressing rooms. The costumes might already be inside.

We both disappear into our dressing room. I look at the clothes hanging there. I again wear an utterly black costume. The focus has to be on Sloane again.

I quickly change and leave the dressing room. Someone is in the fitting room with Sloane. Giggles can be heard as they put on her costume. Irina is putting a red rose into the pocket of my shirt. So this is the look.

Sloane is going to match that rose. She is wearing red. The curtain rips away, and she steps out. I look at her, swallowing the lump down my throat. God, I have never seen something that stunning. Her outfit is revealing, and it's undoubtedly doing things to me. I can feel my heart racing inside my chest. My dick is hardening as I look at her. I wish I could look away, but my eyes are glued to her. She is wearing a red costume with an embellished bra top. It's god damn revealing.

„It's perfect and fits like a glove once again!" Irina is more than happy with it.

„Go and get changed. I'll get everything ready at the checkout. We're taking the costumes with us now, " Irina tells us, and we nod. I am still staring at Sloane.

„You don't have to help me. I am sure I can take it off myself," Sloane tells the sales assistant. And with a nod, everyone disappears to the front.

Sloane turns back toward me. She smiles sweetly as she comes closer.

„What are you doing?" I ask her as she slowly pushes me toward my dressing cabin. The cabin is not big, and I am sure everyone will notice if we're disappearing into the same one.

„You have a situation going on there," she points to my crotch, still moving toward the cabin.

„I am well aware of that, " I reply. My answer is coming out in a small breath. She drives me absolutely insane.

„I can take care of that," she whispers, closing the curtain behind us.

„We'll get caught, " I reply slowly. I am not really sure what we're doing here. I don't want to get noticed, especially not by Irina. She'll kill us, and I am sure that we don't need the costumes then. We won't skate together when someone finds out what this is between us.

„No one is going to notice if you keep quiet. I'll be quick," she winks at me, already unbuckling my pants. I can't say no to her anyway. Everything she does is making me harden even more. I want her pretty lips wrapped around my dick. God, I would do everything for them right now.

She slowly slips her hand inside my pants before pulling them down. She is pumping me slowly.

Then she finally pulled down my pants, freeing my cock. And from that moment on, she doesn't waste any time. She wraps her lips around me, pleasuring me most deliciously.

Her tongue licks the underside of cock, while she sucks on it. She circles the tip every now and then, which drives me absolutely crazy.

I keep every sound inside. Even when I wish I could moan her name right now. I want to tell her how good she makes me feel right now.

She knows exactly where to touch and lick. It's embarrassing how quickly she can make me come. But I can't stop it. It feels too damn good.

She looks up at me as she swallows everything, looking so innocent that it tips me over the edge even more. She wipes her lips as soon as she is done, smiling sweetly. I pull her in for a kiss. A kiss not lasting long enough.

„That was fun. I start liking that whole hiding thing," and then Sloane leaves my dressing room to go into her own. She leaves me behind, still panting. I'm still catching my breath.

„Asher, are you ready?" Irina yells just minutes later. There is no way that Sloane has already left her cabin that quickly. That means it only took a couple of seconds for her to change. Less than a minute.

I quickly change back into my regular clothes. Holding the costume tight to my body as I leave the cabin. I hope that no one noticed what just happened.

„There you are!" Irina smiles at me. Sloane standing next to her, her hair now in a ponytail. She smiles as well.

I hand back my costume. They're putting it into the same bag as Sloane hers.

„Great, I'll see you guys tomorrow!" Irina tells us. Our way part in front of the store. We're walking back to Sloane's car, and Irina walks toward her.

„Do you want to go skating?" I ask Sloane slowly. I want to get rid of the tension I am feeling right now. If I am not getting rid of it, I might do some things to her. I am not sure if she wants it. I don't want to use her for sex. It's not the main thing about our relationship anymore. It's about much more, and I don't want to screw up. I want to make this work.

„Sure, why now?" She shrugs her shoulders as she starts the engine. Our next stop is now the rink.

61
SLOANE

Asher and I are on the ice again. The rink is open for everyone right now. This means that no one is using it for training. But the tricky thing is that we have to skate around other people. I don't know why it is so full today.

We indeed can't practice our performance here. Instead of that, we're skating around, trying some easy elements. We can't try a lift, there isn't enough space for us. I surely don't want to knock out a skating person on the ice.

„I forgot how full it is when it's opened for everyone," Asher sighs. He clearly is annoyed. I know he doesn't like being surrounded by so many people.

„It's not that bad. I love to watch them sometimes." I smile back at him. He isn't smiling. He is not even smiling back.

„Look at the children, how hard they try to learn something. It reminded me of myself when I was younger. I can see the looks on their faces when they're watching us." I gush about the children. It is the cutest thing. The girls try to learn something new, dreaming about being an ice princess, just like I did when I was little.

Like this, most children aren't afraid of getting hurt at a young age. They are eager to try something new.

„We could maybe teach them something?" I ask Asher. But his mood seems to be too bad for it.

„I don't care about the children. I wanted to skate with you," he grumbles, making me laugh.

„We can skate when everyone is gone. You know we are allowed to use the rink after it's closed for the public." I remind him, and I skate toward the little girls.

I want to help them. Maybe, if I teach them something new, I wake the desire for more. Perhaps they want to be like me and skate professionally. This could be the next generation. I am eager to help with that.

„Do you want to learn some really cool things?" I ask them, smiling brightly at them. I can feel Asher his eyes on me. He is watching me, still standing on the edge.

He doesn't care to join me, but he isn't moving away either. I concentrate on the girls. I show them some easy things, small spins, and easy single elements.

They're learning quickly. Laughing and having fun while doing it. They have to leave as soon as the rink closes. Everyone is leaving now until we're the only ones left behind. I look at Asher, who now seems to be in a better mood.

He skates toward me, a smile on his face as he grabs my hands. It's just us now, and it feels special. No one is watching us, meaning we can kiss every now and then. No one here can see us.

It feels great to skate with him, even though he takes it a bit too seriously. We're rehearsing more than in our regular training session. He is not even making fun of it.

I stop entirely out of breath, looking at him. „What are you doing?" I ask him, still trying to catch my breath.

„We're rehearsing," he replies slowly. But he is out of breath as well.

„But we're doing fine? I thought this would be fun now, but you're taking this so severe " I look at him, trying to get an answer.

But he grabs my hand, pulling me into the middle again. We start from the beginning.

„We can't rehearse enough!" That is his only reply now.

Again, and again, and again. There is no stop in sight for Asher. But at some point, I have to stop. I am tired, and I can't skate anymore.

„I'll be sore tomorrow. And Irina is not going easy on us. We should stop for today. We're good. I know we will win this competition" I smile at him softly.

But he groans, not being satisfied with what I said. I really don't understand the problem. Why does he want to rehearse that much? I look at him, unsure of what to do now.

„What's going on?" I ask him slowly.

„The tension is not gone," He mumbles. It's hard to understand him, especially it's hard to understand what he means.

„But we just trained for hours," I reply, confused. He has to feel a bit sore by now. There is no way that he doesn't feel a bit. I am exhausted and tired.

„No, not that kind of tension," he replies slowly, avoiding my eyes.

I start laughing. And I laugh so loudly that Asher looks up at me. He seems to be so shocked by my reaction.

„Why didn't you say anything?" I ask him with a laugh. It surprises me even more. I wish he would have told me.

„I don't want you to think I am using you for sex," he replies, and I laugh again.

„What? I know that you're not using me. But if you had told me, you would have known that I would want to go home instead of coming here," I look at him.

„For real?"

„Yeah, I don't say no to releasing some tension" I laugh, and the second I say it, he already pulls me from the ice.

62
SLOANE

Every single day was filled with a lot of training. Asher and I got closer, even though we kept it a secret. I learned from my mistakes, and I told Flynn about it. He will kill me if I keep another secret from him.

First, he didn't like the thought of Asher and me, but I think now that he sees how serious it is between us, he kinda gets used to it. It's hard for him to keep it a secret. Flynn is a person who likes to talk about stuff like this.

But today is the competition, and Irina still has no idea. Luckily. I take a deep breath as I take a look around. The matches are getting harder and bigger, and I am getting more nervous. It's been a long while since I went to competitions this big. Asher is smiling at me. He is holding my hand as we walk toward our seats. It looks like a kind gesture between partners.

This performance is going to be different from the others we did before. I know that everyone will love it, this might be our best. It might be even better than our dramatic performance.

Some people are excited to see us. They want to talk to us. Maybe our chances for a competition in Europe aren't that bad after all. Today is going to be very important for our future careers.

Our performance is in between all the other skaters. I am more than nervous because Flynn and I have never done something like this. Our performances have never been hot and sexy. At least I never saw them like this.

The red costume is also the most revealing one I ever wore. It feels a bit weird, but I feel great as soon as I see how Asher looks at me. The way he looks at me makes me feel desired and sexy. It's been a while since I felt like this the last time. I am truly happy.

Something I thought couldn't be possible after Flynn his accident. I thought the accident destroyed my life in the worst way possible. But Asher is the best thing that happened to me. When I am with him, I am happy.

Flynn and I were a great team. We never made mistakes. Everything was perfect. But we never had this unique chemistry, something I have with Asher. I know what Irina meant the whole time.

I hope she doesn't change her opinion once she knows something is going on between Asher and me. Our personal relationship won't affect our skating relationship, at least not negatively. We're better since we stop avoiding our emotions.

We have to get ready now for our performance. While we're waiting for our turn, we stretch our muscles. My heart is racing inside my chest. I am beyond nervous and scared that we're going to mess this up.

Asher takes my hand, and we're skating to the middle of the ice together. We wave to the crowd, a smile on our faces. After a couple of minutes, everything is getting quiet. Our performance starts, and for a moment, the world stops spinning. I try to forget about the hundreds of people watching us. It's just us right now.

We have our moment here, lost in the performance. I hear the music in the background. I hear the sounds of our skates on the ice. Something I am so used to that I mostly don't listen to it anymore, even though it's one of my favorite sounds in the world.

Asher touches my skin, and it feels like I am on fire. Our movements are smooth and automatic. I could perform this dance in my sleep.

Irina made sure that the choreography was touchy. Even during the most minor elements, we somehow have to touch each other. Every axel jump is a thrill. We're in contact every single second of the performance.

We're sliding forward, slowing down a little after our last jump together. I lean backward into Asher's arm, which is holding me. His other hand is slowly driving down my body. It surprises me because we never practiced this. He starts on my chest, touching my breast swiftly, driving down over my body until his hand disappears.

I cover it up as best I can. No one should know that this was unplanned.

Everyone starts cheering as our performance is over. It feels more than reasonable. It feels like we did everything right.

Asher feels the same way. I can see how he smiles widely at me. He seems to be so happy. I hug him tightly before we leave the ice together.

If every competition feels like this, I never want to miss this feeling. It is the best feeling I have ever had. And knowing that Asher is so happy also makes it a lot better.

We're back in our seats next to Irina. Now we have to wait for the results, as soon as everyone is done. I can't wait to see it. Right now, I don't really feel if we won or not. I really hope that we did. I think that we have outdone ourselves.

Asher softly squeezes my hand, „We did a great job!" He smiles at me.

I nod slowly, „Yes! And it felt amazing! I wish we could do it again!" I reply with an even wide smile.

Sometimes I love the adrenalin rush. I love the competitions and the excitement rushing through my veins. It is truly the best feeling we could ever have. I even love the feeling of waiting for our results. The tingles in my stomach and the way my heart is racing.

The ranking starts from the bottom to the top. With every name, my heart skips a beat. This only means that we're on top of the ranking. The ranking stops at fourth place.

The presenter is going to announce the top three himself. He is building up the excitement. I want him to spit it out right now. I can't wait anymore. I need to know if we did it.

The third place goes to a couple I have never seen before. I think they are not from here, and they don't seem to be happy about it. No one is celebrating. They sadly look to the ground.

Now the presenter is going to announce the second and the first together. My heart could jump right out of my chest. I am excited and nervous at the same time.

I hear the names. Everyone around us starts cheering and celebrating. But it takes a minute for me to realize what just happened.

We made it. We won the competition and got first place with a phenomenal number of points. No one is even close to us.

Asher wraps his arms around me. We jump up and down together. I smile widely at him. Asher leans in and presses a soft kiss to my cheek. This is the first time that we truly celebrate as a team.

This is the first time everything is truly perfect, and I hope it'll stay this way.

63
SLOANE

With the medals around our necks, we're back home. This is a great feeling. „I can't believe it. Tonight is going to be amazing!" I smile at Asher.

Irina invited us over to her house for dinner. It's not the first time I have been to her place, but it was long ago. She invited Flynn and me after we won the first significant competition. Now she is doing the same with Asher and me.

But until then, we have to wait quite some time. Asher pulls me close before I can think of anything. He presses his lips onto mine, laying his arms around me.

„Before we go to this dinner, I might have an idea of how to celebrate," Asher mumbles against my lips.

„I wonder what this might be," I whisper back, a smirk plastered on my lips.

„How about I show you?" And with that, he already picks me up as if I am light as a feather. He carries me up into my bedroom, where he puts me back down.

Asher slowly unzips my tracksuit jacket. His eyes are glued to my body and the costume underneath the tracksuit.

„God, that costume drives me crazy."

I let the jacket fall to the ground, unbuttoning his costume shirt and revealing his toned abs. He bends down, kissing the skin of my neck. This already got me panting. My breathing gets heavier, and my skin is on fire.

He slowly peels off my clothes. I do the same, slowly getting rid of his costume. I grab the chain of my medal to pull it over my head, but he stops me. „Leave it on."

I leave the medal around my neck, smiling shyly at him. He pulls me to the bed, pushing me down slowly. But this time, I have something different in mind. I switch positions, pressing him into the mattress and straddling his waist.

I sinfully grind against him, the medal hanging around my neck, earning a moan from him, and then I finally sink down on his erection. We both moan out again.

It takes a second for me to adjust until I start moving. I slowly grind my hips against him. Closing my eyes in pure bliss. Both of our breathings are heavy. Asher grabs the chain around my neck, pulling me down to meet his lips.

This moment between us is intense. We're looking into each other's eyes. It drives me mad looking into the green forest of his eyes. It drives me absolutely crazy.

Asher sits up, wrapping his arms around me. My skin is against his hot skin. He is meeting my thrusts, making everything so much more intense. My hand is grabbing his hair, pulling on it, earning another moan. God, the sinful sounds he makes are driving me absolutely insane.

Now that he is thrusting into me differently, he hits every right spot. And every movement brings me closer to the edge. „Asher," I moan out his name.

„Repeat it," he begs, sucking on the skin of his neck.

„Asher," I moan out again, over and over again. „God, you feel so good," I whimper as he thrust into me again.

„You feel like heaven, baby. So good," he praises me, his breath against the shell of my ear.

I can feel his hand sneaking down my body. He starts rubbing my sensitive nub, bringing me even closer. I can feel the knot tighten in my stomach. I come undone a few strokes later, moaning his name in pure bliss. Asher follows after me.

We both let ourselves fall back into the pillows. We're catching our breaths, staring against the ceiling. I look at him with a soft smile on my face. I draw a pattern with my fingertips onto the skin of his chest.

„Round two in the shower?" I ask him slowly. After the competition and our victory, I have tons of energy left.

Asher jumps up, already reaching for the door. I laugh at him, even though I am not as fast as him.

„What are you waiting for?" He asks me, leaving the room and disappearing into the bathroom.

64

ASHER

It's a true miracle that we got ready in time. I couldn't keep my hands off of Sloane. God, and now she is wearing this red dress. I don't even know why we're dressing up. It's only Irina, but Sloane is taking this pretty seriously.

She is looking at herself one last time in the mirror. Then she smiles at me as we open the door and leave the house. She is driving over to Irina her place. Luckily our town isn't that big, so her place isn't that far from Sloane, her home.

I am a bit nervous about having dinner with Irina. What if she is now going to notice that there is something between Sloane and me? Maybe this will be the last time we sit together as a team. I doubt that Irina would be very fond of the thought of us.

But Sloane is pretty calm about this. She greets Irina with a huge smile. They even hug, and then Irina hugs me. For the first time, she seems to be relaxed and happy. She isn't in a bad mood and isn't strict with us.

It's a relaxed evening, nothing business-related. I realized really quickly that this was a dinner between friends. Irina gestures for us to sit down at the dinner table. She has already prepared the starters for us. And this is something I learned about Irina today. She loves cooking, and she also is pretty good at it. The food she is serving looks phenomenal.

And tonight, I got to know her a lot better. Maybe this is a good sign. She is opening up to us as well.

„I started skating when I was five. I always dreamed of going to the Olympics. Being the best." She starts her story.

„I was good at the Olympics, and right then, when I was at my highest, I had this accident. It was similar to Flynn his. The doctors told me that I couldn't skate anymore. A world broke down as they told me that I am risking my life if I would continue doing it," she sighs, and she looks at us with a sweet smile.

„And what happened then?" Sloane asks her curiously.

„Well, I have never been as responsible as Flynn. I didn't listen to the doctors and continued skating until I had an accident again. I couldn't feel my legs for a month. They thought I could never walk again. This was the worst time of my life…" she seems lost in her story. She notices what she just said, and it looks like she told us too much.

„And then?" Sloane insisted on hearing more.

„And then I got help, and I became a coach. Being a coach is better than not being able to skate at all. I can see the joy of skating through my students. And years ago, I had the pleasure of becoming your coach," she smiles at Sloane.

She just skipped a whole point of her story. But no one dared to ask about the help she got. Irina is a single woman who isn't married and never talked of a partner.

I look at Sloane with a smile. Irina is right about her. Sloane is a talented skater, the best I know. She is going to win everything. Irina possibly knew that from the beginning.

„I am thrilled you both went through your difficulties and got over them. Now that everyone is getting along, it is much better. Also, your skating improved. As I said from the beginning, you both are a great team. I can see you coming very far," Irina gushes about us.

„We hope that everything is working out well for us. It would be great to go to the Olympics one day. Maybe we'll be able to win them" Sloane smiles, deeply in her dreams.

I am dreaming about this as well. I always dreamed of this, but it never seemed possible until now.

We're enjoying our dinner with Irina. She is telling us even more about her experiences as a skater. It's interesting to hear about her history. She went through a lot, and she is a great role model.

„And your partner Andrew? Are you still in contact with him?" Sloane asks her. But I notice that this question might not have been the best.

Irina tenses up as Sloane mentions her partner. Maybe something happened between them. It doesn't seem like they are still in contact.

„No, he had a new partner after me. I never heard of them again. Which might be the best thing possible," she replies quickly, hoping there won't be another question.

Sloane looks at me, shocked that Irina switched her mood that quickly. As if she just flipped the switch.

„I'm sorry that I asked," Sloane replies quickly, and Irina shakes her head quickly.

„It's okay. You're just curious."

„I am because this is the first time you open up toward me. Why?" Sloane has a lot of questions now. Which I can totally understand. She has known Irina for a long time now. But it seems like they never really actually talked.

„Well, I thought you deserved to know this. You saw my competitions, and I know you might have already had some of the information. You both are having a great time, and opening up could tighten our bond. Maybe it's also a chance for others to open up," Irina looks at me, her eyes full of hope.

She wants me to talk about my past. Maybe she wants to know what is going on with my dad.

„There is nothing I have to talk about. I handled my situation," I reply with a quick nod.

She doesn't have to worry about a single thing anymore. Thanks to Sloane, I don't have to worry about anything.

„Okay, I would never force anyone to talk," she replies with a smile. I nod, thankfully. I don't want to talk about it. I don't think that I'll ever be ready for it.

„But I am happy that we're talking. I feel like everything is perfect right now," Sloane says happily. She is genuinely excited about everything going on right now.

„I would be happy if there were no secrets between us." Irina smiles sweetly as she hands us the desserts.

No secrets… this sounds like she knows something. This truly makes me believe that she knows about Sloane and me. I feel unwell when I look into the round.

„There are absolutely no secrets," Sloane smiles innocently at her. I am surprised that she can lie that easily to Irina.

„You sure? Don't you want to tell me why Asher is staying with you?" Irina asks us, and I tense up automatically. Sloane, on the other hand, seems to get angry. I can see it on her face.

„Did Flynn tell you this?" She asks our coach.

She immediately shakes his head, „No, he didn't say anything. He knew it?" Irina shakes her head again, in disbelief maybe.

I look at Sloane, not sure what to say. I never thought that Irina would actually ask us about it.

„I'm not stupid. I see how you arrive together and leave together. I know that something is going on between the two of you." She starts, and I jump in before she can make any conclusion.

„Yes, I am living with Sloane. I had some problems at home, and she offered me to stay with her until I find something on my own," I explain quickly.

„That's why I said, you don't have to worry about anything anymore. I don't have any problems at home because I am not living there," and this is everything I want to say.

This is everything that she has to know about it, and it seems to satisfy her. She nods, not asking any further questions.

„I better hope nothing is going on between the two of you. I told you what I think of relationships between partners, " Irina replies, and with that, the conversation died.

65
SLOANE

Irina is paying attention to a lot of things. I never thought that she noticed something between Asher and me. She surprised me at the dinner, and I am happy that Asher saved it.

Irina never asked another question. I think that she believes us for now. She would surely freak out if she found out about the truth. I don't know what she would do, but I don't want to risk it. The worst thing that could happen is that she kicks Asher out, and I get a new partner.

Luckily she gave us a day off. Asher has to work today. He couldn't work the past few days, so he has to work the whole day now. I received a message this morning from Flynn. He asked me to meet him. He needs to buy something in town, and I should accompany him.

I got ready right after Asher left for work. It is a weird feeling to spend this day without him. It's been a while since we have actually been without each other. We nearly spend every single day together. But I am happy that I will spend this day with Flynn. We haven't really spent a lot of time together lately.

I wonder what he has to buy in town. I can't think of a thing right now. That's another reason why I want to be on time. He is already waiting for me, and he seems more than nervous next to everything.

He can't stand still and looks at me like he is in a hurry and I am too late. I wonder what is going on. I hug him quickly with a soft smile.

„Hey there! What's the plan for today?" I ask him curiously.

He looks at me, totally freaked out about something. Now I am getting nervous as well.

„I need to talk to you," he starts slowly, making me absolutely nervous. I don't know what is going on, but it seems serious.

„You're scaring me, " I whine, looking at him for some explanation.

„You don't need to be scared. I thought about something, and I need your opinion on it, and then I need your help," Flynn tries to explain what is going on, but he doesn't really explain it. I look at him even more confused.

„I'm totally freaking out right now. What are you trying to tell me?" I ask him. Flynn needs to tell me what is going on.

„I am going to propose to Gregg," he finally spits out, leaving me completely speechless. I thought about a million things, but this wasn't one of them. I am happy but also shocked about this exclamation.

„That's absolutely amazing!" I screamed out as soon as I found my voice again. I hug him happily and pull him as close as possible.

„And you want me to help you prepare everything? Do you already have an idea? Oh my god! I am so excited!" I can't stop the words from escaping my mouth. I am so happy for my best friend.

He and Gregg have been together for a long while now, and it was clear from the beginning that they would marry one day. It makes me happy that Flynn is talking to me about it.

„I do have a plan, and I thought you could come with me and take pictures… but secretly?" He asks me, earning eager nods from me. I am more than excited to be a part of this.

„Of course, I'll do whatever you want me to," I tell Flynn with a smile. I don't know what he has in mind, but I am here.

I'll do whatever he wants me to do.

„Okay, I want to buy a ring for him, something very simple," he tells me, and as soon as he says it, I grab his hands and pull him toward a store.

We shouldn't waste any time. I am so excited that I can't wait for this moment anyway. I look at Flynn while he nervously tries to pick a ring. I don't even need to help him because he exactly knows what he is going for. Flynn knows his boyfriend best, so I am sure he picks the right ring.

„It's going to be amazing! And it's undoubtedly going to be the best wedding" I clap my hand excitedly together as he gets a ring.

„What if he says no" Flynn seems to doubt the answer of his boyfriend. This is absolutely crazy because I am sure that Gregg would never say no.

„He is totally going to say yes! I am so sure. Gregg absolutely loves you. You're meant to be together," I smile at my best friend.

He nods slowly, but I can see that he is still nervous. I can't imagine what it feels like.

I can't even think of marrying someone right now. I love Asher, and we're definitely far from getting married. I believe that we both need tons of time until we get there.

„Thank you," Flynn smiled at me.

„For what?" I ask with a laugh. There is nothing he could possibly thank me for. I am just being his friend right now. It's something natural.

„For being here with me and for helping me."

„I still do have this camera. I promise you you'll get the best proposal pictures ever!" I squeal happily. I want to see them both happy. I want them to have tons of memories to this day. This is the least that I can do.

My dad took tons of pictures of us skating, he bought a good camera for this, and I am sure this camera is still in our house. I will ask my dad, and I am sure the pictures will be phenomenal with it.

„That would be amazing! I'll think about a day, and then I'll send the details to you" Flynn smiled happily.

I nod, knowing that I'll be wherever he wants me. „You can also take Asher with you if you want to," Flynn adds with a smile.

I don't really know how to reply to this. I haven't thought about bringing Asher with me.

„You both are together, right?" Flynn asks me curiously. I know he kind of waits for some news, but there isn't much to take. We keep our distance again, especially after the conversation with Irina.

„Kind of. The dinner with Irina was weird, she warned us of being together, and it freaked us out," I sigh and shake my head again.

I know that Flynn has his opinion when it comes to this. My best friend is strict, and he told us several times that we shouldn't be together. Or at least tell Irina about it.

„I am sure you both will get through it and make it. Irina has to accept it if you both take this seriously. There is always a risk, but tons of other things could happen. I mean, look at me" he laughs, and I nod. Right, but a relationship is preventable. I am sure that an accident is not.

„I hope that Irina is going to be okay with it. We have to tell her. Otherwise, she is going to be even more furious at us. I already feel so bad because we kept it a secret for so long," I sigh and look at the redhead.

„The longer you keep it a secret, the more disappointed she'll get," he tells me with a nod. I know that he is right. But telling her seems to be the hardest thing ever. I don't know how to do it.

Irina has always been a part of my family, but she is very strict, and there are some things that I would never tell her.

I know what she would think. She would hate us. I don't want this to happen.

„I'll tell her when it's the right moment," I promise Flynn, or it's more a promise to myself.

66

ASHER

Ever since that dinner, it's weird between Sloane and me. We try to hide that the conversation did something to us, but we can't. Everything might be fine at home, but as soon as we see Irina, it gets more awkward. It feels like she is watching us. It's like she is watching every move we make.

I think that she is suspecting something. Maybe she already knows it. She just doesn't have any proof. We will deny it, so it wouldn't make sense to talk to us. I totally get why Sloane is kind of scared to tell her. Even I am afraid now.

Irina is obsessed with our training sessions. It seems like she is even more strict now. We have to work hard, but Irina is a bit too obsessed with training.

She is yelling around, even though we don't have a new choreography now. We're rehearsing the essential elements, and then we have some training off the ice. No one is really talking. The atmosphere is tense.

„Everything good?" I ask Sloane as we walk into the small gym. She smiles softly at me, nodding.

„Yeah, why are you asking?"

„I don't know. It feels so weird today. I mean, it feels strange since the dinner. Do you think she knows something?" I ask her slowly. My voice is low that no one can hear what we're talking about. She shrugs her shoulders,

„I don't know. But if she knew it for sure, she would kill us. Maybe she suspects something, but she doesn't have any proof," Sloane replies slowly.

It's just as I thought. Maybe Irina knows it deep down. It's hard to miss that there is something between us. I can't really hide my feelings for Sloane. I never felt like this before, and I think I can't control how I look at her.

We're stretching our muscles while Irina is watching us intently. She talks about Europe now and how we're not allowed to mess anything up. Going international is a huge thing. We all know that. Every pair of eyes would be on us, affecting the media. Everyone would post about us, and we might be on the news then. I can't imagine that this might really happen. I can't believe we brought it this far after a short time.

It's only been a couple of months with Sloane together. Everything is moving so fast. We went from hating each other to loving each other. We went from being a lousy team to being an excellent team together.

„And Paris is the first international step?" Sloane asks our coach. We're excited and curious. There is nothing we want more, I think.

„Yes, Paris, Poland, or Norway. I will try to get us into one of the competitions. They're in the next couple of weeks, and it's hard to get into them," Irina explains, and we nod quickly.

„I hope that we can do it. It would be amazing to finally go international," Sloane smiles, and I look at her with a nod.

I know that Flynn and Sloane once tried to go international. They had a couple of competitions in Europe. But then the accident happened, and Sloane started again together with me.

She knows at least a bit about what it feels like. I don't know much about going to Europe, traveling and all those kinds of things.

„Do you think we have a chance?" I ask Irina, knowing that she will give us her honest opinion.

She would never lie to us or give us false hope. I know she is working hard to reach her goals, and she is always honest with us.

„After the last competition, I think we have an excellent chance of getting into the contest. We have to work really hard to keep up the score," she smiles, and I nod slowly.

She is right. Our last victory has also been the best. We have had the highest ranking in our skating history so far.

„And now back to work, let's concentrate" Irina changed her tone of voice. She is back to her stern and firm voice.

67
SLOANE

We're rehearsing every day. Irina is quick in creating new choreography for us. We don't even know which competitions are coming next. But Irina is so energetic that she is sure the next thing will be important.

But today is going to be evenly important. I asked my dad for the camera, Flynn was done planning the proposal, and today was the day. We're going to meet in the park, where he and Gregg first met. My heart is racing uncontrollably.

I am so excited for them both. I am sure that they both are going to be really happy. Flynn sent me the location of the exact spot where we have to wait for them. I set up the camera and everything that I might need. My dad explained how the camera works, and I think I can do it. Even though I am still scared that I still mess up.

I take a look around, trying to spot them both. „Stop being so nervous. I think you're getting more anxious than Flynn himself," Asher laughs.

I quickly shake my head, but I know that he is right. I am beyond nervous and happy for both of them. Maybe I am really as tense as both of them.

I look at Asher and shake my head again, „I am just happy for both of them. I mean, how can I not be happy for them?"

„Take a deep breath. Otherwise, you're going to mess up the photos," he smiles at me, and I nod again. He is right, I only have this one job, and I surely don't want to mess this up.

„Thank you for being here with me. I would totally freak out alone," I smile at him. Asher wasn't really fond of the idea. First, he thinks that Flynn doesn't want him there. They don't know each other well, and a proposal is enormous.

But Flynn told me myself that I could bring him with me. And it is making things easier for me. He calms me down, even though I am not calm at all.

„I don't want to know how much you would freak out then. You're already freaking out," Asher chuckles about it.

„Well, it would be much worse without you," I tell him, giggling about that.

„Oh god," he laughs.

I quickly check the camera one last time. Flynn sent me a quick message that they're on their way. I am sure that it won't take that long now. And I am more than nervous.

I am sure that Gregg is going to accept. There is no other way. But still, I am nervous. I want them both to be happy. They're young, and maybe this is something that scares Gregg.

„Look! There they are!" Asher points to the couple. They're walking toward the lake with bread in their hand. They came here feeding the duck. I can't believe they met like this. It is absolutely the cutest story I have ever heard in my entire life. I remember that day very well. Flynn came to see me. He couldn't stop talking about the cute guy he had just met. It was shortly after he came out to me.

I would have never thought they would end up like this together. They hadn't talked that day, but they returned the next day, hoping they would see each other again.

And here we are, years later, and Flynn is proposing to him today. I get the camera ready, already taking a couple of pictures of them feeding the ducks. They look so happy. Both of them are smiling at each other.

I think they're now sharing their memories of their first meeting. I can see how they look at each other, the sparkle of love in their eyes. I could really get jealous if Asher didn't sneak his arms around me, pulling me closer to him.

He is holding me close to his body, looking at the pictures I am taking now. It is absolutely perfect.

My heart skips a beat as Flynn reaches out for Gregg his hands. I don't know what they talk about. I can't hear them. I can barely see his lips moving from that far.

But then he drops to one knee, grabbing the ring box from his pocket. He drops the question. Just like Gregg, his jaw drops down. I can see the excitement in his eyes, and I am more than happy to catch this moment with the camera. Those are memories forever.

I can see how he nods wildly. I know that he is saying yes right now. Flynn put the ring on his finger, and they kissed.

Asher presses a kiss to my cheek at that right moment. I smile softly at him, wondering if he thinks about proposing one day. It's still early. We're not even officially together.

After a while of hugging and kissing, Flynn points toward us. I am done taking the pictures of the moment. I got many good ones, and I think they will both like it very much.

They walk toward us with huge smiles on their lips. I don't think that something could destroy their mood right now. They are beyond happy, which is totally understandable right now. Even I am more than happy for them.

„Congrats!!" I smile, hugging them both. Asher is doing the same. We're both curious to hear what Gregg tells us about the proposal. It makes me happy to hear that it has been a complete surprise, he wasn't expecting this in the slightest, and I think this is a good thing. I nod slowly, listening to him sharing his thoughts.

They are both having the same opinions about the wedding. As I can hear so far.

„What about going out to eat something? You can share your thoughts about the wedding! It's on me," I suggest, and everyone agrees quickly.

We agree quickly on a restaurant. The four of us came in two different cars, so we met at the restaurant again. Asher and I are walking back to my car.

I am still talking about the proposal. Flynn and Gregg are the loveliest couple, and I couldn't be happier.

Asher is not interrupting me for once. He is listening to me patiently. Even though I start talking about my own proposal wishes. I don't want to freak him out, but I am in my feelings talking about all of this.

I look at him with a sweet smile on my lips. „I'm sorry, I'm talking too much," I laugh, apologizing.

He shakes his head quickly, „No, no, it's okay. You're so happy. I love listening to you. And honestly, I might have to take some notes on your wishes," he laughs.

I am surprised by this. It seems like Asher is already thinking about the future. My heart skips a beat.

„But we still have time." I reply slowly. I don't want him to feel like he is under pressure.

„I know. We should concentrate on our career," Asher tells me with a smile, and I nod. He is correct; we both have goals and should do everything to reach them. Skating has always been our priority, and this shouldn't change.

At the restaurant, we hear everything about Flynn's and Greggs's plans for the wedding. They have the same taste, and it seems like they want to wait around a year until they get married. I look at Asher and smile.

Maybe we'll be in this position in a couple of years. Perhaps we're sitting here talking about our wedding while these two are already married.

Flynn is also talking about his college plans, and I am truly happy that it seems like he finally has a real plan. His life was a mess after the accident. I am so glad that everything is better now. He has a plan and a perspective for his future.

He seems to be so excited and happy about it. I never thought that I would see him like this again. Maybe he doesn't miss skating that much anymore. He could always come back and start coaching, even though he had already decided against it.

I think that the door is always open for him. He was a fantastic skater. Some could only dream of being that good.

68
ASHER

Everything is fine again. The proposal gave me a sight of a different future. I never thought about marrying or having a family. I always thought that it might never happen. I promised that I would never fall in love and have a girlfriend. Now I am sitting in the house of my secret girlfriend. Sloane is my savior. She saved me from the situation at home and gave me a chance for a better life and career. I have so much to thank her for, and I think I could never make up for that.

We're getting ready for our training session today. Irina might already wait for us. I open my closet to pick my training outfit for today. It doesn't matter what I am wearing. I mostly have the same stuff.

Sloane might take a bit longer than me. She always has to put her hair back. It takes a long time for her to put her hair up. This means I have tons of time to get ready.

A soft knock on my door let me look up. I just wanted to take off my shirt, but now I take a look at the door. „Come in," I yell.

The door opens slowly, and Sloane peaks her head inside. She looks kind of worried, and she is still not ready.

She closes the door behind herself, coming closer. „I need to talk to you," she tells me, patting at the space on the bed next to her.

I am more than confused because I can't remember anything happening. Maybe Irina knows everything, and now she doesn't want me to return.

„What happened?" I ask her, worried, sitting down where she told me to.

I look at her, waiting for her to open up. But this takes longer than I want to. It seems like she is trying to find the right kind of words. Sloane struggles. I see her struggle to find the right words for the first time. She talks a lot, especially with people she is comfortable around.

„Well, I just got a call. I'm so sorry, Asher, but the police just called," she tells me slowly. Then she takes my hand, but the words she just said are not making any sense. I don't understand what she wants to tell me. Why should the police call here? They don't have a reason to call here.

Maybe my dad did something? Perhaps they found out what my dad did to me? Or someone told them?

„Is it about my dad?" I ask her, confused. I hope it's not that bad. Maybe he got arrested, but then he finally gets what he deserves. I wish I would have had the guts to go to the police.

„Yes, he died yesterday," she replies. Her words seem to be so far away. I look at her, my eyes filled with shock.

„What?" I ask her, confused as if I didn't understand it. He died? I can't believe it.

„Yes, alcohol poisoning," Sloane. Her voice is quiet, and I notice that she doesn't know how to act. She might be sorry for me. Maybe she thinks that I am sad now that I lost my dad. I am not sad that I lost him. He has never really been my dad. We never did things together. He wasn't there for me. All he did was beating my mom and me. He was a terrible person.

But I feel guilty that he died is my fault. If I had stayed at home… maybe it would have never happened then. I am sure that he would have never drunk too much then.

„Please, say something?" Sloane begs because I just sit there in silence. I stare at her, a bit confused. I don't really know what to do. I don't really know how to react right now.

„This is all my fault, " I whisper, not knowing if I should cry right now. I feel more like I want to break something.

„It is not your fault! What are you talking about?" She tries to calm me down, stroking my back up and down.

It's not helping. I am more than sure that this is my fault. I could have prevented this. I made the decision to leave him.

„It is my fault. I left my father. I never even checked on him. I always cared for him, made sure that he isn't killing himself," I tell her, tears are filling my eyes. I don't even know why I am crying right now. I hated my dad. He wasn't even really a dad.

„No, you couldn't have done anything to prevent this. It is not your fault," Sloane says again.

I don't think that anything can change my opinion. It is definitely my fault. I kind of killed my father because I left him. He told me not to go, and I did. I never cared, so I just left him.

„Can you please leave me alone?" I ask her calmly. On the inside, I am everything but not calm. I want her to go. Right now, I need to be alone, even though it might hurt her.

„Of course, tell me if you need anything. I'll call Irina and cancel training for today" she smiles softly at me. She slowly presses a kiss on my cheek and then leaves.

It's somehow terrible to be alone, but it's also what I wanted. I don't want Sloane to see me like this. There is also nothing that she could do to make me feel better.

I know that it is my fault that my father is gone. No one can tell me otherwise. This is the only reason why I am sad. Or am I sad?

I feel guilty, but somehow I am also relieved. It makes me a terrible person for thinking like this, I know. But I am relieved because he can't hurt anyone anymore. He can't hurt me anymore. This is the most selfish thought I have ever had. My suffering is over now. He is gone. He can't hit or kick me anymore.

There is nothing that he can do, and this makes me happy. God, I am such a terrible person.

Maybe I am just like him. This might be the start of me becoming him. And it scares me.

I don't want to hurt anyone. I don't want to hurt Sloane or put her in danger.

But my thoughts are scaring me. My father just died, and I am happy about it. I feel guilty but also relieved. I am terrible.

69

SLOANE

I am worried about Asher. He isn't leaving his room. It's been days, and I don't think Irina will be patient with him anymore. He doesn't want to come to training. I don't want to leave him alone. I try to stay with him, but he doesn't want me near.

It's terrible to see him like this. I wish I could help him, but he isn't listening to me no matter what I say.

„Asher?" I knock on his door again. I don't wait for his reply this time. I open the door slowly and step inside the room.

„Irina called. She wants to see us. We have ten minutes to get there," I tell him, hoping he won't argue with me. He doesn't even look at me. I think he couldn't hear me, but I know well that he did.

„Come on. I don't want to lose my career. I know you're grieving, but Irina just wants to talk. No one is forcing you to go back on the ice today," I tell him slowly, and this finally makes his move.

He looks at me, nodding. I quickly grab my stuff, staying in my comfortable clothes. Asher is not talking. I haven't heard his voice in days, and I miss it. I sometimes bring him food and water, but he barely touches them.

I know that he never had a good relationship with his father. His father was a terrible person, but I know that Asher is somehow grieving on the inside.

Maybe he still thinks it's his fault, and I don't know how to help him.

Irina is already waiting for us. She quickly talks to Asher about his loss. But as soon as she realizes he doesn't want to talk about it, she drops it.

„I called you here to see how you're doing. You are missing a lot of important training days." She starts, and I quickly gesture for her to drop it. This is not the right topic for today. I know that Asher is not ready for this conversation now. He needs some more days, and I accept it.

„I know you still need some time, but I got you into one of the European competitions. We're traveling to Poland in two weeks," she tells us slowly.

It takes everything inside of me to keep it inside. I am happy and excited about it, but it is definitely the wrong moment to show that. I know that Asher might not be that happy about it. I look at him, worried about his reaction.

I understand that we don't have much time left. I know that we have to practice a lot and that we have to learn the new choreography.

Asher turns around without saying anything. He walks straight out of the building. I follow him right away.

„Ash, please talk to me!" I beg him. But he doesn't turn around. I already miss his voice. He is like a shadow of himself.

I understand it is hard for him, but I want him to talk to me. Maybe I can do something for him to ease the pain. Perhaps I can somehow help him.

„I don't want to do this anymore!" He tells me. His voice is broken and quiet.

„What? Skating?" I ask him, confused. I never thought that he would want to quit. There is no way that he is retiring, but he nods. He doesn't look at me. He looks to the ground. This is an impulsive decision, something that he might regret later.

„You don't mean it. Let's go home and rest. Tomorrow you might think differently about this," I tell Asher, leading him toward my car.

But he shakes his head. He isn't walking with me. Asher is standing there in the middle of the nearly empty parking area.

„I don't deserve to go to Europe. I don't deserve to skate. I am not good enough for you or for anyone. I go back inside and tell Irina I am not doing this anymore," Asher tells me again.

I wonder where he got those thoughts from. It's total bullshit, and it breaks my heart that he says something like this.

If someone deserves it, it's him. He deserves everything good. Asher deserves it to reach every goal he dreams of and see the world. He is a fantastic person. I wish he could see himself through my eyes.

„Bullshit. You're coming with me. If you want to still quit tomorrow, you can do this. But you won't quit today," I grab Asher's hand, pulling him to my car. There is no way that I let him quit.

He is going to regret this decision. I know that he would hate me for letting him quit. So I won't do it. I won't let him quit. Not today, at least.

„I'm sorry," he whispers on our way home.

It is driving me crazy, the way he is behaving. I know it's the grieving process, but it makes me insane.

„For what? You don't have to be sorry for anything," I reply quietly. At least I am trying to be patient with him. I really do try my best, and eventually, it's working.

„I am sorry that I can't go to Europe with you. I know how happy you were when Irina told us. First, Flynn had this accident, and now I am bailing on you," and then he starts crying.

Good lord, I am the worst person at comforting others. I never know what to do. I failed with Flynn, and now I don't know what to say to Asher. Why is he saying something like this while I am driving?

So I don't reply while I am driving. And the minute we're home, I get Asher out of the car and back into his room. There he is, laying down, turning away from me. But this time I won't leave. I sit down right next to him.

„You're not bailing on me. Flynn didn't either. He had an accident. And this accident made us skate together and look at Flynn. He is happy again," I start slowly.

If Asher is quitting now, he is totally bailing on me. But I won't tell him that because he won't quit.

„Nothing can make me go angry. I am here, and nothing can make me run away. If you really don't want to skate anymore, I'm here," I tell Asher slowly.

I hate saying this. I think a part of me would hate Asher for stopping skating. If he really wants this, I accept it, though.

„But I know that you don't want to stop. Skating is your one and only passion. It's what you always wanted to do. So you maybe shouldn't make that choice while grieving," I tell him slowly.

Asher is back in his usual position. He isn't looking at me, and he isn't talking to me. He is staring against the wall, avoiding my eyes.

„Let's make a deal?" I suggest. Maybe this is getting his attention. I won't give up that easily. I have to get him back onto his feet. There must be something that I can do.

„What is it?" Asher asks me slowly.

I don't really know what to say now. I wouldn't have thought that Asher would reply so quickly. I try to come up with something as fast as possible.

„You go to your father's funeral, and if you need something from your old house, I'll bring you there one last time. After that, I'll bring you to an exceptional place, and you'll do whatever I want you to. And if you still want to quit then, I'll let you, " I suggest, hoping that he would seal the deal with me.

I might have an idea how to bring him back. The funeral is in two days. I think that Irina might be okay with that. If everything is working out perfectly, we could still make it.

We lost tons of time, but I know that we could still win this competition in Europe.

„Deal," Asher replies quietly.

I smile at him softly, noticing that he slowly falls asleep. I carefully drive my hand through his curls. Then I finally stand up and pull the blanket over his body.

I hope that he can close the chapter with the funeral. Maybe it might be easier for him to talk to someone.

Asher went through a lot with his father, and he never talked about it. He always kept it a secret.

70
ASHER

I hate today. I wish I could just stay in my room. But now that I want to quit skating, I feel bad staying here. It doesn't make any sense.

„I don't want to go. Can we stay here?" I ask Sloane one more time. She is tightening my tie. Sloane looks gorgeous in the black dress she is wearing for the funeral.

She is sure this will give me some closure. But I don't think it'll help. I look at her, still skeptical.

„No, we won't stay here," she replies slowly.

And I really can't make her stay home with me. She drags me out of the house, sitting me in the car. I'm grumpy today, not in my usual numb mood. Everything is bothering me, and when I say something, I'm only complaining.

I wonder if someone is going to be there. I can't remember that my father had any friends. We also don't have any family left. One part of me is scared of going there.

I don't need to say goodbye to my asshole of a father.

Sloane is holding my hand as we walk to his grave. There will be a small ceremony. I know that Sloane wants to stay for the whole ceremony. I couldn't actually care less.

I can already see from afar that there is no one. I don't think that anyone would actually come. My father spent his life at home after my mom died.

There is a preacher. He waits for us to come closer. And then he starts with the small ceremony. He doesn't look up as he reads down the lines. The ceremony is quick. I haven't listened to a word anyway.

There aren't any flowers, and I begged Sloane to not bring any. My father doesn't deserve flowers. It shouldn't look pretty. He won't be missed, and I don't want to make it seem like it.

„Are you feeling a bit better?" Sloane asks me as we're back in the car. She looks at me, waiting for my reply before starting the vehicle.

„No, now I am angrier than before," I tell her slowly, taking a deep breath.

„What? Why?" Sloane asks me, surprised. She really thought that this would help me get over my father. Maybe she thought that I would feel a lot better.

„The coward took the easy way out. He never got punished for the terrible things he did. Now he is dead, resting in peace…." I try to explain. I don't know if that makes sense, but I think he needs to be punished.

I wish he would have spent his life in jail, not for hurting me, but for making my mom's life a living hell. She died because she was sick, but he beat her even though she wasn't already feeling well. He never cared for her.

„I know. But you don't have to be scared anymore. He can't hurt anyone anymore," Sloane replies slowly. She is right. This is the positive side of his death.

He can't hurt someone anymore. I don't have to be scared, even though I don't think the nightmares will ever go away. One part of me will never forget the days with him.

I nod slowly, and she starts driving. Our next stop is my old home. It's not mine. The house doesn't belong to anyone anymore. No one can pay for it, and I don't want to live there anymore.

I have nowhere to go. I don't have a home anymore. I lost everything with his death. I can grab some things that I might need. The rest will get sold. I think that they maybe have an auction with all the items. They do not worth much, though.

„Should I come with you?" Sloane asks me as we're right in front of the house.

I quickly shake my head. Hoping that she won't come with me this time. I am not even sure if I really want to go there. I wish I don't have to come back here ever again.

„It's okay. I'll just grab some things," I tell Sloane and jump out of her car. I don't exactly know what I am looking for now.

Maybe I don't want to grab anything. Most of my clothes are at Sloane her place. There is nothing else.

But I still take a walk through the house. It's a mess, and it smells so bad in here. No one ever cared about cleaning.

There are still empty bottles in the living room. The kitchen is a dirty mess. The sink is full of rotten dishes. There are takeout containers everywhere.

There is nothing in the living room that I like to keep. No pictures on the wall, nothing personal.

My room is totally destroyed. My father had one of his crazy episodes after I left. He destroyed everything in this room. The clothes I left here are ripped out of the closet. They are lying chaotically on the ground.

My bed is broken. I think he kicked against the wood until it totally broke down. He ripped the pillow and the blanket. The mattress is also thrown into the middle of my room.

I don't have many personal things. There is only one thing I can think of that I might want to keep. I quickly look for a bag in my closet, something I can put my belongings in.

Then I walk over to my broken desk. I open one of the drawers. I am surprised that he never touched my drawers. In the last one, I kept a small book. I grab it and stuff it into the bag.

Then I leave my room behind. A place where I always felt fear, anger, and loneliness. I am happy to leave it behind.

I never thought that I would actually leave it behind one day. And now I am entering a room I never dared to enter in my entire life. My parent's bedroom.

I think my father never slept in it again after my mother died, and even before, he rarely entered it. He mostly dozed in his armchair in the living room.

I wasn't allowed to go in here. He would have killed me if I ever tried to open the door. All of my mother's belongings are here. Everything that is left of her.

The bed is untouched, which makes a shiver run down my back. Everything here is dusty and dirty. No one touched it for a long while. I don't know what I am looking for, but I want to remember the good thing of my childhood before leaving everything behind.

My mother always tried to protect me. She always had been there for me. She wanted me to start skating, and she supported me when I decided to do it. Even when she was sick, she tried her best for me. I never really understood why she died. I was young and always thought it was my father's fault.

I partly think it is. Maybe if my father didn't beat her and give her the medical care she needed, she would still be alive.

I open some of the drawers to look inside. I don't want to keep clothes from her, it's weird, and they are old and dusty.

My mom also never had many personal things. My father spent all the money we had on alcohol. She wasn't allowed to buy anything for herself.

But she has a small box full of jewelry pieces, things she bought secretly. She hid the box from her husband, hoping she would at least have something for herself.

The box is still here because my father never went into this room. I slowly open it, having a look inside. It's not much, but I keep the box and the things inside. I slowly put it into my bag and finally left everything behind.

71
ASHER

I never thought I would feel better after visiting my parent's house. Somehow I do feel better now. It gives me peace knowing that I had been there one last time.

Sloane is now driving to a secret location. I promised her to do this for her. I am not allowed to ask questions, and I won't. I don't want to talk to her right now. I am not ready to let the words leave my mouth. Simply because I don't know what exactly to say.

Sloane accepted that I am not talking much, so she isn't either. She parks the car at our destination and then grabs something from the trunks. Sloane is clearly hiding something from me, but I follow her quietly.

I don't know where we are. I have never been here before, so I can't tell what we're about to do here.

„Change your shoes," she tells me, handing me my skates. I am confused. I can't see any ice here, and I don't want to go back on ice. She knows it. But I don't have the power to argue with her.

So I change into my skates and look at her. She does the same.

She leads me further, and I finally understand where we are. Sloane brought me to Canada's famous skating trails. There are many of them, especially in bigger cities. I never knew that we have one as well. But now we're quietly skating next to each other.

I love the feeling of ice beneath my feet. It's a familiar feeling, something I never wanted to miss.

I am lying whenever I say that I want to quit. I don't want to actually quit skating.

I have nothing left except skating, nothing else I want to do in life. Sloane knows this because she knows me better than I want to admit.

I look at her. She is the best thing that happened to me in a very long time. I would even say that she kind of saved me. I have been terrible to Sloane the past couple of days, but she never left. I somehow expected her to leave or to kick me out. I thought maybe her parents would do the job for her. But everyone has been more than understandable toward me. They cared for me, and Sloane always ensured I had food and everything I needed.

„Thank you," I whisper.

She isn't replying. First, I thought she hadn't heard me. Maybe I was too quiet. But then she looks at me, taking my hand. Our fingers intertwine, and I know she doesn't have to reply.

„Do you feel better after today?" The blonde girl asks me, worried. I know that she wants me to feel better. And I do nod. She helped me a lot today. I think I might have overreacted the past couple of days. I can't tell what I was going through, but today helped me let go of a piece of my past.

„I do feel better, " I reply slowly.

„Do you want to talk to someone?" She asks me carefully. I know she doesn't want to hurt or freak me out. Sloane already spoke to me about therapy. I never dealt with my trauma. I never talked about what I went through.

„I haven't thought about it. Maybe?" I shrug my shoulders, not really knowing what I should do.

„But I thought about skating. And I believe that Europe might not be a good idea. I know you have been so happy about going there, which is a huge step. But I don't really know if we're ready...." I start.

I am sure that I don't want to quit skating. But I don't think that we should take significant steps like this. I am not ready. I don't even know if I can return to a training schedule like before.

„If you don't want to, it's okay," Sloane replies slowly.

I know that she always wanted to make that step. I wanted it as well. We both wished for a chance to go to Europe.

„I know we worked hard for this…."

„And we can still do it! Don't you think we should try it? It doesn't matter if we're winning this." Sloane interrupts me.

„I will think about it," I reply slowly.

It's not the right time to start this conversation. I am also a tiny bit scared that we will fight about it. I don't want to fight with Sloane. Not right now.

So we stopped talking. We made the first real step by starting to talk. And it feels good. It feels more than good to speak to her again. I still need some time. There is a lot to deal with now, but I know I'll get through it with baby steps.

We picked up food on our way home. It's the first real meal I have eaten in days. It kind of feels good. It feels like I am earning back my strength. I don't feel that helpless anymore.

„Are you coming with me? I want to show you something," I smile, taking Sloane her hand.

I lead her up into my bedroom. I said goodbye today, and it was time to share something with her. I grab the bag that I got from my old home. Two items are in there.

Sloane never asked me what I got. She never asked me about the items. But it's something that I want to share with her.

„Thank you for taking me to the house. It helped me." I smile at her, grabbing the book first.

It once belonged to my mother. I stole it from her room after she died. My father freaked out that I had been in there. He beat me that night. I never dared to open the door to her room ever again. I was so scared that he would beat me to death if I did.

But I grabbed the book, which would always remind me of her. Now I hand it to Sloane.

She carefully takes it, opening it. It's a photo album filled with photos of my life.

Pictures of me as a baby, some with my mom, and me as a kid when I started skating.

271

„My mom always told me to open this whenever I am sad. Because the pictures are showing happy moments, some moments without my father's anger," I tell Sloane as she turns the pages.

My father is in none of the pictures; he took some but never wanted to be in them.

There are not many pictures. Most of the book is empty.

„My mom died when I was young, so no one took pictures anymore. And there haven't been many happy moments. I glued some of my skating victories in it. But there are not many," I explain.

I tried to glue happy moments there, but my old partner and I weren't winning much. Sometimes I forgot it, or my father threw away the newspaper, and I couldn't cut out the picture.

„Your mother was so beautiful, and you're the cutest little kid I have ever seen," Sloane smiles at the pictures.

She looks at me, and I think I can see tears in her eyes.

„Thank you for trusting me. This means a lot to me," she tells me happily.

I pull her close with a nod, kissing her passionately. What did I do to deserve her? I had to go through hell all my life, and then she came and changed everything.

„There is something else…." I take the book from her, putting it on my nightstand. Then I grab the box from my bag.

I handed it to her, so she could open it. There are a couple of items in it. I want her to look at them.

„This belonged to my mom. These are the only personal items she had, next to the photo book," I explain.

Sloane looks at the box. It's like she is afraid to touch the items on the inside. I carefully take out a pair of earrings and a matching necklace.

My mother told me so often about the pieces. That's how I know them and their worth.

„This belonged to my grandmother, then to my mother. My mom always told me that I should give this to someone extraordinary one day." I explain to Sloane as she sees the gold necklace with a teardrop-shaped blue gemstone and the matching earrings.

„And I want to give them to you." I finally tell her.

I knew it the second I picked up the box. I knew that I would give this to her.

„What?" She replies, evenly shocked and surprised.

„There is only one person I could think of when I saw this box. The other things are probably not worth much, but I want you to have this box. And I want you to have my grandmother's jewelry because there is no single person in my life as important as you. There never will be a single person more important than you." I tell her, opening the necklace.

I carefully lay it around her neck, putting it on. She carefully touches the jewelry with her fingertips. Her eyes are glued onto me.

„I know this is a foolish moment. I have been a dick the past few days, and I shouldn't say something like this when I am a mess. But I love you, Sloane."

I never said those words to anyone. I never thought that I would say them. I never even knew what love was until now....

72
SLOANE

I can't believe what is happening now. I think that I could move something today. Asher is different since he left the house this afternoon.

Maybe it really helped. I partly gave up hope after the funeral. I can't help someone that doesn't want help. Now we're sitting here, and he is so lovely and cute. He showed me the pictures of his childhood.

Then he pulled out a box that once belonged to his mother. He gave it to me, and I opened it pretty confused. Pieces of jewelry inside. I don't really know what he wants me to do with them.

He should keep them. They belonged to his mother. It's something personal from her, the last pieces he has left of her.

But the whole story went a lot crazier the second he grabbed the pieces which belonged to his grandmother. God, I thought I couldn't understand him correctly. But he really is saying this.

He really tells me that I am important to him, and he is suddenly talking a lot. *I love you, Sloane.* This is what he told me just a second ago after he put his grandmother's necklace around my neck.

I look at him in pure shock. I indeed wasn't expecting this. My heart is racing nervously inside my chest, or is it excitement?

This is the weirdest moment, and I am scared to say it because he is now emotionally confused. Maybe he is still grieving.

But I also loved to hear it. It makes me happy, even though I wasn't expecting it.

„Asher…" I start slowly, still unsure what to say. His face drops. My reply is taking too long. But there is only one reply for me. There is only one thing that I can say right now.

„I love you," I finally reply, which makes him breathe out, relieved. And then he already pulls me close. He kisses me so hard that I struggle to breathe. He pulls me against his body, holding me close.

And after he broke the kiss, he hugged me so tightly. It's filled with so much love that my heart could burst.

„I will go to therapy. I'll talk about my trauma, hoping to get better," he tells me.

This is surprising me even more. Where does the sudden change come from? But I am happy to hear that.

He wants to change something, and this is an important step.

„What if we talk to Irina? Maybe an honest talk with her would help your decision about Europe?" I suggest slowly.

I don't want to give up hope entirely. We have been working so hard, and going to Europe would be a big step. Maybe we won't get this chance again, indeed not in this season.

I look at him hopefully.

„Let's take baby steps, okay? We can talk and see how everything is working out," he calmly tells me, and I nod.

I hope that everything is working out somehow. I know that we can do everything together as a team.

„Of course, we don't have to rush" I smile at him, softly kissing his lips.

I wouldn't do anything to make him feel uncomfortable. He is going through a lot. I think he is still grieving.

„Thank you for everything" he smiles at me. His voice is soft and calm. I don't really know what he means right now.

„For what?" I ask him slowly.

„For literally everything. You're always there for me. You didn't even leave me alone the whole time. I appreciate that you brought me food and water. Even now that I am telling you that I might not want to go to Europe, you accept it" he smiles at me.

„Of course. There is not a single reason why I shouldn't do it. Asher, I love you, and I would do everything for you," I smile softly, pressing a kiss to his cheek.

„Everything, mhm?" Asher asks me teasingly with a smile.

„Yes, everything," I tell him again.

„Okay, then I want to watch a movie with you and snuggle up underneath tons of blankets."

„Absolutely. I'll get us some popcorn while you decide on a movie" I smile at him. And with that, I quickly leave the room and go into the kitchen to prepare some snacks.

I'll call Irina tomorrow morning to inform her about everything. Hopefully, she can talk to Asher.

73
SLOANE

Irina agreed to meet us in the city diner. We just wanted to talk about everything, and Asher decided to open up to her.

It might be possible for her to understand him a little bit better. I can see how nervous Asher is. He barely touched his breakfast this morning.

„You don't have to tell her if you don't want to," I tell him again as we leave. He can't keep himself still, and I wonder what he might think about right now.

„I want to tell her. It'll be okay," Asher says with a nod. He takes a deep breath. He is absolutely nervous.

I am here to support him. He made this decision for himself, and I am proud he wants to take this step.

Irina is confused that we want to talk to her. I think that she is expecting the worst. After the past few days with Asher, she might think we want to give up. Maybe she thinks that Asher really is quitting.

„Is everything okay? I am worried about you," Irina tells us after we sit down. I look at Asher. He should start this conversation.

„No need to be worried. I wanted to talk to you," Asher tells Irina with a smile, and after he takes another deep breath, he starts his story.

He tells Irina everything from the beginning, from the first moment they met. Asher tells her about his father, about his financial problems.

It's a lot to process for someone who hears it for the first time. But this might distract Irina from the fact that Asher and I are together. She now knows why I offered him to stay with me.

She nods slowly, „If you need more time, it won't be a problem. I trust you, and I think we can still do it with tons of practice."

Irina wouldn't say we can still go to Europe if she doesn't mean it. This gives me hope, and I look at Asher with an encouraging smile.

„I don't think this is a good idea…." Asher starts.

I look at our coach. If she agrees now, it's over. There might not be another chance for us to take such a huge step. But she shakes her head eagerly.

„I signed you up for the competition. If you quit now, you get kicked out entirely. I think that we should at least try it. I have a lot of faith in you two, and I wouldn't say that I think you can win if I wouldn't mean it," Irina smiles at us, taking our hand.

„Okay, so we start training like right now?" Asher asks her carefully. I think that he doesn't want to start today. Maybe he is not ready for it.

Irina shakes her head slowly, „No, I think tomorrow is a better day for that."

She smiles. I have never seen her this emotional. I can see that there is something different behind her eyes. Something that she isn't telling us. Maybe she feels sorry for Asher. At least she can understand everything a bit better.

And while we're eating something, she tells us about the competition in Europe. She mentions every positive aspect to make it sound nicer to Asher. I know that she wants us to go there. It is also a big deal for her as a coach.

It's her birth country. I know that she is excited to go back there. Now she is a successful American figure skating coach. I bet that everyone is very proud of her.

„My family is throwing a big party for you. So I would like to invite you two to my home…." Irina smiles at us.

This completely surprises me. I would have never thought Irina would want us to meet her family.

I don't know much about Irina. She never really opened up that much. But right now, she is sharing a lot. We should even meet her family. This is absolutely crazy to me.

„A real polish party? I am so here for it!" I smile excitedly at her.

Asher nods, agreeing with me. This makes me even more excited for our Poland trip. I bet it is going to be amazing.

Maybe we could also do some sightseeing. I want to discover this new place with Asher together. I have never been to Poland before. There is a lot that I want to see if we're staying in the capital city.

„I don't think that you'll like it that much. Polish parties are crazier than the American ones," my coach laughs.

„I know, and I can't imagine something better. Also, I am meeting your family. I have known you for so long, and I can't wait to meet a part of your life" I smile at her.

Irina has always been one of my role models. I always looked up to her. Now I actually see something from her life. I got to know her a bit better.

This is what I have been dreaming about for years. I always wanted to get to know her better. Now it is finally happening.

74
ASHER

Maybe throwing myself back into work was the best decision I could make. Now it is sure that we're going to Poland. There is no going back. I want to win this competition.

Irina is going to introduce us to her family. This makes me nervous because I don't know Irina very well. I don't know much about her. She doesn't know much about me.

I just told her a massive part of my life. Now she is asking me daily if I am doing good. She cares about Sloane and me.

It feels like our bond is getting stronger, which is really good for our team.

I went to my first therapy session this week. I don't really know if it is helping. I feel a lot better after I talked a bit about it. We're moving in small steps. It takes some time until I am entirely doing fine.

There is a lot that I have to talk about. A lot of trauma that I went through.

But for now, everything seems to work out again. We're working hard for the competition in Poland. Irina created new choreography for us. I love how she always comes up with different kinds of things. The last time was a sexy performance, something filled with desire. This time it's a happy and fast dance.

It's something different from all the performances we had before. But I sure like it. Irina already told us what the costumes should look like.

She is sharing every thought with us. This is giving me a good feeling. Maybe we're actually doing fine.

One part of me thinks we can't win first, but maybe we'll still make it onto the podium. It would be amazing.

It is our first international competition, this could be the start of something big. It's the first step.

I look at Sloane with a smile. She saved me, over and over again. She is the only person who ever chose me. Sloane had the opportunity to turn on me, but she never did. Not even at the beginning when we hated each other.

Now she is helping me overcome my trauma, and I try for her. I want my life to work out for her and for myself. It's the first time I can imagine a future next to skating.

Even though skating is our priority now. Skating, and the success that comes with it, is our first and only goal for now.

Maybe we can really make it. All the way up to the Olympics. We're trying our bests. There is not a single day that we're not on the ice. Irina is working hard with us. There is no stop in sight.

„Okay, this is looking pretty good, actually! You're doing fine!" Irina praises us with a smile on her face.

She is trying to take it easier on us because of me. I know that Irina is trying her best to understand the situation I am in now. But she sounds hopeful as she tells us we're doing a good job. This kind of gives me hope.

Maybe we can really do it. I know that Irina would always be honest with us.

„Really? You think that we can win this?" Sloane asks Irina while putting her hair up into a ponytail.

Irina nods slowly. „Yeah, of course!"

This gives me hope. Maybe for once, my life is working out. Maybe for once, I'll get what I want.

„I am excited. This is a big step for us" I smile at them. But suddenly, the conversation is over. They are cautious when it comes to me. They don't want to say anything that might upset me. I wish they would treat me normally. It just might take a while, though.

We continue our training session for a couple of more hours. There is still a lot that we have to practice. Everything has to be perfect, and the choreography is a bit more complex this time. It is harder to perform a dance like this, something faster. The movements still have to be perfect, but they happen much quicker than in the other performances.

„Can you treat me normally again, please?“ I ask Sloane as soon as we're sitting in her car.

„What do you mean? I treat you as usual,“ she replies, a bit confused. As if she doesn't know what I am talking about.

„No, you are not. I understand that you don't want to say anything wrong. But please treat me normal again. I won't be upset.“ I tell her slowly.

„I just want you to feel good. You're going through something right now. You shouldn't worry about anything else,“ Sloane tells me with a soft smile on her face.

„But I would feel much better if you treated me normally. It would make things a lot easier,“ I tell her slowly.

Sloane nods. She probably tries to remember this from now on. I don't think this will work, but it's essential to talk about it.

„Okay, I'll try my best,“ she tells me, pressing a kiss to my cheek after she parked the car in her driveway.

„Thank you,“ I reply, putting a strand of her hair behind her ear.

„No, thank you for talking to me.“

75

ASHER

Only a couple more days until we leave for our journey to Europe. I have never been so nervous in my life.

Luckily today, we only have the costume fitting on our schedule. Sloane begged Irina for half a day off. It seems like she needs some things for our journey, so she has to go shopping.

I don't actually know if I need something specific for this journey. Irina cares about all the paper stuff, and I think I will pack my back just like the last time. Some clothes and my hygienic products will do.

But before Sloane and I go shopping, we must get through the costume fitting. Irina already chose a costume for us. We just have to try it on today.

Everyone is greeting us happily. We're always visiting the same store. I think the owners are good friends of Irina. Whenever we're here, they talk loudly and happily. Everything around us is happening so quickly. My costume is again black.

I think that most of the male costumes are black in general. But this time, the shirt is a black sheer see-through shirt. My chest is visible, and the cutout is deep and wide.

I quickly try on the costume, leaving the small cabin again. Irina nods proudly to herself. I love that she is creative, coming up with everything. I know that every small detail and idea is coming from her head.

Everyone is turning their heads to look at Sloane. She looks absolutely fantastic.

Sloane wears a green and gold costume, tassels and fringes, and sparkly emerald-colored crystals. This fits the dance perfectly. Even though I think this costume might be hard to grab when it comes to the spins and lifts.

It's definitely a challenge that I accept. I would never let Sloane fall or let anything happen to her.

„It's absolutely perfect!" Irina claps her hands together, nodding to herself. This costume might really be perfect.

Now Poland has become realistic. In only a couple of days, we are there. We'll skate against fantastic skaters from all over the world. It's a heavy weight on our shoulders now. Everyone can watch us live on tv. This feels more than unrealistic to me.

There is no going back now. We have to bring on the perfect performance. It feels like we're not allowed to fail in any way. Everyone is counting on us, and this makes me beyond nervous.

„I like this costume," Sloane giggles as she twirls around one more time, making the tassels and fringes fly around her body.

She could wear anything and still look like a freaking angel. God, I am falling so deeply for her.

„Great, this is it! You're free to leave as soon as you take this off, " Irina tells us with a smile.

I think that she is taking the costumes with her. We'll get them back as soon as we're in Poland. That's when we need them the next time.

I look at Sloane. She nods and then disappears into her dressing room. I do the same, taking off the costume and putting on my regular clothes. I hand the outfit to one of the workers.

Then I wait for my girlfriend. Well, my secret girlfriend because no one knows that we're together.

But as we're leaving the store, she takes my hand for the short walk back to her car. I am surprised, but I don't mind that slight physical touch right now.

Sloane knows precisely where she wants to go.

„I need some things from Walmart. They have everything. I guess that's our only stop. Or do you need to go somewhere else?" Sloane asks me with a smile. She is looking ahead. Right now, she seems so happy and peaceful. I know that she wants nothing more than this trip.

„No, Walmart is fine," I reply with a short nod.

„Do you think I need to buy something? I never traveled that far…." I ask her carefully. Somehow I am embarrassed about this. She has seen already so much of our world. She knows exactly what to pack and what we might need. But I don't have a clue. I don't know a single thing about traveling that far.

„We'll see. Probably just some new hygienic products," she tells me with a soft smile.

I know I don't have to be embarrassed about anything. She is the most understanding human being. At least she tries to understand me.

And as we're walking through the store, she is not making another comment as she puts products for herself and me into the card. „Do you think you need a pillow for the flight? Or maybe something else to get you comfortable?"

It's going to be a long flight. Maybe a pillow isn't a bad idea. „I think a pillow is excellent " I smile at Sloane, and she puts it into the card.

I sat in an airplane before, but not for that long. At least I am not entirely in the unknown.

I look at Sloane as she puts her beauty products into the card. I love to see her that excited. Maybe it really was the best decision for us to go to Poland.

„You know I am more excited to get to know Irina's family than about the competition," she giggles, and I nod.

„Just imagine they are all just like her," I tell her, and we both look at each other. We burst into laughter just a second later.

That would be really chaotic. Irina is a complicated person, she is very strict, and she is also very Polish. She loves to cuss, and she is brutally honest. Sometimes she is even lovely, somehow emotional.

I imagine a whole family like her, and it's absolutely chaotic.

„I bet it is going to be amazing!" Sloane smiles. She presses a soft kiss onto my cheek.

This journey feels personal. Maybe this is where the line between work and emotions is washing away. We promised each other that this couldn't happen. Simply because we can't mix these two lives together.

But I think this is something we should worry about after the competition. We should put everything into the competition right now. There is nothing more important.

„I feel this is going to be unique," the blonde girl smiles, slowly leaning into me. I lay my arms around her for a moment.

She looks me right into the eyes, and I stare back into the blue that I could get lost in instantly. Then she leans in, kissing my lips right here in public. It feels good to have an ordinary couple moment right now. We don't have a moment like this very often. We're mostly staying at her house or on the ice. There is nothing else existing in our life. And I don't think that there ever will be something else.

But I love my life just like this. With Sloane by my side, the both of us skating.

76
SLOANE

I'm proud of the progress Asher makes every day. It feels like he finally feels better himself. This is all that matters to me.

I know he is still grieving, but he is still trying hard to continue his life. I smile at him as we're waiting in line for the security check. He is nervous about the upcoming flight. Even I am a little scared now. It's been a while since I have been to Europe and even longer since I went to the competition.

This makes me the most nervous right now. The competition is unbelievably close. I don't know if we even stand a chance to stay in the ranking. We're now risking everything.

I am not even sure if Irina gave us the strongest performance. Maybe our choreography from the last competition would have been better than a fast and happy dance.

No one is talking right now. Irina is nervous about seeing her family again. Asher and I are anxious about everything, especially the competition.

I know that Asher is feeling the weight on his shoulders. He thinks that we have to win, but we don't. It's sad if we're not in the ranking anymore. But it indeed is okay. We could try again next year.

I'm baffled by myself. My priorities changed so quickly. Skating became one of the less important priorities in just a couple of months. My top priority is the well-being of Asher right now. There is nothing that I care more about.

I would risk starting again next year if Asher were more comfortable with it. It would be hard to accept, but I would indeed accept it.

I look at Asher as soon as we're sitting on the plane. The two of us sit next to each other while Irina sits two rows in front of us.

„She is going crazy," I whisper carefully to Asher. I don't want her to hear me. Otherwise, I have no idea what would happen.

„I think it is because of her family," he replies calmly, and I nod. Irina is not telling us everything about her family. Meeting them again is making her more than nervous.

I don't really know what to expect from meeting them. I don't even know how big her family is or what they're like. I don't even know if we're speaking the same language. Maybe they never learned how to speak English. This would be a bit difficult because I can't speak Polish.

„She'll be okay once it is over," I nod slowly. I at least hope that she is feeling a lot better once we're back in Canada. I hope that we'll return home with some excellent news.

„Everything is going to be okay," Asher assures me as if he just read my thoughts.

„I can see you thinking. I know you worry about the competition and everything else," Asher adds quickly before I can say anything.

„I just don't want to fail. It feels like this performance is not our strongest, and all the other couples are so good," I think out loud. But Asher takes my hand into his. He smiles at me so sweetly.

„No one is better than you are. This might not be our best performance, but we'll be fine. I can feel that everything is going to be okay," Asher smiles.

„Woah, where is this coming from?" I ask him with a soft chuckle. To me, he changed a lot in the past couple of days. He visits therapy quite often, making him a lot calmer and much more relaxed.

„I don't know, I just want to enjoy my time. It's my first time in Europe. This has to be good!" Asher smiles, pressing a kiss to my cheek.

I carefully look at Irina, it's stupid, but I have to ensure she isn't looking at us. I have to make sure that she can't see us here. As soon as I see that she is looking ahead, I turn to Asher with a massive smile on my lips.

He makes me unbelievably happy, and I wish we could be like an average couple no matter where we are. I guess that we're both scared of Irina her reaction. We both know this has consequences, and we're not supposed to skate with each other when we're in a relationship.

It's this or that, and not both of them. Irina always told us. I am surprised that she never suspected anything before. Or she is just not saying anything because right now, everything is fine.

I don't think that it will ever change. I can't imagine that Asher and I will ever split up. It wouldn't make any sense if I thought so. We are happy and understand the responsibility of being skating partners.

„You worry too much," Asher whispers.

I nod slowly, „I know, and I am sorry," I reply quietly.

I can't help it now, but I overthink everything. I am worried that something will happen, and we must give up something we love.

„Don't do it. Everything is fine," Asher drives his hand through my hair, pushing it away from my face.

I smile softly and so sweetly at him. My heart could burst from all the love that I receive right now. I have never felt that way. I have never been in love before. Not like this.

„I love you," I whisper back, thankful he is here calming me down on the inside.

„I love you," he replies, then quickly steals a kiss. As quick as it comes, as quickly it is over.

I lean into him, closing my eyes. Now we have a long flight ahead of us. And as soon as we land, a new step in our career starts.

77

SLOANE

I am exhausted as we arrive at the hotel. I forgot how tiring it is to travel that far. I absolutely can't wait to sleep for a couple of hours. Irina isn't tired at all. She is thinking about the upcoming competition. At least, this is what she is non-stop talking about right now. She explains everything that we have to know.

Irina even set up a schedule for the next couple of days. We only have one day off, a day we can spend exploring the city on our own.

I am sad that we don't have more time to explore the country, but I take what I can get. I smile at Asher, nodding. We can make this work. Maybe we can win this competition and take the next big step.

„And don't forget, we'll see my family for dinner and some sort of celebration after your training session tomorrow," she tells us nervously. Before we can reply to anything, she disappears to check us in.

Irina is weird whenever it comes to her family. I know that it makes her nervous to see them again. But suddenly I feel anxious too. I don't know anything about her family. I don't even know if we should bring a gift. They are kind to invite us, and we appear without anything.

I look at Asher, but he is only shrugging his shoulders. He hasn't slept the whole flight. He must be tired, and it seems like he doesn't care about anything else.

„Here are your keys," Irina quickly hands us the cards for our room. Without saying anything else, she turns around. She heads toward the elevator and already presses the button.

We're following her quickly. For the first time, I have a look at my room number. Looking onto the board next to the elevator, I see my room is on the seventh floor.

I quickly glance at Asher's card, seeing that his room number is very different from mine. His room is on the fifth floor. Knowing that he is two floors away from me, my heart breaks a little. I wish we would at least be on the same floor.

Irina takes a look at her number. She is one floor above mine, the eighth floor.

It's not like we could at least leave the elevator on the same floor now. Not that I want to do that. I am sure we can survive a couple of days without being in the same room. Or more like sleeping in the same room.

„Good night," Asher smiles awkwardly, and then he leaves. Irina and I are left. No one is saying another word.

I can feel how tense she is about being here. Something is going on right now. I don't know what she feels, and I am sure she doesn't want to talk about this.

I would ask her, but I admit I am a little scared of her reaction.

„Good night," I smile at her, leaving the elevator. I quickly look for my room. I can't even describe the feeling inside of me right now. I am just so happy as I open the door.

The bed is the first thing I am going for. I just really want to sleep right now. I don't want to change my clothes or unpack my bag. The only thing that I can think of right now is sleep.

But before I can let myself fall onto the bed, someone knocks on my door. I am confused because I surely don't know who it could be.

I carefully open the door, revealing a smiling and tired-looking Asher in front of it.

„What are you doing here?" I ask him slowly. He changed his clothes. At least he is wearing something different now.

„I don't want to sleep alone," he replies, entering my room. This is great because I don't want to sleep alone either.

He pulls me to the bed. We're both stripping off our clothes, except the underwear, and then move underneath the covers.

Asher instantly pulls me closer. The warmth of his body welcomes me. Right now, I feel so comfortable that I fall asleep as soon as I close my eyes.

I feel so exhausted from the long journey that I can't stop myself anymore.

78

ASHER

I slowly open my eyes, bright daylight streams into the room. It takes me a minute to understand where we are.

Sloane and I are really in Poland. We're here for the first international competition. I can't believe it. I take a look around, seeing Sloane sleeping peacefully next to me.

This might be the perfect start for our journey. This brings me to the thought that we have our first training day today. I turn around slowly because I don't want to wake my girlfriend.

I lift my phone from the bedside table to check the time. As soon as I see the time on my phone screen, a loud „Fuck, no!" escapes my lips.

It's loud enough to wake Sloane up, not in a gentle way. She sits straight, looking at me alarmingly. „What happened?"

I can see that she is still putting everything together. The jet lag is hitting us badly right now.

„We forgot to set the alarm. Irina is going to meet us in two minutes," I tell her, already jumping out of bed.

I try to put on my clothes as quickly as possible. I have to return to my room and get my training clothes and the skates.

„Shit, I wanted to take a shower!" Sloane whines as she jumps out of bed, opening her luggage.

There is definitely no time for a shower now. „I'll see you in the lobby," I tell Sloane, leaning down to kiss her lips.

I nearly forgot my room card as I left. My heart is racing. Irina is going to kill us when we're too late. I press the button for the elevator multiple times in the hope it will arrive faster.

But as the doors open, I wish it would have never arrived at all. Irina is standing inside, looking at me, evenly surprised. She knows that this isn't the floor I'm staying on. I'm also not wearing the clothes for training.

„Good morning," I smile at her as if nothing happens. And I sure as hell try everything to not look like I just got caught doing something forbidden.

„Good morning, Asher. Where are you coming from?" Irina asks me curiously. Something in her voice is off. Maybe she already thinks that I came from Sloane, her room.

„I checked out the gym. I am so sorry. I lost time because I was talking to the staff there," I tell Irina.

I see that the gym is on the seventh floor with a quick look at the board. It sounds logical, and I hope that Irina believes the lie I just told her.

„I hope the gym is good. Is it big?" She asks me curiously. Now my heart is racing inside of my chest. I can't lie about this. Maybe she wants to check it out herself.

„I don't know, actually. It sounds stupid, but I didn't check it out thoroughly. I talked to the guy at the register. As soon as I saw how late it already was, I left," I explained, hoping I didn't say anything wrong.

God, I hate lying, and I am bad at it. I lied about my life all the time. This here is different. It wasn't about something like this. It never mattered that much and would have affected my career.

„Sounds like a lovely guy you talked to." Something in her voice sounds off again.

„I'll change, and then we'll meet in the lobby, " I tell her, leaving the elevator as quickly as possible.

Now I feel fucked. This can't be anything good.

Maybe she already knows that there is something between Sloane and me. Perhaps this was some kind of confirmation for her.

As soon as I am in my room, I freshen up quickly. Brushing my teeth, washing my body as fast as possible. Then I get dressed, grab my stuff, and leave.

I hope that Irina won't be mad at me. I can't stand her lousy mood for the whole day.

79
SLOANE

As soon as I was downstairs, the mood between us was awkward. I could tell something had happened, and I was too scared to ask Asher. I don't know what happened between him and Irina, but he will surely tell me if I have to know.

Right now we should concentrate on our training session. The ice arena is vast, maybe the biggest I have been in. We are skating against a lot of other couples. It's going to be the biggest competition so far. Perhaps it'll take the whole day.

We have two hours of training because the others want to see the arena. We can't skate simultaneously, which is actually something good. No one can see our choreography, and we can't see the others. It would make me nervous to know how good the others are.

Irina even allows us to skate one time with our costumes on. She thinks that we need to get a feeling for them. She had never done that before, but everything had to be perfect this time. It is more important than any other competition.

I know she doesn't want to mess up in her home country. Maybe her family is coming to watch us, and I understand that she doesn't want to fail more than anything else.

I don't want to fail either. I have a massive problem with not being the best. There is no excuse for us to not win this.

We rehearse the performance again, and again, and again. There is no stop for us in these two hours. We're trying our best, hoping it'll calm Irina at least a bit.

She is freaking out because of the party tonight. Her mood is terrible, and it is awful to be in a room with her. She is freaking out over the most minor things.

Now that we're in Poland, she is cussing in English for once. This is a different side of her, something I never heard coming out of her mouth. I didn't even know that she knew many curse words in English.

I flinch whenever I hear her voice rise. And I can't even describe the relief I feel as soon as we're done. Asher and I excuse ourselves because we're leaving in a different car. We want to buy something for Irina and her family later.

I think that as a guest we should bring something for the host. They don't know us, yet they want to invite and talk to us. I think that we should give them something small.

I don't know if you actually do this in Poland. It is complicated because I want them to like me. I want Irina to be happy with me.

I could ask her, but she isn't in the best place. So asking her might not be the best idea.

„What if we get them something like the gift baskets we have? I am sure they have them here too," Asher suggests as we leave the cab.

I think this is actually not a bad idea. Every country might have a gift basket, and they could maybe use everything that's in one.

„And flowers!" I add with a smile.

First, I thought we would meet Irina's mother, but I remember Irina telling me her mother isn't alive anymore. I don't know who we will meet from her family, but I am sure there is someone we could give a bouquet of flowers.

It is actually hard to find the right store. My orientation sense isn't working as good as I thought it would. I try to use google maps as a bit of help, but it doesn't bring us any fast to our destination.

I don't know or understand how we make it back to the hotel. But now we don't have that much time left.

I don't know how we're always doing this. We are constantly in a hurry. I wish we could enjoy our days here a little more.

„Okay, if we hurry a bit, we could still take a shower together," Asher whispers into my ear.

„Only if we do some stress-relieving. I'm feeling a bit tense," I chuckle. With that, we hurry toward the elevators.

80
ASHER

Sloane looks absolutely stunning in the sparkly purple dress that she is wearing. It's hard to keep my hands from her. But now, I have to constantly remind myself that she is just my partner now.

We don't have any feelings for each other. This is what others have to believe tonight.

I hold the flowers in my hands and Sloane the basket as we meet Irina in the lobby. She is looking a lot different. I think that she is wearing a lot more make-up and a dress. I have never seen her in a dress before.

„Oh good, you got gifts. They'll love this," Irina's Polish accent seems to be stronger now. Her voice is shaking, a sign that she is nervous.

No one is saying something as we hop into the cab. Irina tells him the address, and from that moment on, everyone is silent. It's tense, and I know I would rather spend the night in my room, but this is impossible. I have to do this for Irina. I have to somehow make her proud.

We have two more days until the competition. I at least hope that Irina is in a better mood tomorrow. Maybe she is just nervous and tense because she will see her family. That's what I am at least hoping so far.

The car stops in a neighborhood that seems normal to me. It's not luxurious, but it is also not as bad as the one I lived in. The street is empty and quiet.

My heart is racing. I don't know why I am suddenly nervous, but I feel a bit unwell. It doesn't seem to be the right thing for me to be here. I barely know Irina, and this here seems too personal. But we already rang the doorbell. There is no going back now. Simply because someone is already opening the door seconds later. It's a small woman. She is smiling so brightly.

She starts yelling something in Polish, hugging Irina happily. I guess they are all happy to see each other. Even though it is a bit weird that this is the first time they see each other again.

I wonder why Irina hasn't seen them without us first. After a while, her relative turns to us. She hugs Sloane and me tightly. And as she lets go, another person steps in, hugging us. This continues for what feels like an eternity. Everyone is coming outside to greet and embrace us. It's horrible for me. I hate hugging strangers, which is the most uncomfortable thing now.

As we step inside, we give away the basket and the flowers. „Oh, this isn't necessary," the woman who turns out to be her sister smiles at us. Her accent is much stronger than Irina's, but she is fluent in English.

Some can't speak English, and some only a little. This is going to be a chaotic evening.

On the other hand, Sloane seems so happy about everything that she starts a conversation right away. She tries to ask everyone as many questions as possible.

She is just as interested in everyone here in this room as everyone is in us. They want to know everything about us and our skating history.

„They are my pride and joy," Irina smiles proudly. It feels like she is showing us off right now. I don't really have a problem with that, but it kind of feels wrong.

It feels like it's making the weight on my shoulders heavier. Maybe, she is telling us that we have to win the competition. God, I don't want to know what happens if we don't win.

Right now, I am happy that Sloane is doing the talking. She is telling them everything she needs to know.

Irina is not talking either. And her mood is making everything at the table a lot more awkward.

My feeling tells me she doesn't want to be here at all. I look at her every now and then, but she avoids everyone's eyes. She is just as happy as I am as we start eating dinner.

I thought it might get quieter as soon as everyone started eating, but I was wrong. A lot wrong. Now that everyone has a plate in front of them, they seem to get louder.

Everyone is chatting happily, laughing, and making jokes. I am amazed at how well Sloane is doing. I remember meeting her the first time. I thought that she wasn't the most open person.

„Asher, now we know what Sloane thinks about you, but what do you think about your skating partner?" One of the girls asks me. She barely has an accent, which hints that she speaks English more often.

I look at her, surprised that she is even talking to me. It's been what? An hour? This is the first time someone actually talks to me.

I look at her, unsure of what to say now. Everyone wants to have the perfect answer right now. Sadly I haven't heard what Sloane told me about me.

„I have the best partner. Couldn't wish for someone else. Sloane is the best figure skater I have ever laid eyes on," I reply. This is the truth only. But the girl seems to be unsatisfied with my reply.

She shakes her head, a frown on her face.

„Yeah, that's so something everybody could say. Come on, dig a bit deeper."

„Look at her. She is absolutely brilliant, kind-hearted, and absolutely astonishing pretty. And she is the best skater you'll possibly ever meet," I reply again, hoping it'll be enough this time.

The girl nods, not saying anything else. She looks at Sloane, pure admiration in her eyes.

Everyone adores her. She comes into a room, and everyone looks at her. Mostly because she is so damn pretty. She has the perfect body, long honey blonde hair, and bright blue eyes.

I bet all the girls want to be just like her. They must burst from jealousy.

I smile proudly because she is mine. No one knows it, but Sloane belongs to me. She loves me, and I love her more than anything else. I carefully lay my arm around her, resting it on the back of her chair. I bet that no one notices this small gesture.

Irina is too far in her thoughts, and everyone else is deeply engaged in a conversation.

And a couple of minutes later, I remove my arm again. There is still some food that I have to try on the table. I had never had Polish food before, and it felt like everything was on this table. Irina's family really tried their best for this evening.

Everyone is so kind to us. They tell us that they saw us on tv and how much they love to see us skating.

The more they gush about us, the more relaxed is Irina. She just wants to make her family proud.

I have never seen her like this. I thought she didn't care about other people's opinions, but she did care about it.

This makes her only more human.

81
SLOANE

Irina's family is funny. I love them, and I love the time here. Everyone is asking about us, gushing about our skating skills. It's a nice feeling. Her family is funny, and everyone is in a good mood, except Asher and Irina.

But I don't bother. I bet their mood lights up as soon as the dinner is over. The music is louder now, everyone is drinking alcohol, and some are dancing. They yell and laugh. It is fun. I have never seen a family party like this, but I love it.

Soon after the real party started, a young girl dragged me to the middle of the room, which was now some dance floor.

I laugh as they make me twirl around. I don't know what Irina feared, but her family is fantastic. I love how they celebrate. I love how kind and funny they are.

It's unusual to see someone party like this, and I am not used to the amount of alcohol they are drinking. I only drank a pin for courage, but other than that, I stayed away from alcohol. Asher is not drinking as well, for a different reason, though.

I know he wants to stay away from alcohol because of his father. Maybe, this is why his mood is that bad right now. He sits there all grumpy, not talking. He doesn't even smile.

So I grab his hands and pull him with me onto the dance floor. Irina's family is trying so hard for us. They try to make him laugh or offer him all kinds of stuff to make him happy. It is Irina her choice if she wants to be grumpy. It's her family, after all. But we're the guests. We should at least try to be happy.

„Smile a bit! And try to enjoy this evening at least," I yell over the loud music.

I look at Asher. His face isn't changing. There is still no sign of a smile on his face. I wonder what he is thinking about right now.

„Try for me," I beg him. And then something moves. A forced smile appears on his face. It is the worst forced smile I have ever seen in my entire life. But he is at least trying.

„It's just weird to be here. They are strangers, and Irina is in a bad mood. I want to go back to the hotel," he replies grumpily, making me laugh.

I look at him and shake my head, but before I can reply anything, he leans in, whispering right into my ear, „I'd rather rip off that dress than be here. I can't even kiss you in front of them," he sighs, which makes me bite my lip.

I wish he could kiss me right here. I wish we could now go back to the hotel. I look at him and shake my head.

„Don't you dare repeat something like this!" I reply slowly. God, I want to go back to the hotel so severely now. But we have to stay here and celebrate with them.

And I am even more surprised that Asher is relaxing after some time. He even smiles at the others.

The party goes on for hours. My feet hurt from all the dancing and my cheeks from all the smiling. I am surprised that Irina didn't drag us to the hotel way earlier. She sat in the corner all night long, not really happy about anything.

I don't really know if she doesn't like her family. I can't tell if there is bad blood between them, but it's also not for me to know.

„That was a charming evening," I tell her with a smile as we return to the hotel.

Her sister offered to stay with them, but we have a training session tomorrow morning. I don't know how we're supposed to get up that early.

Irina isn't replying to anything, and I wonder what she thinks now.

„Your family is really lovely. Thank you for taking us with you," I try again.

Maybe, she is just tired. It was nearly five in the morning, and she looked tired all night. Perhaps, she just wants to go to bed.

„Yeah, they are nice until I fail. Right now, my family thinks that I will win everything with you. But that's not how life is working," she replies grumpily.

This is the most honest thing she could say right now. I understand her struggle, but it makes me feel bad about the competition. This means we're not allowed to lose. I don't want to disappoint Irina, and I don't want her to feel bad about anything.

„We won't lose," I promise her. This is not my call to make, but I will surely try my best.

„The chances of winning are low. I don't think we'll win," Irina shrugs her shoulders before the cab stops. She is paying the driver to leave right away.

Irina isn't looking back at us. She is heading toward the elevators right away. I don't think that Irina wants us to follow her quickly. Maybe she just needs to be alone. At least we know now that she won't be in a better mood until the competition is over.

I look at Asher. He is just shrugging his shoulders. He seemed so tired in the cab, but now all of this is gone. He smiles brightly at me. „Can I rip off your dress now?" He asks me, his voice husky.

I am surprised that he is still thinking about it. But I honestly want nothing more than that. I nod eagerly.

Asher doesn't waste any more time. He grabs my hands, leading me to the elevators. Irina is already gone. She won't notice that we're both disappearing into Asher his room.

82
SLOANE

We thought the competition day was the first day we saw Irina smile. It is a forced smile for the media, but it is a smile. And she isn't yelling anymore. She looks around, making sure everything is perfect. Irina is fumbling around with our costumes and makeup, which she never did before. I can see her hands shake as she fixes my hair.

I slowly grab her hands. Maybe she is going to hit me for this. But I stare right into her eyes. „Calm down. It's going to be okay," I tell her calmly. I try to stay as calm as possible. I try for her to remain calm. Everything inside me is beyond nervous. I am more scared of failing than ever before.

I don't want to disappoint anyone, and I know that Asher feels the same. I look at Asher with a smile. He nods slowly.

Everyone is hoping that today is going to be a good day. We're nervous, and no one is really talking much. This is the first time seeing our competitors, and they all look stunning. I believe that each of them is absolutely good at skating.

We have already received a ranking of the performances. We're somewhere in the middle, closer to the end than the beginning. We have to wait for a long time. Watching the others is going to make me even more anxious.

I think that everyone is going to be better than us. We made it here with struggles. Asher didn't want to be here in the first place. I kind of forced him. Well, Irina kind of pushed him.

I feel like this might be too big for him. It feels like I forced him to do something he never wanted. Or at least not in this season. Being healthy and happy is more important than success.

This is what Irina told us after Flynn his accident.

There is no going back right now. We're already here, and we have to skate now. I hope for the best result possible.

We're perfectly performing our dance. I am sure that we might make it onto the podium. As I watch the other couples perform, my doubts are growing bigger. Everyone is absolutely perfect. They don't make mistakes.

The skaters are from all over the world. It feels like only the best are here. We have to stay in the ranking. Otherwise, we'll never make it to the Olympics.

„Everything is going to be okay,“ Asher whispers as he looks at me. But I am unsure if he is telling me or trying to calm himself down. The Toronto competition a couple of weeks ago has been tremendous, but this here is another level. It is terrifying. There are all kinds of media running around here. I am sure that Flynn can watch us live on TV at home.

God, thinking about this makes me even more nervous. I bet that everyone is watching us. I don't know why it makes me so nervous. I don't understand why Irina is so anxious. We went through this before. Flynn and I were in Paris, we won the competition there. There were cameras everywhere. People even threw flowers onto the ice after our performance.

I have never been scared of failing because I never did before. I never lost a competition with Flynn. We have been together since we were kids. But with Asher, everything is so much different. We are skating for a couple of weeks only. And we made it so far. Other couples would need years to make this progress.

I guess that Asher and I are unique. This is why we deserve to be here. We deserve it as much as everyone else to be here.

„Everything is going to be okay, “ I nod.

I smile softly at him as he takes my hand. He slowly squeezes it, looking back at me. It comforts me the way his eyes get lost in mine.

I would never change this moment right here. I enjoy it way too much to be here with Asher. It feels so damn right to skate with him. This is how it is supposed to be.

We get up. There are two performances before we get onto the ice. We need to stretch our muscles and warm our bodies a bit. The nervous feeling in my stomach is not leaving. Now it's mixing with the rush of adrenaline. I love competitions for this. I love the cheering crowd and the spotlight while I am skating.

We practice some easy things as our warm-up. Also, it's to make the time fly until we're up. There are no mistakes allowed now. Irina is following us with every step. She makes sure that we're looking good and that the costume is just the way it should be.

I look at her with a smile. The last couple had already left the ice. Now they get everything ready for us to enter. The voice introducing us is a blur in my ears. Everything is happening so quickly right now. All I can hear is the beating of my heart.

The cheering of the crowd is in the background. We're skating to the middle of the ice, waving in every direction. I look at Asher with a smile. He nods encouragingly.

Then the music starts, and so do we with our performance. The performance starts slow with the music, but as the music gets faster, we do too. I hear the crowd cheer in the background as I land our first jump.

The atmosphere is different here. The audience is loud and cheerful. They love to watch, and it gives us as the skater a different feeling. I love it more than anything right now.

The performance could last forever, and I would not get tired of it. I feel like I could do this forever, without ever getting tired. The nervous feeling is gone. I feel free and happy on the ice.

Asher is smiling so widely, but this isn't the smile for the audience. His natural smile indicates that he is just as happy as I am.

I can hear the ice as we slide over it. I always loved the sounds.

But the performance is over way too quickly. The song ends, and we're taking our final position. Our breathing is heavy, our smiles wide.

I could do this all day. God, it was perfect. We bow for the audience, and then we leave the ice. I throw my arms around Asher as soon as we're back on solid ground. He pulls me in, in an even tighter hug. His arms are wrapped around me, picking me up from the ground.

I wrap my legs around his waist. We did a great job out there, and I am proud of that. We made it so far. I love seeing that we're not giving up no matter what is happening.

What feels like minutes later, I'm back on my feet. We go back to our seats and sit down. We have to wait for a very long while now.

83

ASHER

The performance wasn't as bad as I thought it would be. It was actually pretty good. I am happy that we're here. Poland isn't bad, and the competition is a good idea. I thought it would be too early. The other couples are perfect. Everyone has an entirely different performance. We had tons of different and complex elements, and each element gave us the points we needed. It felt perfect while we were doing it. Maybe it was enough for the judges.

Now we sit here and wait. I am not really thinking of anything as we look around. The time is flying terribly slow. I wish it would go by a lot faster.

I want to know the result right now. Irina would deserve a good rating. She worked the hardest. We all worked as a team for the first time, and I tried everything to get us here. A victory would be excellent.

I look at Sloane with a smile. She takes my hand and squeezes it slowly. We both don't really believe that we won. Neither is saying it, but I know that we both think about it.

Everyone here is good, and others might have had a better performance. It's hard to tell because we can't see ourselves perform. It felt good, but next to the others, we seemed like fools.

Irina is not saying a word. She wasn't talking for the whole day. Irina just shifts around nervously. I know that she just wants to win. There is nothing more that she wants right now.

I wish to know what is going on inside of her. Even though I think to understand that this is about her family.

The presenter starts talking again. It's hard to focus on his speech. He is currently talking about the event today and the skaters in general. Nothing exciting. Of course, he is avoiding the most exciting part. He is avoiding what this is really about. I know this is supposed to build up some tension, but it is absolutely freaking me out.

My heart is racing. I need to know now where we are in this ranking. Maybe we come back home, and we're done for this season. It would be terrible to know that we would have to try again next season. Maybe we come home, still in the ranking but somewhere in the middle. This would mean we could still skate in competitions, but not good ones like these. Or maybe we come home victors. This is highly unrealistic, but we could try to climb higher. We come closer to our goal.

Sloane and I are holding hands, hoping for the best to happen. Irina is standing behind us. All three of us are now watching the board. Slowly the names appear on it. Couples we had never heard of. And so far, we're not on the board.

This is a good sign because the higher it gets, the better. We're still not on the board as they announce the top five.

We are better than I thought we were, making me absolutely happy. I look at Sloane with a smile. The top three are on.

Even though everyone is already dying to know, the presenter builds up more tension. I just want to see if we made it. I want to know if we really reached another step closer to our dream.

„And the third place goes to…." He yells out, calling the names right afterward. It's not us. The third place goes to *Josephine Winfrey & George Miller* from England.

I keep thinking about how crazy all of this is. It feels more than crazy to be here in Poland. We're just two people from a tiny town in Canada.

Skating partners from all over the world are here to try their luck. Now we're in the top two. We made it so far. And it feels like a dream to me. I was so distracted as the crowd erupted in cheers.

Everyone is cheering and celebrating. Sloane is throwing her arms around me, and I think she is crying.

„WE WON! WE WON!" She yells, jumping up and down on the same spot. I look at her, more than shocked, then I look back to the board.

We won!

We really won the competition. There it is, *Sloane Griffin & Asher Williams from Canada* in the first place.

It takes way too long for me to realize. But now, I throw my arms around Sloane pulling her closer to my body. I hug her as tightly as possible for a second. Without her, I wouldn't be anywhere. It's all thanks to her.

My life changed to the best possible after meeting her. And so I do the only thing that comes to my mind. I totally forget how I should not be doing this. I press my lips onto hers, kissing her so deeply. Right now, I don't really care who is seeing us. I don't care that Irina is standing right behind us. I just need to feel her lips on mine. And then it is too late. I kissed her right in front of the whole world. Cameras are pointed at us. I never realized that really everybody knows now.

As we part, she looks at me, so shocked. I surprised her with my action, but the smile on her lips told me she wasn't angry.

We hug again. And then we finally turn to Irina. First, I prayed that she didn't see it. Maybe, she was looking away right at that second. Of course, she wasn't. She looked at us the whole time.

The smile on her lips is now forced, the hug even more. I think this is the time that is going to kill us. Well, not in front of everyone, but as soon as we're going to be alone.

I don't know what is going to happen now. Irina seems so calm, even though she is not talking to us.

Luckily we got separated right away. They want to interview us. We need to get to the podium for the medals. And this might take enough time.

I don't think that she is going to forget what just happened. But it would be more than nice if she would. Maybe we're lucky for once.

I look at Sloane. She is only shrugging her shoulders. But I can tell that she is now thinking about something else. She is not thinking about Irina or what might happen as soon as we're alone with her. She is in the moment right now.

84
ASHER

We're still alive. Even though we still haven't been alone with Irina yet. She is quiet on our way back to the hotel. She hasn't spoken to us, and I hope she won't. The worst thing is that she never said anything about the victory.

I know that she is mad. She doesn't have to say it. We both know that she is angry. Sloane is cautious with what she says, so she doesn't say anything. She is quiet, too quiet in my opinion.

We leave the cab as soon as it stops in front of the hotel. And as we're in the lobby, Irina finally turns around.

„We'll talk about this when we're home. Don't you even dare think that I'll forget about it," Irina warns us, and then she storms off. She doesn't say anything else.

A part of me is happy about that, but another part wishes that we would get over it. I know that Irina is probably going to yell at us.

„It could be worse. Irina wants to calm down before she is talking to us," Sloane sighs. She shrugs her shoulders as we slowly walk toward the elevators.

„I don't think that she is going to calm down. It is Irina we're talking about," I reply, skeptical. I believe that she is going to kill us either way.

„Yeah, true, but Irina can't split us, at least. Everyone saw the kiss. They know now that we are together. If she is separating us now, everyone is coming for her." Sloane thinks aloud, and I look at her, confused.

„Do you mean that partners are allowed to be together?" I asked her because I thought it was a skating rule that you could not be in a relationship with your skating partner.

„What? Yes, I know tons who got married in the history of skating. It's just Irina her rule. She never wanted her partners to be together because mixing emotions with work may complicate some things," Sloane explains.

She pulls out the elastic and opens up her golden hair. She drives a hand through her hair to loosen it up a bit.

I look at her even more surprised now. I never thought about it, so I thought it would count for everyone. No one ever told me anything because they thought I'd be sleeping my way around anyway.

It has never been true, but I never cared about a girlfriend. I have never been interested in finding someone before.

„So I don't know if Irina cares about other people's opinions," I slowly start, but Sloane is already shaking her head.

„Oh, she does! I mean, look how she acted the last couple of days. She might pretend to not care, but she actually does. So she won't separate us. And I'll talk to her. Maybe it won't be that bad" she smiles at me, and I nod.

Maybe, it won't be that bad. I can't really tell because Irina is hard to see through. I don't know what she thinks or how she feels. But she indeed feels some kind of betrayed by Sloane.

We lied to her, as we denied being together. I think that this is sure for her now. Maybe she is angry at us because of that.

We might have lost all her trust and need that as a team. We need to trust each other.

I am scared that she doesn't want to be our coach anymore. She is the best we could get and our ticket for anything coming in the future.

But Sloane doesn't seem to worry about it at all. She even sent Irina a message if we were still having dinner together.

The dinner was already planned before we went to the competition. But we said that this is going to be our kind of celebration.

No, you both can go alone.

This is the reply we receive from her. But we don't feel like going alone. We know we did something wrong, and it feels even worse to go to dinner without Irina. So we order something up to my room. And after we ate, Sloane left to go into her room. We indeed feel guilty even though we pretend like nothing happened.

It is all my fault. It would have never happened if I hadn't kissed Sloane. Now I feel more than guilty because I never wanted to ruin anything.

85
SLOANE

It's been days. I haven't heard anything from Irina. She doesn't want to meet us, and now this is getting me worried. She is ambitious. I know that she is eager to win. But now she doesn't want to see us.

Can we talk?

This is the third time I am sending her a message today. I feel so stupid because I am running after her. It was a damn kiss, and she was freaking out. We haven't even told her everything.

I don't want to lie to her anymore. She can't forbid our feelings. I am sure we can work together even though we're in a relationship. I know that it can work out.

We'll see each other tomorrow. at 11 a.m. at the rink.

She finally replies after a while. This makes me feel at least a little bit relieved. I am happy that she isn't completely ignoring us. But there is still worry inside of me. Worry that she is going to quit. I'll never find a new coach. No one was as good as her, to say the least. I hope that we can talk about everything tomorrow. Maybe it won't be that bad.

„Hey, can I come in?" Someone says in front of my door. It takes a while for me to notice that it is Flynn.

„Oh, yeah, come in!" I tell him, my eyes already glued to the door.

He first peaks his head inside, making sure that I am alone. And as soon as he sees me sitting on my bed, he enters.

As always, there is a huge smile plastered on his face. There has only been a short time in his life when he lost his smile. I am more than happy that he got it back.

„Where is your boyfriend?" My best friend asks me with a smirk.

„He is working, and after his shift, he has a therapy session," I reply, my heart jumping as I think of Asher.

„Oh well, how mad is Irina?" Flynn asks me. I haven't told him about the kiss yet. So I wonder who told him? Maybe Irina did? I wouldn't be surprised if Irina asked him about us.

„What?"

„Oh sweetie, it was all over the internet. I saw it on live television," Flynn replies. The grin is getting wider.

I can't believe what he is saying. I haven't seen anything about the kiss on the internet. And I haven't seen anything on television. But now that Flynn is mentioning this to me, I'm slightly worried.

„Here, have a look" my best friend hands me his phone. He has already opened a Canadian newspaper website. We really are in the news. *Canadian figure skating couple is also a couple in real life!*

Canadians, newcomer number one, are dating?!

This is really bad. Irina is not going to like this. At least now I understand why she isn't talking to us. I wouldn't speak to me too.

„Oh, this is bad," I hand Flynn back his phone.

How haven't I seen something like this before? Well, I haven't checked the news. And I haven't been much on my phone.

„Irina is avoiding us. She just replied that we're going to talk tomorrow. But I don't think it will be good," I tell the redhead as he sits next to me.

I am scared that we just ruined our careers. I knew that Irina never wanted this to happen. She told me years ago that this is an absolute no-go for her. I ignored her as soon as I met Asher. We crossed a line.

„Nah, she'll get over it," Flynn shrugs his shoulders. But he knows as well as I do that Irina won't get over it quickly.

„Yeah, maybe she'll quit tomorrow."

„No, she is too good to quit. She wants to win, and she knows that you both are her only chance. I think she'll continue, but it won't be easy to work with her." Flynn tells me.

He might be right. Irina won't find skaters like us. But maybe she wants to try it. I don't know what will happen, and this freaks me out.

„I don't want to say it, but you should have told her the first time something happened. Maybe it wouldn't have been that bad. I mean, now you probably destroyed her trust in you."

„Thank you for your encouraging words," I sigh. I know that Flynn is right, and I must hear that.

I really destroyed everything. I shouldn't have kept it a secret, but I knew Irina her rule, and I disagreed. I wanted Asher, and I still want him. Nothing can change that, especially not her stupid rule.

„She can't separate," I whisper.

„I don't think that she'll try. But her rule was for your own good. She told you what could happen if you mix emotions with work. She told us all the time…" Flynn reminds me.

And this is when I realize something. „Do you think that it happened to her? She always said that she knows someone."

I remember when she told me about her skating partner. We had dinner with her, I was curious, but she wasn't open to talking about him.

„Maybe… That's not for us to know." Flynn replies.

And this is probably why he is Irina, her favorite. He never asks too many questions. I think that he never cares about her personal life. Flynn never asked much about her or her skating history. It was enough for him to google her Wikipedia page.

„But Asher and I are different!" I exclaim immediately. I know that we are different. We won't break up.

„How do you know that? No one knows, and Irina just wanted to protect you both from that. It is easier to separate that, you know that"

Of course, I know that. But I don't want to think about it. It indeed is too late for that. And I don't think we could have separated that from the beginning. Asher is the best skater that we could find. And I can't change my feeling for him.

„Maybe, it is not going to be as bad. Just wait for tomorrow and see," Flynn smiles at me.

I know that he is seeing everything super positive. He always did. Flynn never had a problem with anyone. Irina loved him, and it was always easy for him. I am the black sheep of the two of us. I always had been the troublemaker.

Now I crossed a line. I know that Irina is disappointed, making me even more scared of tomorrow. I never meant to disappoint her. I never meant to hurt her feelings.

I have looked up to her ever since I started skating. I wanted to be just like her, just as good as her. My worst fear, next to failing, was to disappoint her.

Irina is like my second mother. I spent more time with her than with my mother, which is sad, but I never mind. I love her, and I am stupid to betray her so badly.

86
SLOANE

I couldn't sleep that night. All I could think about was Irina. I am way too scared that she is going to quit. I don't think it is a good idea, but she is angry and might not think straight.

I had seen her in rage before, even though it was always different than this time.

She is way too calm right now. It seems like she is thinking about her actions. This gives me hope that she actually just wants to talk. I have the hope that it won't be bad at all.

But the worry still leaves me sleepless. I am not hungry the following morning, so I pass on the breakfast.

„It can't be that bad, right?" Asher looks at me, pretty concerned. She is worried about me and about the whole situation. He still thinks it is his fault. But it is actually all mine.

I should have told Irina about everything. We wouldn't have a problem if I were honest. It is obviously too late for that. The worst thing is that we weren't honest with her, and then we publicly kissed each other. We made her look like a fool. This is what she hates most. And I know that we made a mistake. We made a really huge mistake with that.

I can't take this back now. But maybe I can explain everything going on in my head. I will apologize to her, hopefully making many things better between us.

I want everything to be just like before. We had a fantastic time in Poland, and even before that.

It felt like we were finally a real team. I missed this feeling for nearly half a year. I never thought that I would get it back after Flynn his accident.

„I don't want to lose Irina or my career. I don't want to lose anything" I sigh as I stand up to get ready. I don't know if I should get prepared for training. Usually, I would, but I don't know and understand if we continue our training sessions.

Even if we won't, I still need to go onto the ice and skate for a while. It calms me down. It always brought me peace.

We should be celebrating right now. Our victory in Poland is a huge step. And I never thought that we actually would win. This is something massive.

Now we have nothing but drama. There is no happiness about the victory. I don't know if we will continue skating like we did before. Maybe Irina thinks that we shouldn't be part of competitions anymore. I can't blame her. We made a fool of her in front of everyone.

I know that people talked to her about us being a couple. I know that she probably had to do some explaining.

Asher and I weren't talking the whole way to the rink. No one is saying a word, and I can feel how anxious he is getting now. He still thinks that Irina is going to say something about that kiss. But this is obviously not going to happen. It's more than the kiss for her. She is going to say something about the whole relationship.

I can already see her as we walk inside. She sits down on the bench she usually sits on during training days. Her eyes are fixed on the empty ice.

No one is here except for us. This is good because I don't want anyone to hear and see what will happen now.

„Hey Irina," I greet her politely. I look at her, even though I want to avoid eye contact.

I won't show any weakness or fear. Irina hates this, and there is no need to. We never did anything wrong. I should be afraid of what I am feeling.

„Right on time, that's good," Irina sighs as she looks at us.

I can't tell what she is thinking right now. Her facial expression gives nothing away.

She is good at hiding her feelings. She always had been. It is something terrible because I need to know what will happen now. I want to predict it.

„Irina, there is a lot I have to say. But first, I am so very sorry," I tell her, but before I can say anything else, she cuts me off.

„I don't want to hear it," she spits out. I flinch at her harsh tone.

„You both lied to me. For how long has this been going on?" Irina is still looking at us.

I hoped she would never ask this question. She is going to be even more furious at us when she knows.

She looks at us, waiting for a reply. Asher shifts uncomfortably next to me. „A while. I can't tell precisely when it started," he replies slowly.

„And you just decided to lie to me?" Irina fires back. I can feel her anger rising even though she is holding it back. I know that she doesn't want to make a scene here.

„No, I never wanted to lie to you. But I knew your rule, and I was scared of what was going to happen," I reply quickly before Asher can say anything. This is on me.

„Yes, and I stand by this! Look where we are now. If you would just easily follow my rules, this would have never happened," Irina starts yelling at us. Something that we can't avoid.

Irina yells mostly. She has a loud voice. I am used to it, but now it is a lot different. Something is off in her voice, and it kind of scares me. I am afraid that something terrible is going to happen now.

„I can't change what I am feeling, and Asher can neither," I reply, trying not to yell. I wonder if she had never been in love. Doesn't she know what it feels like? I can't ignore these feelings.

„I have seen what it does. I have seen the worst thing that could possibly happen. I never wanted it to happen to you! Love is not meant to be mixed with a business relationship," she replies.

„I have seen how it got mixed. They thought that it would last forever. Nothing could break their bond because skating together made them stronger. But this is a lie! As soon as she couldn't skate anymore, he let her fall. He turned on her, not only when it came to skating but also in their relationship. You'll not only lose one thing, but you'll also love everything!" She yells, and this is the first time I realize she is talking about herself.

It seems to be a sensitive topic for her, always had been. But that doesn't mean it will happen just like that again. Asher and I are not Irina and her partner.

„You made a fool of me in Poland. I had a lot of explaining to do, pretend like I knew it"

„I am so sorry," I reply again. But I think that it doesn't matter. No matter how often I say it, it doesn't matter.

„You know that this is putting me into a very complex situation," she sighs, and I wonder what she will do now.

Is this the moment she is going to quit? I don't want anything to change. I don't want anything to be different. Even though it is going to be very much different now.

„We have to continue, even though it is going to be a lot different from now on," Irina tells us, and I breathe out, relieved.

She isn't quitting, at least. It would be the worst thing that could have happened.

„I am so sorry. Irina, I know that everything can go back to normal. We just need a little time," my voice is low. I am scared of hearing something different from her.

I am scared that she will disagree with me.

„I am sorry too. This is all my fault. You gave me the best chance in my life, and I betrayed you," Asher says.

But Irina is just looking at us, not saying anything. For a moment, I think that she isn't going to reply. She turns around, grabbing her iPad.

„We'll start with the training today. I signed you up for another competition in a week," Irina tells us. With that, the other conversation is over.

She doesn't want to talk about it. And it seems like she doesn't care at all about our apologies.

There is nothing more that I can do. There is nothing to prove to her that I really feel sorry. We somehow have to deal with it right now.

She'll see that nothing is going to change between Asher and me. Everything is going to stay the same. No one is getting hurt or heartbroken.

And as soon as she sees everything is okay, I can regain her trust. Maybe everything can be back to normal after a while.

87

ASHER

It's different now. Everything is different now. Sloane and I don't have to hide anymore. We can be an average couple, doing usual couple stuff.

We come to training as a couple. There is no secret anymore, and this part really feels good. I hate it to be a secret. I never wanted it to be a secret.

But now that it is out, there is also a bad side to the whole situation. Irina is treating us a lot differently. I understand that she is still mad. Hell, I would be angry too.

There is no personal relationship anymore. It doesn't feel like a family anymore. It's just us as business partners. She treats us like we don't know each other. She isn't talking to us anymore. And it seemed like she became stricter. It feels weird, and I miss the time we had before. It was nice to have a personal relationship with everyone.

Flynn isn't allowed at training sessions anymore. No one is allowed to watch. I guess it shouldn't feel like fun to us anymore. It's just our job.

Irina tries to make this our real job. Not only bringing us to higher competition and getting us a marketing deal. Something like this.

I have absolutely no idea about all of this. I never even thought about being seen in a commercial. I never thought that it would be important for us. But apparently, it's worrying now that everyone knows we're a couple.

Tons of people saw us on the news, which means we can now be commercialized as a couple, not only as skaters.

This worries me a bit because I wanted this to be about skating. Not about my relationship. Sloane seems to be skeptical too. But this is not for us to decide. Irina made it clear.

All we have to do is obey and skate.

„I can't do this anymore. And it has just been a week," Sloane whines as she takes off her skates.

The competition is tomorrow. We can't talk to Irina now, but I understand what she means. It's exhausting. Irina is taking every single bit of energy from us. She makes sure that all we do is skate.

„Irina has always been my role model. I looked up to her because she, some kind of always, had been my second mother. But now she just changed, like she flipped a switch."

I know that this is a lot harder for Sloane. Irina watched her grow up. She never had a different coach. I don't know what it feels like. I never had a deeper bond with my coach. I could get used to it because I would focus on skating. But if Sloane feels like this, it is getting harder. I want her to be happy, and now I can see how hurt she is.

„Maybe you should talk to her. But wait until after the competition," I suggest with a soft smile.

There is nothing else that we could do. We could maybe try and talk to Irina. Or maybe Sloane should do it alone. I have never been close to her for long. Sloane knows her better, so it might be best to talk with her.

„I might do it right after the competition," she smiles.

„Good," I reply with a smile. I put on my shoes, still looking at Sloane to ensure she was doing fine.

„Just imagine, we could really enjoy all of this. Like being a famous skating couple. This is what I always wanted. I wanted the media's attention. I wanted to be the best. It would be so lovely to celebrate that with everyone, especially Irina. I would have never done anything without her," Sloane smiles.

I know that we both want to enjoy our victories. We worked really hard for everything. I understand that she wants to share this happiness.

Now I look at her with a nod.

„One day, we can enjoy all of it. Everything will be back to normal," I tell her with another look. I know that everything will be okay in the end.

88

SLOANE

We won another competition. Adrenaline is still rushing through my veins. A smile that can never be wiped off plastered on my face. This is nearly perfect.

Well, it would be perfect if everything were normal with Irina. I look at her with a smile, trying to get some emotions out of her. But she is stone cold. She isn't even looking at us.

It takes a while until we're ready to leave the venue. We have to get through interviews, take pictures, and talk to many people. This is what we do now. We do famous skating people stuff.

It still feels like a dream to me. Everything was happening so quickly. I would have never thought my life would change that much in just a year. And it hasn't even been a whole year.

„Can we talk?" I ask Irina as soon as she walks away from her last conversation. I can't wait anymore. I miss her as my friend. I want the relationship that we had before back.

But she looks at me, trying to think of some way to say no to me. This hurts. I wish it would be easier. This is not how I wanted everything to turn out. I never wanted to hurt her.

„I give you five minutes," she tells me. At least she is not saying completely no to me.

„But I want to talk to you alone," I reply because there is no way I am doing this in front of everyone here.

She slowly nods. This is not what she was expecting. Maybe she thought that I would just try it right now. She could quickly decline everything here.

I wouldn't get loud or beg because everyone else could hear us. „Okay, we'll meet at the café tonight?" Irina gives in, and I nod with a smile on my face. This is the best I could get.

But now I have to wait, which is the hardest thing I have ever done. I can't wait anymore. I want to talk to Irina right now.

So I get ready as early as possible and try to take as much time as possible. I'll probably be too early in the café, but I don't care. I am nervous about doing this without Asher. He could be my emotional support, but I know I must do this alone. I have to talk to Irina alone.

I can't believe she is already waiting for me as I arrive at the café. I am early, so it surprises me that she is already here waiting for me. I look at her with a smile. „Thank you for seeing me here," I tell her.

We sit down, and before we start talking, we order a drink. A coffee for me, and a tea for her. Now I don't know where to start. There is a lot that I need to tell her, but my head is suddenly empty. I can't form a thought anymore. I don't know what to say.

„I am so sorry for everything that is happening. I just want you to know that I really regret it. I would turn back time and tell you everything from the first second on if I just could do that, " I tell her. And I guess this is a good start.

Irina is just looking at me. I wonder if she is going to say anything about it. I can't sit here and just stare at her. I need her to say something, even if she wants to yell at me. Right now, I would be okay with it.

„I know that you were talking about yourself when you told us that you saw the worst that could happen. And I am sorry that you went through so much. But that won't happen with us. I can't promise that but we have been a great team so far, and I don't want to give that up. You are a big part of our team, and nothing is working anymore because we miss the way it was with you before," I try again. Maybe this will bring her to talk to me.

I want her to say anything. I might have crossed a line by talking about her past. I know that she hates that.

But now she is staring at me again. This is driving me crazy.

„You don't understand. I wanted to protect you. You betrayed me,"
Irina replies, and her words hurt me. I never meant to hurt her, and
now I can hear the pain in her voice.

„I know, and words can't describe how sorry I am. I will never do
this again."

„You can't promise that. And I can't believe it. Too many people
told me this, and they still did it" it sounds so bitter when she says
it. I never knew what she was going through. I never thought about
it before.

Now I regret even more that I haven't been honest with her. If she
could only know what I feel right now.

„No, I mean it. You are like a mother to me, my biggest role model.
I would never do anything like this again. I would never betray or
fire you or whatever you might think of. I need you, not only as my
coach but also as my friend as my family."

Irina is important to me. She is part of my family, and I can't
imagine life without her. I always wanted to make her proud. I
knew she could never skate again, so I wanted her to see herself in
me. I wanted her to be proud of me.

„Really, I love you, Irina. And I don't want anything bad between
us. I can't handle that I disappointed you." I continue. I would even
beg for her forgiveness if I had to.

„Sloane, you know that I love you too. And this is why it hurt me.
But I think I understand. I just want to protect you," she replies,
much calmer than before. This might be the first step right now.

„I understand that, but we can't choose who we fall in love with. I
obviously would have never thought I would fall in love with
Asher. I knew your rule, and I was scared you would separate us, "
I explain. Because that was my worst fear at that moment. I
thought that she would split us.

Asher is the best skater, and he is my best chance for the Olympics.
I only thought about reaching my goals.

„I don't know what I would have done. This is a really sensitive
topic for me. But I want this to work between us. You're still my
favorite student, Sloane. But I hope that you'll never do something
like this again."

THE ICE BETWEEN US

This sounds really good. It sounds like she is ready to get over it. Maybe we'll really make it work somehow. I would love to go back to normal. We had a great team dynamic before Poland happened, and I want that back. I loved the team we were before.

„I won't. I absolutely promise." I quickly reply because I have never been so sure of something.

„I'll try my best to get over it. I just need some more time until it goes back to normal," Irina replies. And this, I think, is the first real step back.

I love that she will try. I love that she is giving in at least a little bit. I smile, standing up from the table. There is only one thing that I can think of right now. So I wrap my arms around her and hug her so tightly. I haven't done this often enough.

Irina is my coach. She is strict and very professional. But for me, she is also family, and this is where the professional line fades. She is more to me than just a coach.

I think that sometimes I should tell her this. I should have told her that more often. It seems like she needs to know that she is important to me.

I don't know what she is dealing with. She doesn't have to tell me if she doesn't want to. But I will think of that. I will treat her more like family now.

„But don't you think I'll go easy on you now" Irina laughs, and I shake my head. She would never go easy on me. She never went easy on me before, so I didn't expect something different.

„Nope, we'll be on time tomorrow." I reply with a laugh.

She can go as hard on us as she wants to. I'm here for it, as long as we are a team.

89

SLOANE
ONE YEAR LATER

I always wanted to visit Paris with Asher. I have been here a couple of times already. But this time, it is unique. We are here because of the competition, and I am pretty sure we will win this one too. It's been a year with him as my partner, and we haven't lost ever since that Poland competition. We are improving ourselves each and every day. I am grateful to be here today with him and Irina.

Even Flynn and Gregg are here with us. Paris is a magical city, and I am experiencing this with the most important people by my side.

The competition is tomorrow, but we decided to do some sightseeing today. It is essential because Asher needs to see the city.

So we hurried to the city to see the Louvre, the triumphal arch, and much more. We tried authentic French macarons and other famous French dishes. I love it here. A while ago, I could even imagine living here. It was my dream to come to Paris.

But this is long ago because I can't imagine living anywhere else but home right now.

„We should be rehearsing right now," Irina whines. She is not entirely okay with the plan for today.

She takes the competitions very seriously. She wants us to win and reach our goals even more than before.

I look at her and shake my head, „Come on! Have some fun. Everything is going to be okay tomorrow," I smile at her.

We all know that everything is going to be okay. We definitely have control of everything.

So this is also Irina's day off, and she should enjoy it to the fullest. I even planned something unique. I haven't told the others about my little surprise. But I told them we would have a fancy and memorable dinner.

We all get ready, wearing something incredible to our night out. I want it to be special because I don't think we'll have this again. It's a rare moment with everyone that I love. With the family, I chose myself.

„Where are we going?" Flynn asks me with a huge smile plastered on his face. He is excited to see what I planned. I haven't even talked to him about it.

But now, I am confidently leading them to a restaurant at the Eiffel Tower. We will dine there and have the most beautiful view in Paris.

„Tadaa," I point out with an even wide smile on my face. Everyone is looking up to the sparkling Eiffel Tower. I love how it shines at night.

„Okay, before we go into that Restaurant, I need a picture," Flynn exclaims.

And this is where it starts. We have a massive photo session in front of the Eiffel Towers. And this for sure is one of my favorite memories of all.

We're laughing and joking around as we take pictures in front of the sparkling tower. We even manage to take a group photo of ourselves. „Okay, now Slo and me," Asher smiles, handing the phone to Irina so she can take the picture.

Irina is now okay with our relationship. She changed a lot in the past couple of months. She even opened up about her past toward us, which I think is a massive step for her.

Now she is smiling at us as she tells us where to stand so it'll be the perfect picture. She gestures us to move a little to the left, and as it is perfect, she points her thumbs up.

I smile at the camera, knowing I'll frame this picture. But right then, Asher grabs me, pulling me closer to him. And as I turn to the side to look at him, he leans in and kisses me. He kisses me right underneath the sparkling Eiffel Tower.

Isn't that on everyone's bucket list? Kissing the love of their lives underneath the Eiffel Tower. Now the city of love really does have a new meaning to me.

It's not only the first time I have had a great time with the people I love. It's the first time I have come here more than happy, in love, and as a victor.

We also leave the city as a victor. There is no other way than to win the competition. This is my life now. And it still seems pretty crazy to me.

And who knows, maybe one day we'll stand on the podium of the Olympic Games.

EPILOGUE
ASHER

It's been years together with Sloane, professionally and privately. We made it, like for real. We finally made it. My heart is racing as I look at the ice for the first time. The Olympic Rings are shown everywhere. Today we're representing our country in the Olympic Winter Games.

This is what we always wanted. This is our dream coming true right now. The smile can't be wiped off our faces, even though the weight on our shoulders is pretty heavy.

I look at my girlfriend. We went through everything together, every high and low.

I learned a lot in the past couple of years. Sloane taught me a lot, and I am thankful for her every single day.

She taught me that I deserve happiness and am not like my dad. I can have a different life. Maybe one day, I'll show my children to grow up differently.

She made me happier than I have ever been. I now not only have a girlfriend, but I also have a career. Because of Sloane, I have a future.

Skating at the Olympics comes with a lot of pressure. I guess that we're all thrilled when this is over. We hope to be the victors of today. We tried being here before. We haven't been that lucky before. But now we can make our dreams come true.

We're next. My heart is racing. The choreography of today is the one we already know. It was our first successful performance. The drama performance we once absolutely hated. I am excited to perform the choreography this time.

We have nearly the same costumes as years ago. This gives me flashbacks.

I smile at Sloane as I take her hand so we can skate to the middle of the ice together. We wave to the audience and bow to them.

Then it's starting. The song slowly starts. It's the same as years ago. Sloane starts as she skates around me, she takes my hand, and we start gaining some speed.

We got better compared to the last performance. We learned some things, and now our performance is more complex than one year ago. We added some new, more complicated elements to it.

I think that we're doing well. This has some great potential. Even though Germany has the highest rating right now. Their performance was absolutely perfect, and with the number of elements they had, their performance was hard to beat.

But we're here to try. With a smile on my face, we slide over the ice. The audience claps and cheers every now and then. We land every element perfectly, just like we practiced it.

We never worked as hard on anything as on this. We knew that this had to be absolutely outraging.

Everyone can see our ratings right now. With every element, the points are getting higher. They see which place we're at right now. But Sloane and I are so focused on our performance that we have no idea what is happening right now.

There are two more couples after us. They still have the opportunity to win. But being first would already mean a lot right now. It'll be hard to beat us then. Germany is already hard.

The song ends, and we're in our final position. My face is buried in Sloane's neck, where I press a soft kiss onto her skin. Our breathing is heavy, and adrenaline is rushing through our veins.

This was something different. It felt more than great to me.

With a huge smile, we wave to the crowd again. We look around until we finally see our ranking. A small screen shows us how many points we gained with our performance.

My heart stops for a second to see that we did it. We beat Germany, which means we're now in the first place. For right now, we're the winners.

This is everything I ever wanted. Well, this is nearly everything I ever wanted.

I hug Sloane tightly, pressing a kiss onto her lips. It might take some while to really realize that we won this. I don't think that the other two couples can be better. The rating is too high right now.

We have a little team booth where we sit down again to watch two couples. Irina hugs us tightly, a massive smile on her face. It is a huge accomplishment for her as well. She waited just as long as we did for this to happen.

So Irina is just as excited as we are as we really win. No one can beat us. We have the highest rating, and we win the Olympic Games.

It is a great feeling. I would have never thought that this would actually feel like this. It feels like a dream, and tomorrow when I wake up, I might not realize that this happened.

I look at Sloane. She is crying about our victory, wiping away the tears of happiness. Now we have to celebrate.

Everyone that we love came here to celebrate with us if we won. And now we really did, which means we have to party tonight.

But before that, we have to take tons of pictures and get interviewed. We talk to tons of people and answer questions. It takes a while until we leave the venue.

I am still nervous. My heart is still racing inside of my chest. There is still something for me to do.

I take Sloane's hand as we leave the venue. Every person that came here to watch the games is already gone. Now the athletes are leaving with their teams.

I stop right in front of the building, showing the Olympic Rings. I look at Sloane with a huge smile, „We should take a picture to remember this day," I tell her.

This is the perfect photo location and would be a perfect memory. Flynn is quickly there with his phone in his hand. He kneels down a bit for a better angle.

„You know today is a dream coming true for both of us. This is what I always dreamed of. I always wanted to win the Olympic Games. I never wanted anything else," I start a little speech.

I prepared this in my head, even though none of my thoughts are really making sense now.

„But then I met you. And I quickly realized that there was something that I wanted more than skating. I now know there is something I want more than winning the Olympics, and I have known this for a long time now. I want to spend the rest of my life with the woman I love. You changed my life completely a couple of years ago. You made me the happiest man on earth by giving me your love."

I smile at Sloane as I slowly kneel down to one knee, taking in every slight reaction she gives to me. My hand reaches into my pocket to get the small ring case. I open it, showing Sloane the diamond ring inside.

„Sloane, will you marry me?"

I finally asked the question. I watch every tiny movement of Sloane. I try to take in every detail that I can get.

She sucks in a breath as she sees the ring. Tears are filling her eyes once again as she looks at me. She takes a step back, a hand covering her mouth. This is a total surprise to her. Everything is exactly how I wanted it to be. I thought about it a millionth time, trying to make everything perfect.

My heart is pounding so heavily that it nearly is the only sound I'm hearing. I am scared that Sloane might reject me. Maybe marriage is not what she wants in life. Even though I know that she wants to get married, we discussed it before.

She slowly lowers herself until she is at the same height and starts nodding eagerly. „YES! YES! YES!" She yells.

Sloane wraps her arms around me, burying her face in my neck. I stand up with her in my arms, twirling her around.

Now, it is the best day of our life. We not only accomplished the most significant thing in our career. I now will marry the love of my life.

I kiss her, pressing myself into her. And then I finally slid the ring onto her finger. She is mine, forever.

ACKNOWLEDGMENTS

This is absolutely crazy! I can't believe how quickly everything is happening right now!

I had this idea long ago, yet I wrote it down quickly. It happened so smoothly!

A huge thanks to everyone who was part of my writing process. All of this really couldn't happen without the support.

This book exists because figure skating was what I wanted to do professionally when I was a little girl. Sadly that didn't work out for me, but I am more than happy to fulfill a little dream with this story.

I am absolutely in love with Sloane and Asher, and I hope my reading community loves their story as much as I do!

A huge thanks to everyone who is reading and liking my books! You mean the world to me, and I'll forever be more than thankful to have you.

Thanks to my best friend Poppy, who is always by my side. She is my most immense support while writing a book, and I am thankful to have her.

Huge thanks to my friends who read my book beta for me. This wouldn't happen without you! Thank you for being there for me and for supporting me!

Thank you!

MORE FROM THE AUTHOR

Holding on and letting go
Godless
Senseless
Heartless

Printed in Poland
by Amazon Fulfillment
Poland Sp. z o.o., Wrocław

93421366R00197